PENGUIN ENGLISH LIBRARY

THE CHRISTMAS BOOKS · VOLUME ONE

CHARLES DICKENS

Michael Slater is a Lecturer in English at Birkbeck College,
University of London, and has been Editor of the *Dickensian*
since 1968. He has edited a collection of centenary essays
entitled *Dickens 1970.*

CHARLES DICKENS

THE CHRISTMAS BOOKS
Volume One

━━

A CHRISTMAS CAROL

THE CHIMES

━━

Edited with Introductions and Notes
by Michael Slater
and original illustrations by
Leech, Maclise, Doyle
and Stanfield

PENGUIN BOOKS

Penguin Books Ltd, Harmondsworth, Middlesex, England
Penguin Books Inc., 7110 Ambassador Road, Baltimore, Maryland 21207, U.S.A.
Penguin Books Australia Ltd, Ringwood, Victoria, Australia
Penguin Books Canada Ltd, 41 Steelcase Road West, Markham, Ontario, Canada
Penguin Books (N.Z.) Ltd, 182–190 Wairau Road, Auckland 10, New Zealand

—

A Christmas Carol first published 1843
The Chimes first published 1844
Published in Penguin English Library 1971
Reprinted 1972, 1974, 1975

—

Introduction and notes copyright © M. Slater, 1971

—

Made and printed in Great Britain by
Hazell Watson & Viney Ltd,
Aylesbury, Bucks
Set in Monotype Fournier

The illustrations for this book have been taken from the
Oxford Illustrated Dickens edition of *The Christmas
Books* and are reproduced by permission of
Oxford University Press

CONTENTS

INTRODUCTION

I wonder if you have ever read Dickens's *Christmas Books?* ... they are too much perhaps. I have only read two yet, but I have cried my eyes out, and had a terrible fight not to sob. But oh, dear God, they are *good* – and I feel so good after them – I shall do good and lose no time – I want to go out and comfort some-one – I *shall* give money. Oh, what a jolly thing it is for a man to have written books like these and just filled people's hearts with pity. *Robert Louis Stevenson to an unidentified correspondent*[1]

WE can, I think, be fairly certain that the two Christmas Books which moved Stevenson to such an enthusiastic response were the *Carol* and *The Chimes*. Both these little books, products of the Hungry Forties, overflow with benevolence towards the poor and appeal urgently to the reader's charitable feelings. Both are distinctly seasonal, the *Carol* having a Christmas setting and *The Chimes* a New Year's Eve one. In both stories the supernatural plays a crucial part, the main character being converted by its means from an undesirable state of mind to a joyful and generous one. All these features reappear in the last of the Christmas Books, *The Haunted Man* (1848), but the two intervening ones, *The Cricket on the Hearth* (1845) and *The Battle of Life* (1846), must have puzzled Stevenson if he ever got round to reading them. The *Cricket* has a winter setting but nothing particular to do with Christmas; the supernatural element is reduced to pretty embroidery; and there is no direct appeal to the reader's social conscience. This book does, however, share with its two predecessors a special intimacy of tone, a style more colloquial than that which Dickens usually adopted in his big novels, and, like them, it could be described as 'a whimsical kind of masque', the phrase which Dickens applied to all his Christmas Books when he wrote a general

1. Quoted in the *Dickensian*, vol. 16, 1920, p. 200.

preface for them. *The Battle of Life*, on the other hand, seems to have no feature at all in common with the other volumes in this series, apart from the emphasis it lays upon family love and the delights of home (a motif which runs strongly through all five books), and appears as nothing more nor less than a savagely foreshortened Dickens novel.

We might conclude, then, that these five stories have nothing in common apart from the family-love motif already mentioned (and this is, after all, ubiquitous in Dickens's work) and the fact that they were all written for the Christmas market and published in the same format. There is, however, one interesting theme which is found in them all, to a greater or lesser degree, and that is the theme of memory and its beneficial effect on the moral life. Scrooge's conversion begins when he is forced to contemplate scenes from his past life; in *The Chimes* Mrs Chickenstalker's kindness to Meg and her ruined husband in Trotty's vision of the future is prompted by her memory of them in the bright and hopeful days of their courtship; John Peerybingle in the *Cricket* is prevented from committing murder by the memory-pictures of his happy life with Dot which the fairies call up; Marion in the *Battle* keeps in her heart all the signs which she alone perceives of her sister's silent self-sacrifice and it is the thought of them that in the hour of crisis strengthens her to match such generosity of spirit; and in *The Haunted Man* Redlaw is made to learn that memories and feelings of compassion are inextricably intertwined in the human psyche.

A hint of this theme appears in the first piece Dickens ever wrote for Christmas, a sketch entitled 'A Christmas Dinner', published in a newspaper eight years before he wrote the *Carol* and later collected in *Sketches by Boz*. The matriarch of the family depicted in this sketch is reconciled on Christmas Day to the daughter who had displeased her by marrying a poor man. The mother finds she cannot deny her child a place at the hearth 'round which she has sat on so many anniversaries of the same day, expanding by slow degrees from infancy to girlhood and then bursting, almost imperceptibly, into a woman'. But Dickens does not yet admit what is to become important in the *Carol* (and central to the idea of *The Haunted Man*): that painful memories may have an even more salutary effect on the moral life than pleasant ones. 'Look on the many faces of your children . . . as they sit around the fire,' he urged his readers in 'A Christmas Dinner'. 'One little seat may be empty; one slight form that gladdened the father's heart and roused the mother's pride to look upon, may not be there. Dwell not upon the past. . . . Reflect upon your present blessings. . . '. Scrooge, however, was to be made to dwell, not only on but in, his past, reliving painful as well as pleasant experiences, and to see in his vision of a possible future Bob Cratchit admonishing his children after Tiny Tim's death: 'I know, my dears, that when we recollect how patient and how mild he was; although he was a little, little child; we shall not quarrel easily among ourselves and forget poor Tiny Tim in doing it.'

The 'Chrismas Dinner' sketch anticipates the *Carol* in another way. It shows children and adults mingling on equal terms in their enjoyment of games and feasting. 'It is good to be children sometimes,' Dickens observes in the *Carol*, 'and never better than at Christmas when its mighty Founder was a child himself.' Bob Cratchit going down 'a slide on Cornhill, at the end of a lane of boys, twenty times, in honour of its being Christmas Eve and then [running] home to Camden Town as hard as he could pelt, to play at blindman's-buff' epitomizes for Dickens the right approach to Christmas. He made it the very keynote of what is undoubtedly (the *Carol* apart) his most famous celebration in print of the Christmas season, 'the good-humoured Christmas chapter' of *Pickwick Papers*, published in December 1836, describing the Pickwickians' holiday visit to Old Wardle at Dingley Dell. The only representative of actual childhood at the Dell is the somnambulist and gormandizing fat boy but Mr Pickwick and his friends do not need the company of actual children to show them what Dickens sees as the right way to celebrate Christmas – 'happy, happy Christmas, that can win us back to the delusions of our childish days'. They throw themselves into a round of games and feastings and story-tellings with all the energy and innocent joy of childhood (Sam Weller being always at hand to see that everything goes smoothly) and Dickens, through the zest and vigour of his prose, creates one of the most memorable idylls in our literature:

The paths were hard; the grass was crisp and frosty; the air had a fine, dry, bracing coldness; and the rapid approach of the grey twilight (slate-coloured is a better term in frosty weather) made them look forward with pleasant anticipation to the comforts which awaited them at their hospitable entertainer's. It was the sort of afternoon that might induce a couple of elderly gentlemen, in a lonely field, to take off their great-coats and play at leap-frog in pure lightness of heart and gaiety; and we firmly believe that had Mr Tupman at that moment proffered 'a back' Mr Pickwick would have accepted his offer with the utmost avidity.

What is missing from the Pickwickian Christmas but strongly present in at least three of what I may call the four 'genuine' Christmas Books (for *The Battle of Life* must always be considered as standing somewhat outside the genre) is the appeal for charity, the urging of the need to carry the Christmas spirit out of the happy family circle into the world of the poor. Abundance rejoices but Want is not keenly felt in Dingley Dell for it is indeed an idyllic place, remote from the everyday world. It contains a 'benevolent old clergyman' but the only objects for practical benevolence who appear in it, Wardle's poor relations, are presented as comic supernumeraries, strenuously eager to please (in the game of blind-man's buff they 'caught the people who they thought would like it, and, when the game flagged, got caught themselves'). The question of charity, therefore, simply does not arise. Gabriel Grub, the misanthropic sexton, who is the hero of Old Wardle's Christmas story, is punished by the goblins for unsociable and unseasonable behaviour rather than for lack of charity – sneaking off to drink by himself on Christmas Eve he knocks a boy on the head for singing a Christmas carol – and Dickens tactfully leaves vague the manner in which Gabriel's reformation manifested itself. To show him at the end of the story, when he has learned 'that men like himself, who snarled at the mirth and cheerfulness of others, were the foulest weeds on the fair surface of the earth', sharing his bottle of Hollands with a party of boon-companions would hardly have had the effect that Scrooge's dispensation of turkeys and largesse has in the finale of the *Carol.* We should note, however, that the most detailed part of Gabriel's visions in the goblins' cavern does concern a poor but loving and united family and the way in which its love and faith enables it to sustain the death of its youngest member. But this is all presented at two removes from Mr Pickwick and his fellow-celebrants of Christmas. In the *Carol* Dickens brings this family into the mainstream of his narrative by making its head an employee of Pickwick's anti-self, Ebenezer Scrooge, and is thus able to forge together into a wonderfully effective literary whole what should be, he feels, the two great qualities of Christmas, domestic joy and practical charity towards the less fortunate outside our doors.

*

Details concerning the origin, composition, publication and reception of the individual Christmas books will be found in the separate introductions supplied for each book. I want here to say a little about the literary qualities they exhibit before commenting finally on the interest that they have, as a group, from the point of view of Dickens's novelistic career as a whole.

The first and greatest of the series, the *Carol* is, considered from a literary point of view, first and foremost a triumph of *tone.* This tone is quickly established in the first few paragraphs of the story as that of a jolly, kind-hearted bachelor uncle seated across the hearth from his hearers on some festive domestic occasion. The joke about 'not disturbing the wisdom of our ancestors or the Country's done for' in the second paragraph gives us a hint, too, of a rather sharper tone which the bachelor uncle can command; one cannot imagine Old Wardle making such a crack. The story proceeds in this colloquial style, laced with jokes and puns and lip-smacking descriptions of gastronomic delights or plump female charms and when, in Stave Two, Dickens writes, 'Scrooge ... found himself face to face with the unearthly visitor ... as close to it as I am now to you, and I am standing in the spirit at your elbow ...' his comparison is both justified and effective because the reader has already received, through the style of the book, such an overwhelming impression of the story-teller's physical proximity – an impression which this passage, of course, strengthens.

Dickens's choice of style is ideal for the presentation of Scrooge:

Oh! But he was a tight-fisted hand at the grindstone, Scrooge! a squeezing, wrenching, grasping, scraping, clutching, covetous old sinner! Hard and sharp as flint, from which no steel had ever struck out generous fire; secret, and self-contained, and solitary as an oyster:

and it is not long before Scrooge's zestful malice is delighting us as much as Quilp's does in *The Old Curiosity Shop*; 'If I could work my will,' he growls at his nephew, 'every idiot who goes about with "Merry Christmas" on his lips, should be boiled with his own pudding, and buried with a stake of holly through his heart. He should!' His determined attempts to treat the disagreeable apparition of Marley's ghost with the same briskness that he had displayed when routing his charitable visitors provides some splendid comedy: 'You may be an undigested bit of beef, a blot of mustard, a crumb of cheese, a fragment of an underdone potato. There's more of gravy than of grave about you, whatever you are!' Even when the ghost (surely one of Dickens's finest grotesque creations – that detail about its removing the bandage round its head 'as if it were too warm to wear indoors', thereby causing its lower jaw to drop on to its breast, has exactly the right comic/horrific touch) has brought Scrooge to his knees in terror and dismay, he is not altogether squashed: 'Don't be flowery, Jacob! Pray!' he urges as the ghost intones its solemn exhortations, and later, when told he will be visited by three Spirits, he tries to bargain for a minimum of disturbance – 'Couldn't I take 'em all at once and have it over, Jacob?'

The bachelor-uncle tone of the *Carol* deepens into a much grimmer register at the end of Stave Three when Scrooge beholds the two 'yellow, meagre, ragged, scowling, wolvish' children, Ignorance and Want. The Ghost of Christmas Yet to Come whose appearance follows swiftly is, appropriately, a far more mysterious and alarming apparition than its predecessors and the dramatic tension of Stave Four, where the reader is ahead of Scrooge in grasping the full horror, for him, of what he is being shown, is admirably maintained. But after the scene in the graveyard Dickens has no difficulty modulating back into the genial basic tone of the story as the phantom, imploringly grasped by Scrooge, shrinks and dwindles into a bedpost and we find ourselves back in a bright Christmas morning.

The apparition of Ignorance and Want is not to be seen as a gloomy digression in the *Carol*, however. These wolvish children are essential not only to its Christian message (compare Dickens's words about the poor in Chapter Three of his *Life of Our Lord*: 'If they are bad, think that they would have been better, if they had had kind friends, and good homes, and had been better taught') but also to its effectiveness as a piece of literature. The shame and horror of desperate poverty, and the danger to society it represents, must be vividly evoked in the book if we are to feel the fearfully urgent need for Scrooge's conversion and hence respond with joyous relief to the ebullient manifestations of his changed heart at the end. For Scrooge, of course, is more than a character in a story about a skinflint employer and his clerk. He also embodies all the selfishness and indifference of the prosperous classes who parrot phrases about the 'surplus population' and think their social responsibilities fully discharged when they have paid their taxes.

The management of the allegory is indeed one of the finest aspects of the *Carol*. Nearly every picturesque detail about the ghosts and about Scrooge's dealings with them is full of meaning which the least sophisticated reader can hardly miss. The chain dragged by Marley's ghost was forged by the living man and is made of 'cash-boxes, keys, padlocks, ledgers, deeds and heavy purses wrought in steel'. The Ghost of Christmas Past 'fluctuates in its distinctness' and can only be perceived at all by the 'bright clear jet of light' which springs from the crown of its head while under its arm it carries a great extinguisher for a cap. Scrooge, the man who has ruthlessly suppressed all memories of the past, has at his first sight of this apparition 'a special desire to see the Spirit in his cap; and [begs] him to be covered'.

The supernatural elements in Dickens's next Christmas Book (it might perhaps be more properly called a New Year's Eve Book), *The Chimes*, do not form the basis of any sustained allegory. They are church-bells, but Dickens is certainly not writing about the benign influence of institutional Christianity. The Chimes do not, in fact, relate to anything in the moral world any more than do the goblins who carry off Gabriel Grub. Nor does the story's leading character, Trotty Veck, transcend a richly realized individuality to become a part of all of us in the way that Scrooge does (in common with all the great 'Dickens characters' – Pickwick, Micawber, Pecksniff and the rest). In this book Dickens appears less concerned with moral allegory than with political satire and the very intensity of its topicality has meant that (like the writings of the radical journalist, Douglas Jerrold, whose influence may be clearly seen in the book) it has not worn so well as literature. It contains some fine things such as the powerful opening description of the night-wind in a church, the tender little scene between

Trotty and his daughter when she brings him his breakfast
in the street, and the grotesque outbursts of Mr Filer which
one can enjoy even if one knows nothing about the political
economists whom Dickens was satirizing:

Tripe is without an exception the least economical, and the
most wasteful article of consumption that the markets of this
country can by possibility produce. The loss upon a pound of
tripe has been found to be, in the boiling, seven-eights of a fifth
more than the loss upon a pound of any other animal substance
whatever. Tripe is more expensive, properly understood, than
the hothouse pineapple. Taking into account the number of
animals slaughtered yearly within the bills of mortality alone;
and forming a low estimate of the quantity of tripe which the
carcases of those animals, reasonably well butchered, would
yield; I find that the waste on that amount of tripe, if boiled,
would victual a garrison of five hundred men for five months of
thirty-one days each, and a February over. The Waste, the
Waste!

But, considered as a fable in the same genre as the *Carol, The
Chimes* suffers not only from its topicality but also from the
fact that elements of traditional Dickensian plot begin to
appear – Cute and Bowley are connected through Fern,
Mrs Chickenstalker turns out to be an old friend of Lilian's
mother, and so on. The cast of human characters is enlarged
for this second Christmas Book and, instead of the simple and
terrible vision of Ignorance and Want we see a number of
individuals – Meg, Will Fern, Lilian, Richard – becoming
involved in the crimes and miseries of the Victorian poor –
sweated labour, prostitution, drunkenness, suicide, infanticide. This produces, I think, a very different effect on us, one
of gloomy reflection which is not really dispelled by the
sudden burst of merry-making at the end of the story. The
conclusion, one contemporary critic wrote, 'is huddled up
under a grand flourish of trumpets'[2] and we do not feel
that, because Meg and Richard decide to proceed with their
marriage after all, everything will be well with them, still

2. The *New Monthly Belle Assemblée*, February 1845.

less with the Ferns, for ever afterwards; Cute's dismal prophecies about their future have not been truly exorcized.

For all this, I feel that the current of passionate anger which runs through *The Chimes* can still take hold of a modern reader and make him respond somewhat as he responds to the passion behind *Hard Times* or behind Dickens's apostrophe to his readers after Jo's death in *Bleak House*. The insolence of office is powerfully evoked in Alderman Cute's brutal bantering of Trotty, and Sir Joseph Bowley, MP, 'floundering now and then, as in the great depth of his observations', can hold his own in Dickens's gallery of fatuous politicians. Most effective of all, perhaps, is the way in which Dickens conveys to us, through the character of Tugby, the vicious hatred which the casualties of society can arouse in the petit-bourgeois:

'O!' he said softly. 'You have come back?'
She looked at the child, and shook her head.
'Don't you think you have lived long enough here without paying any rent? Don't you think that, without any money, you've been a pretty constant customer at this shop, now?'

The fierce satire of *The Chimes* is not relieved by any glowing set-piece such as the Cratchits' Christmas dinner or Fezziwig's ball and, as if to compensate his readers for this, Dickens filled his next Christmas Book, *The Cricket on the Hearth*, with geniality to the exclusion of almost everything else, except a touch of melodrama with Tackleton's temptation of Peerybingle to jealousy as a sort of pantomime or puppet-show echo of *Othello*. The 'bachelor uncle' voice tones to pathos occasionally and also to mystery ('what was that young figure of a man, which the same Fairy Cricket set so near Her stool, and which remained there, singly and alone?') but never strikes the grimly prophetic note that we hear in both the *Carol* and *The Chimes*.

The greatest shift in tone comes at the end, after the grand finale, when Dickens adds a wistful little coda which excellently evokes the feeling he mentions in 'A Christmas Tree', his first Christmas Story (written for his journal *Household Words* in 1850), the 'dreary sensation' of returning to everyday life after an evening of willing participation in the glittering delights of a pantomime – 'wanting to live for ever in the bright atmosphere I have quitted ... doting on the little Fairy, with the wand like a celestial Barber's Pole and pining for a Fairy immortality along with her'. This is exactly the mood conveyed by the epilogue to the *Cricket*:

But what is this! Even as I listen to them, blithely, and turn towards Dot, for one last glimpse of a little figure very pleasant to me, she and the rest have vanished into air, and I am left alone. A Cricket sings upon the Hearth; a broken child's-toy lies upon the ground; and nothing else remains.

The broken toy is a beautifully apt touch here for in the *Cricket* we have found ourselves in a world of toys. The characters are animated dolls, pretty or homely or grotesque, and their little houses are full of playful objects, singing kettles or 'convulsive little haymakers' on the top of Dutch clocks. Dot has 'a very doll of a baby' and the kind-hearted little toy-maker, Caleb Plummer, lives in his 'little cracked nutshell of a wooden house' surrounded by 'little tumblers in red breeches, incessantly swarming up high obstacles of red tape' and 'innumerable old gentlemen of respectable ... appearance, insanely flying over horizontal pegs, inserted, for the purpose, in their own street doors'. Here he conjures up a make-believe world of delight for his blind daughter and shields her as best he can from the Mr Growser of this Toytown, Tackleton the toy-merchant, 'a domestic Ogre, who had been living on children all his life, and was their implacable enemy'. Tackleton, like the 'hideous, hairy red-eyed Jacks in Boxes' that are among his favourite merchandise, enjoys spreading alarm and despondency among his fellow-dolls, and clouds with care the honest wooden carrier's face with as much zest as when delighting to 'insinuate grim expressions in the faces of brown-paper farmers who drove pigs to market'.[3] But he proves to be powerless against the good fairies and eventually arrives, converted, to take his place in the joyful *pas d'ensemble* with which the story ends.

Apart from the general charm which Dickens diffuses throughout this story (which was, not surprisingly, more eagerly seized on by the theatres for turning into a Christmas *divertissement* than any of Dickens's other Christmas Books) there are two main sources of pleasure for the reader – the incomparably fine portrait of Boxer, the carrier's dog (a creation well worthy of Landseer's pencil), and the good-humoured, clumsy nurse, Tilly Slowboy, whose engaging antics with the doll-baby culminate in a splendidly Dickensian detail:

Miss Slowboy ... wept copiously for joy, and wishing to include her young charge in the general interchange of congratulations, handed round the Baby to everybody in succession, as if it were something to drink.

It is through Tilly Slowboy that we get the only reminder in the *Cricket* of the theme which had been so prominent in the *Carol* and *The Chimes*: the wretchedness of the poor and underprivileged (the poverty of Caleb and Bertha seem merely part of the fancifulness of their whole conception). Dickens mentions Tilly's

constant astonishment at finding herself so kindly treated, and installed in such a comfortable home. For the maternal and paternal Slowboy were alike unknown to Fame and Tilly had been bred by public charity, a foundling; which word, though

3. Dickens reverts to the terrors of the toy world in 'A Christmas Tree', in a passage to which Angus Wilson has recently drawn attention (in his *The World of Charles Dickens*, 1970). He describes there a number of frightening toys which have the true Tackletonian trade-mark, e.g. the cardboard man 'who used to be hung against the wall and pulled by a string; there was a sinister expression in that nose of his; and when he got his legs round his neck (which he very often did), he was ghastly, and not a creature to be alone with'.

only differing from fondling by one vowel's length, is very different in meaning, and expresses quite another thing.

Much development of this subject would, however, have been ruinous to the atmosphere of this 'Fairy Tale of Home' and Dickens saves it for the presentation of Mrs Snagsby's skivvy, Guster, in *Bleak House*.

In his next Christmas Book, *The Battle of Life*, the England of the Hungry Forties disappears altogether and Dickens gives us instead a middle-class eighteenth-century setting and a story which dispenses entirely with the supernatural element and does not relate in any way to Christmas, despite the snow-scene at the end of the second part. The 'bachelor uncle' tone is dropped too, while the powerful quality of the prose of the first few paragraphs (which Mr Emlyn Williams has recently converted to a very effective item in his repertoire of Dickens readings) is not sustained. The book remains an interesting failure, Marion's behaviour foreshadowing both that of David Copperfield's Dora on her deathbed and of Sidney Carton in *A Tale of Two Cities*. The only successful feature of the story is the character of the homely devoted nurse, Clemency Newcome, long recognized as the forerunner of Peggotty in *David Copperfield*. Her mate, Britain, however, unfortunately does not have anything like the imaginative appeal of Peggoty's Barkis.

One can understand why G. K. Chesterton completely ignored *The Battle of Life* in his introduction to the Everyman edition of the Christmas Books but it is less easy to see why he also ignored the last of the series, *A Haunted Man*. In this book, which is given a very definite Christmas setting, Dickens returns to something like the same blend of features that produced the *Carol* and *The Chimes* – scenes of humble domestic felicity, the conversion of the leading character to a better state of mind by supernatural means and a powerful evocation of the plight of the poor. Redlaw, however, is rather a leaden creation when set beside Scrooge and Trotty

Veck and the good woman who saves him, Milly Swidger, hovers unhappily between human and angelic nature, now talking in the most lofty and exalted strain and now exclaiming artlessly at the results of the healing powers she unconsciously exercises: ' "Oh dear, oh dear!" cried Milly innocently, "here's another one of them! Oh dear, here's somebody else who likes me. What shall I ever do!" '

About the delightfully humorous presentation of the Tetterby family one need make no reservations, yet, because they are imprisoned in a little-read book, they have never been able to rival the Cratchits' popularity (though, free as they are of such insistent pathos as that attendant upon Tiny Tim, one might expect them to be more to a modern reader's taste). Mrs Tetterby's frustration over Christmas shopping ('so much calculating and calculating necessary, before I durst lay out a sixpence for the commonest thing') and little Johnny's devotion to that 'very Moloch of a baby' – no toy-baby like Dot Peerybingle's but a very human one indeed – are excellently done, as is the description of Mr Tetterby's difficulties in getting the family to bed:

Of these small fry, two had, by some strong machinery, been got into bed in a corner, where they might have reposed snugly enough in the sleep of innocence, but for a constitutional propensity to keep awake, and also to scuffle in and out of bed. The immediate occasion of these predatory dashes at the waking world, was the construction of an oyster-shell wall in a corner, by two other youths of tender age; on which fortification the two in bed made harassing descents (like those accursed Picts and Scots who beleaguer the early historical studies of most young Britons), and then withdrew to their own territory.

In addition to the stir attendant on these inroads, and the retorts of the invaded, who pursued hotly, and made lunges at the bed-clothes, under which the marauders took refuge, another little boy, in another little bed, contributed his mite of confusion to the family stock, by casting his boots upon the waters; in other words, by launching these and several small objects inoffensive in themselves, though of a hard substance considered as missiles, at the disturbers of his repose, – who were not slow to return these compliments.

In sharp contrast to the ebullient natural childhood depicted in the young Tetterbys stands the sullen, stunted and ferocious little figure of the starving child of the streets with whom Redlaw is brought into contact, Ignorance and Want made flesh (or rather, skin-and-bone):

A bundle of tatters, held together by a hand, in size and form almost an infant's, but, in its greedy, desperate little clutch, a bad old man's. A face rounded and smoothed by some half-dozen years, but pinched and twisted by the experiences of a life. Bright eyes, but not youthful. Naked feet, beautiful in their childish delicacy, – ugly in the blood and dirt that cracked upon them. A baby savage, a young monster, a child who had never been a child, a creature who might live to take the outward form of man, but who, within, would live and perish a mere beast.

Used, already, to be worried and hunted like a beast, the boy crouched down as he was looked at, and looked back again, and interposed his arm to ward off the expected blow.

'I'll bite,' he said, 'if you hit me!'

The skill with which Dickens juxtaposes his highly cultivated man of science, after he has voluntarily banished all memory of 'sorrow, wrong and trouble', and this terrible child is one of the finest things in *The Haunted Man* (it is underscored by Leech's illustrations – the one of the child before the fire recalls the earlier picture of Redlaw brooding on his hearth and shadowed by his malevolent alter ego). The Ghost enforces the moral of this juxtaposition in a passage in the third chapter which, with its grim foretelling of the ruinous harvest that society is sowing for itself in allowing such horrors as this baby Caliban to come into being, has all the concentrated power of *The Chimes* and looks forward to the achievement of *Bleak House*. This is the aspect of Dickens's last Christmas Book that I think we should emphasize, rather than the possible autobiographical implications his treatment of Redlaw and his brooding over 'sorrow, wrong and trouble' may have, for it is surely here that the real passion of the book is to be found.

*

In a lecture given in 1951[4] John Butt first drew attention to the significance of the Christmas Books as '[marking] an important stage in Dickens's development as a novelist' in that they show him constructing stories with greater care, premeditating the way in which the plot will develop before beginning to write (see his outline of *The Chimes* sent to Forster from Genoa and reproduced in the *Life of Dickens*) and experimenting with effects of contrast, repetition and the like. Writing of *The Haunted Man*, Butt notes:

> The antithesis between Milly and Redlaw upon which the plot turns is presented in the first episode and is carefully developed in those two contrary motions, the wave of destruction which follows Redlaw, and the wave of healing which accompanies Milly.

More recently, Kathleen Tillotson has persuasively suggested[5] that possibly the most important contribution made by the Christmas Books to the novels which followed them 'lies ... in their treatment of time'; by invoking the supernatural Dickens is able to 'play tricks with time, breaking through the barriers of ordinary experience', deepening by these means his presentation of character and its continuity.

From the point of view of the development of Dickens's social criticism as well as of his literary art two at least of the Books are of considerable importance. In *The Chimes* it is to be noted that Cute, Filer, and Bowley are not villains of the Ralph Nickleby stamp; stupid, bigoted and unimaginative they may be, but they all believe that what they are doing is in the best interests of society just as fervently as Dr Blimber,

4. Posthumously printed in *Pope, Dickens and Others*, Edinburgh, 1969.

5. In 'The Middle Years: From the *Carol* to *Copperfield*', *Dickens Memorial Lectures, 1970.*

Sir Leicester Dedlock, Mr Gradgrind and the other more fully developed creators of social mischief in the later novels do. And even if, like Scrooge, they were to have their hearts opened and their imaginations enlarged during the course of the story, what could they do, three individuals, to relieve the enormous and widespread suffering that we have been made aware of (in a much more documentary way than in the *Carol*)? This is very different from the attitude taken in *Oliver Twist*. Here the misery shown in the early part of the book is actually the result of the New Poor Law. This Law was clearly an attempt on the part of the legislators who drew it up, the MPs who voted for it and the Commissioners appointed to administer it, to grapple honestly and efficiently with a huge and complex social problem. But in *Oliver* Dickens concentrates our attention at the other end of the scale where he exhibits in a telling manner the cheeseparing inefficiency of the local Boards and, still more, the unpleasant characters of some officials of those Boards like Bumble and Mrs Corney. So powerful is the odium incurred by these characters that, in the reader's mind, it envelops the whole system and makes it appear as something deliberately organized by a group of evil individuals with malice towards the poor aforethought. Against this sort of evil such champions of good as the Brownlows and Maylies can effectively pit themselves; it is clearly Somebody's fault. In *The Chimes*, however, the ills of society are 'Nobody's Fault' (to quote the discarded title of *Little Dorrit*) and this analysis is carried a stage further in *The Haunted Man* where it is seen that what is nobody's fault must be everybody's fault:

'There is not a father,' said the Phantom, 'by whose side in his daily or his nightly walk, these creatures pass; there is not a mother among all the ranks of loving mothers in this land; there is no one risen from the state of childhood, but shall be responsible in his or her degree for this enormity. There is not a country throughout the earth on which it would not bring a curse. There is no religion upon earth that it would not deny; there is no people upon earth it would not put to shame.'

Thus Dickens arrives at the insight that will provide the very keynote of one of his most devastating criticisms of society, the presentation of the forlorn, harried crossings-sweeper Jo in *Bleak House*.

*

The Christmas Books, then, have great interest for us from the point of view of Dickens's development both as literary artist and as social critic. But at least four of them, as I have tried to show, have sufficient literary merit to be worth reading for their own sake. The traditional judgement, which hails the *Carol* as a masterpiece of 'pop art' and dismisses all its successors as mercenary hack-work, has long been due for revision. Nor, finally, should we forget the very important part played by these books in strengthening and maintaining the unique relationship established between Dickens and his public, a relationship 'personally affectionate and like no other man's', as Dickens put it. Commenting on the 'extraordinary popularity, and nearly universal acceptance, which attended these little holiday volumes', Forster remarks:

> They carried to countless firesides, with new enjoyment of the season, better apprehension of its claims and obligations; they mingled grave with glad thoughts, much to the advantage of both; what seemed almost too remote to meddle with they brought within reach of the charities, and what was near they touched with a dearer tenderness; they comforted the generous, rebuked the sordid, cured folly by kindly ridicule and comic humour, and, saying to their readers, *Thus you have done, but it were better Thus*, may for some have realized the philosopher's famous experience, and by a single fortunate thought revised the whole manner of a life.

SELECT BIBLIOGRAPHY

Forster, John, *The Life of Charles Dickens*, ed. J. W. T. Ley, 1928.

Dexter, Walter (ed.), *The Letters of Charles Dickens*, Nonesuch Press, 1938.

Fielding, K. J. (ed.), *The Speeches of Charles Dickens*, OUP, 1960.

Butt, John, 'Dickens's Christmas Books', *Pope, Dickens and Others*, Edinburgh University Press, 1969.

Collins, Philip, ' "*Carol* Philosophy, Cheerful Views" ', *Études Anglaises*, vol. 23, 1970.

Hardy, Barbara, *The Moral Art of Dickens*, The Athlone Press, 1970 (see particularly Section One, Chapter Two).

Slater, Michael, 'Dickens (and Forster) at Work on *The Chimes*', *Dickens Studies*, vol 2, 1966.

Slater, Michael, 'Carlyle and Jerrold into Dickens: A study of *The Chimes*', *Nineteenth Century Fiction*, vol. 24, 1970.

Slater, Michael, 'Dickens's Tract for *The Times*', *Dickens 1970* (ed. Slater), Chapman and Hall, 1970.

Stone, Harry, 'Dickens' Artistry in *The Haunted Man*', *South Atlantic Quarterly*, vol. 61, 1962.

Stone, Harry, 'The Love Pattern in Dickens' Novels', *Dickens the Craftsman* (ed. Partlow), Southern Illinois University Press, 1970 (discussion of *The Haunted Man*).

Tillotson, Kathleen, 'The Middle Years: From the *Carol* to *Copperfield*', *Dickens Memorial Lectures*, published by the Dickens Fellowship, 1970.

Wagenknecht, Edward, '*The Chimes*', *Dickens and the Scandalmongers*, University of Oklahoma Press, 1965.

*

A facsimile of the manuscript of *A Christmas Carol* with a preface by Frederick B. Adams, Jr, was published by the Folio Press, 1970. A brilliant parody of the Dickens Christmas Book genre will be found in Bret Harte's *Condensed Novels*.

A NOTE ON THE TEXT AND ANNOTATION

THE texts of the Christmas Books printed here are those of the first editions. A few printer's errors have been silently corrected and certain Dickensian peculiarities of spelling, e.g. 'recal', 'pannel', have also been emended. Spellings common in the 1840s, e.g. 'honor', and such forms as 'up stairs' (for 'up-stairs') and 'a going' (for 'a-going'), which appear consistently throughout the original texts have been retained; where, however, the original texts exhibit such spellings and forms only occasionally and elsewhere follow modern usage, the latter has been adopted throughout in this edition.

During the early 1840s Dickens was experimenting with a 'rhetorical' style of punctuation, based on speech-rhythms rather than on grammatical sense. This involved especially the lavish use of dashes, colons and semi-colons. It appears in the first three Christmas Books and was also introduced in the revised version of *Oliver Twist* published in 1846 (see Kathleen Tillotson's introduction to the 1965 Clarendon Edition of that novel, p. 31). In *The Battle of Life* and *The Haunted Man* this style of punctuation was considerably toned down – greatly to the approval of at least one contemporary reviewer.[1] The present edition, which seeks to convey as fully as possible the distinctive flavour of these little stories as they were first published, reproduces the punctuation used in the original printing of each Book.

The manuscript of *The Chimes* is in the Forster Collection at the Victoria and Albert Museum and that of *The Haunted Man* in the Pforzheimer Foundation, New York; the manuscripts of the other Books are all in the Pierpont Morgan

1. See the *Morning Advertiser* review of *The Battle of Life*, 21 December 1846.

Collection, New York. The passages satirizing 'Young England' in the manuscript of *The Chimes* which were cancelled before publication are reproduced in Appendix A by courtesy of the Victoria and Albert Museum; in the text printed here asterisks indicate the points at which these passages were intended to appear.

The Christmas Books were gathered into one volume in 1852 as part of the Cheap edition of Dickens's collected works, and again in 1859 for the Library edition, and finally in 1868 for the Charles Dickens edition. In 1852 and 1858 a few very slight and unimportant alterations were made to the text but the punctuation of the three earlier Books was systematically normalized. For the Charles Dickens edition Dickens also composed a series of descriptive headlines (listed in Appendix B) for the right-hand pages of each book.

T. W. Hill, Hon. Secretary of the Dickens Fellowship 1914–19 and Hon. Treasurer 1932–47, compiled an excellent set of detailed annotations of Dickens's major works, most of which were published in the *Dickensian* between 1948 and 1960. His notes on the Christmas Books were not published, however, but the manuscript was left to the *Dickensian*. I have drawn on this manuscript in my own annotation for this edition and the letter H in brackets following a note indicates where I am indebted to Hill's work for some or all of the information supplied.

M.S.

DICKENS'S GENERAL PREFACES
TO THE CHRISTMAS BOOKS

PREFACE TO THE FIRST CHEAP EDITION

I HAVE included my little Christmas Books in this cheap edition, complying with a desire that has been repeatedly expressed to me, and hoping that they may prove generally acceptable in so accessible a form.

The narrow space within which it was necessary to confine these Christmas Stories when they were originally published, rendered their construction a matter of some difficulty, and almost necessitated what is peculiar in their machinery. I never attempted great elaboration of detail in the working out of character within such limits, believing that it could not succeed. My purpose was, in a whimsical kind of masque which the good humour of the season justified, to awaken some loving and forbearing thoughts, never out of season in a Christian land. I have the happiness of believing that I did not wholly miss it.
London,
September, 1852.

PREFACE TO THE 'CHARLES DICKENS' EDITION

THE narrow space within which it was necessary to confine these Christmas Stories when they were originally published, rendered their construction a matter of some difficulty, and almost necessitated what is peculiar in their machinery. I could not attempt great elaboration of detail, in the working out of character within such limits. My chief purpose was, in a whimsical kind of masque which the good humour of the season justified, to awaken some loving and forbearing thoughts, never out of season in a Christian land.

A CHRISTMAS CAROL

INTRODUCTION TO
A CHRISTMAS CAROL

ON 5 October 1843 Dickens, at thirty-one the most successful and the best-loved novelist of the day, presided at the
first annual soirée of the Manchester Athenæum, an institution intended to bring the means of culture and 'blameless,
rational enjoyment' within reach of the labouring classes. In
his speech he dwelt on the necessity of educating the very
poor. He deplored the mischievous effects of the old saw, 'A
little learning is a dangerous thing', the smallest degree of
education being infinitely preferable to none at all. Describing the sights he had seen in London jails and doss-houses,
he spoke of 'thousands of immortal creatures condemned,
without alternative or choice, to tread, not what our great
poet calls "the primrose path to the everlasting bonfire",
but one of jagged flints and stones, laid down by brutal
ignorance . . .' This whole subject was much in his mind at
this time; the previous month he had visited Samuel Starey's
newly founded Field Lane Ragged School, which was
striving to give some basic education to the local street
urchins, and had sent a 'sledge-hammer account' of it to
Miss Burdett-Coutts, the millionaire philanthropist, to whom
he acted as a sort of unofficial almoner. He offered also to
write an account of the school for the *Edinburgh Review*.
Earlier still during the year, he had been horrified by a
parliamentary blue-book, the Second Report (Trades and
Manufactures) of the Children's Employment Commission
(the document which moved Elizabeth Barrett to write her
famous poem, 'The Cry of the Children'), and had thought
of bringing out 'a very cheap pamphlet called An Appeal
to the People of England on behalf of the Poor Man's
Child'. Now, in Manchester, he was suddenly inspired with
the idea of writing a Christmas story the effect of which, in

33

bringing home to the better-off the plight of the poor, especially the children, would be a thousand times more powerful than any pamphlet. As John Butt has pointed out,[1] he had a ready model for the form such a story might take, in something he had written seven years before: the ninth monthly number of *Pickwick Papers*, published in December 1836, had contained the story of the morose and misanthropic sexton, Gabriel Grub, who was carried off by goblins one Christmas Eve and shown a series of visions which converted him to benevolence and good works.

Returning to London, Dickens fell to work on the story, tooth and nail, in such 'odd moments of leisure' as he could spare from writing the eleventh monthly instalment of *Martin Chuzzlewit*. He wrote to his American friend, Cornelius Felton:

Charles Dickens wept and laughed and wept again, and excited himself in a most extraordinary manner in the composition; and thinking whereof he walked about the black streets of London, fifteen and twenty miles many a night when all the sober folks had gone to bed . . .

By the end of November it was finished and Chapman and Hall published it in a crimson-and-gold binding with four hand-coloured illustrations by the *Punch* artist John Leech, on 17 December, at the somewhat uneconomical price of five shillings. Dickens himself then threw himself into the Christmas festivities like his own converted Scrooge – 'Such dinings, such dancings, such conjurings, such blindman's-buffings, such theatre-goings, such kissings-out of old years and kissing-in of new ones', he wrote merrily to Felton,

never took places in these parts before . . . I broke out like a madman. And if you could have seen me at a children's party at Macready's the other night, going down a country dance with Mrs M., you would have thought I was a country gentleman of independent property, residing on a tiptop farm, with the wind blowing straight in my face every day . . .

1. John Butt, *Pope, Dickens and Others*, 1969, p. 134.

The *Carol*'s appearance was greeted with almost universal delight: 'a most prodigious success – the greatest, I think, I have ever achieved', Dickens called it. By 24 December Chapman and Hall were able to tell him 'that the *Carol* was then in its Sixth Thousand; and that as the orders were coming in fast from town and country, it would soon be necessary to reprint'. Reviewers vied with one another in eulogy, praising above all the little book's humanity and 'beneficial tendency'. The reviewer of the Tory weekly the *Britannia* compared Dickens on 23 December to Dr Johnson in his 'sympathy for human suffering ... not for imaginary and fictitious distresses but for the real grinding sorrows of life'. The *Sunday Times* (7 January 1844) even ventured on the word 'sublime' and other reviewers did not hesitate to invoke the name of Dante in their enthusiasm. Lord Jeffrey, who found Tiny Tim a worthy successor to his adored Little Nell wrote to Dickens:

Blessings on your kind heart ... you may be sure you have done more good by this little publication, fostered more kindly feelings, and prompted more positive acts of beneficence, than can be traced to all the pulpits and confessionals in Christendom since Christmas 1842.

The *Athenæum*, in its review (23 December), spoke of this 'jovial genial piece of Christmas fare' as though it were something good to eat and the succulent descriptions of feastings in Scrooge's visions 'so worked on Carlyle's nervous organization', wrote Mrs Carlyle to Jeannie Welsh on 23 December[2] 'that he has been seized with a perfect *convulsion* of hospitality, and has actually insisted on *improvising two* dinner-parties with only a day between'. Finally, when the little book's fame had 'so spread over England ... that ... not even the godlike and ancient Quarterly itself ... could review it down', Thackeray nobly summed up, in *Fraser's Magazine*, February 1844, by

2. *Jane Welsh Carlyle: Letters to her Family 1839–1863*, ed. Huxley, 1924, p. 169.

declaring that the *Carol* seemed to him 'a national benefit and to every man and woman who reads it a personal kindness'.

It is sad to have to add that, despite this runaway success, the unexpectedly modest profit that he made on the *Carol* proved to be the breaking-point in Dickens's already strained relations with Chapman and Hall, who thereafter ceased to be his publishers for fifteen years: 'I have not the least doubt,' he wrote to his solicitor, 'that they run the expenses up anyhow purposely to bring me back and disgust me with the charges.' But Forster justly points out 'the truth really was, as to all the Christmas stories issued in this form, that the price charged, while too large for the public addressed by them, was too little to remunerate their outlay'. Unsatisfactory legal entanglements following a blatant piracy of the book in a publication called *Parley's Illuminated Library* on 6 January added further to Dickens's *Carol* harassments. But not even all this could really sour a triumph the nature of which was so dear to his heart: 'There poured upon [him] daily,' wrote Forster,

all through that Christmas time, letters from complete strangers to him which I remember reading with a wonder of pleasure; not literary at all, but of the simplest domestic kind; of which the general burden was to tell him, amid many confidences, about their homes, how the *Carol* had come to be read aloud there and was to be kept upon a little shelf by itself, and was to do them no end of good.

Opposite: Black and White facsimile title page from first edition of
A Christmas Carol

A CHRISTMAS CAROL.

IN PROSE.

BEING

A Ghost Story of Christmas.

BY

CHARLES DICKENS.

WITH ILLUSTRATIONS BY JOHN LEECH.

LONDON
CHAPMAN & HALL, 186, STRAND.

PREFACE

I HAVE endeavoured in this Ghostly little book, to raise the Ghost of an Idea, which shall not put my readers out of humour with themselves, with each other, with the season, or with me. May it haunt their house pleasantly, and no one wish to lay it.

Their faithful Friend and Servant,

C. D.

December 1843.

CONTENTS

STAVE ONE
MARLEY'S GHOST

MARLEY was dead: to begin with. There is no doubt whatever about that. The register of his burial was signed by the clergyman, the clerk, the undertaker, and the chief mourner. Scrooge signed it: and Scrooge's name was good upon 'Change, for anything he chose to put his hand to. Old Marley was as dead as a door-nail.

Mind! I don't mean to say that I know, of my own knowledge, what there is particularly dead about a door-nail. I might have been inclined, myself, to regard a coffin-nail as the deadest piece of ironmongery in the trade. But the wisdom of our ancestors is in the simile; and my unhallowed hands shall not disturb it, or the Country's done for. You will therefore permit me to repeat, emphatically, that Marley was as dead as a door-nail.

Scrooge knew he was dead? Of course he did. How could it be otherwise? Scrooge and he were partners for I don't know how many years. Scrooge was his sole executor, his sole administrator, his sole assign, his sole residuary legatee, his sole friend and sole mourner. And even Scrooge was not so dreadfully cut up by the sad event, but that he was an excellent man of business on the very day of the funeral, and solemnised it with an undoubted bargain.

The mention of Marley's funeral brings me back to the point I started from. There is no doubt that Marley was dead. This must be distinctly understood, or nothing wonderful can come of the story I am going to relate. If we were not perfectly convinced that Hamlet's Father died before the play began, there would be nothing more remarkable in his taking a stroll at night, in an easterly wind, upon his own ramparts, than there would be in any other middle-aged gentleman rashly turning out after dark in a breezy spot—

say Saint Paul's Churchyard for instance—literally to aston-
ish his son's weak mind.[1]

Scrooge never painted out Old Marley's name. There it
stood, years afterwards, above the warehouse door: Scrooge
and Marley. The firm was known as Scrooge and Marley.
Sometimes people new to the business called Scrooge
Scrooge, and sometimes Marley, but he answered to both
names: it was all the same to him.

Oh! but he was a tight-fisted hand at the grindstone,
Scrooge! a squeezing, wrenching, grasping, scraping, clutching, covetous old sinner! Hard and sharp as flint, from which
no steel had ever struck out generous fire; secret, and self-
contained, and solitary as an oyster. The cold within him
froze his old features, nipped his pointed nose, shrivelled
his cheek, stiffened his gait; made his eyes red, his thin lips
blue; and spoke out shrewdly in his grating voice. A frosty
rime was on his head, and on his eyebrows, and his wiry
chin. He carried his own low temperature always about with
him; he iced his office in the dog-days; and didn't thaw it one
degree at Christmas.

External heat and cold had little influence on Scrooge.
No warmth could warm, nor wintry weather chill him. No
wind that blew was bitterer than he, no falling snow was
more intent upon its purpose, no pelting rain less open to
entreaty. Foul weather didn't know where to have him.
The heaviest rain, and snow, and hail, and sleet, could
boast of the advantage over him in only one respect.
They often "came down" handsomely, and Scrooge never
did.[2]

Nobody ever stopped him in the street to say, with glad-
some looks, "My dear Scrooge, how are you? when will you
come to see me?" No beggars implored him to bestow a
trifle, no children asked him what it was o'clock, no man or
woman ever once in all his life inquired the way to such and
such a place, of Scrooge. Even the blindmen's dogs appeared
to know him; and when they saw him coming on, would tug
their owners into doorways and up courts; and then would

wag their tails as though they said, "no eye at all is better than an evil eye, dark master!"

But what did Scrooge care? It was the very thing he liked. To edge his way along the crowded paths of life, warning all human sympathy to keep its distance, was what the knowing ones call "nuts" to Scrooge.[3]

Once upon a time—of all the good days in the year, on Christmas Eve—old Scrooge sat busy in his counting-house. It was cold, bleak, biting weather: foggy withal: and he could hear the people in the court outside, go wheezing up and down, beating their hands upon their breasts, and stamping their feet upon the pavement-stones to warm them. The city clocks had only just gone three, but it was quite dark already: it had not been light all day: and candles were flaring in the windows of the neighbouring offices, like ruddy smears upon the palpable brown air. The fog came pouring in at every chink and keyhole, and was so dense without, that although the court was of the narrowest, the houses opposite were mere phantoms. To see the dingy cloud come drooping down, obscuring everything, one might have thought that Nature lived hard by, and was brewing on a large scale.

The door of Scrooge's counting-house was open that he might keep his eye upon his clerk, who in a dismal little cell beyond, a sort of tank, was copying letters. Scrooge had a very small fire, but the clerk's fire was so very much smaller that it looked like one coal. But he couldn't replenish it, for Scrooge kept the coal-box in his own room; and so surely as the clerk came in with the shovel, the master predicted that it would be necessary for them to part. Wherefore the clerk put on his white comforter, and tried to warm himself at the candle; in which effort, not being a man of a strong imagination, he failed.

"A merry Christmas, uncle! God save you!" cried a cheerful voice. It was the voice of Scrooge's nephew, who came upon him so quickly that this was the first intimation he had of his approach.

"Bah!" said Scrooge, "Humbug!"

He had so heated himself with rapid walking in the fog and frost, this nephew of Scrooge's, that he was all in a glow; his face was ruddy and handsome; his eyes sparkled, and his breath smoked again.

"Christmas a humbug, uncle!" said Scrooge's nephew. "You don't mean that, I am sure?"

"I do," said Scrooge. "Merry Christmas! What right have you to be merry? what reason have you to be merry? You're poor enough."

"Come, then,' returned the nephew gaily. "What right have you to be dismal? what reason have you to be morose? You're rich enough.'

Scrooge having no better answer ready on the spur of the moment, said, "Bah!" again; and followed it up with "Humbug."

"Don't be cross, uncle," said the nephew.

"What else can I be" returned the uncle, "when I live in such a world of fools as this? Merry Christmas! Out upon merry Christmas! What's Christmas time to you but a time for paying bills without money; a time for finding yourself a year older, and not an hour richer; a time for balancing your books and having every item in 'em through a round dozen of months presented dead against you? If I could work my will," said Scrooge, indignantly, "every idiot who goes about with 'Merry Christmas,' on his lips, should be boiled with his own pudding, and buried with a stake of holly through his heart. He should!"

"Uncle!" pleaded the nephew.

"Nephew!" returned the uncle, sternly, "keep Christmas in your own way, and let me keep it in mine.'

"Keep it!" repeated Scrooge's nephew. "But you don't keep it."

"Let me leave it alone, then,' said Scrooge. "Much good may it do you! Much good it has ever done you!"

"There are many things from which I might have derived good, by which I have not profited, I dare say," returned the nephew: "Christmas among the rest. But I am sure I have always thought of Christmas time, when it has come round—apart from the veneration due to its sacred name and origin, if anything belonging to it can be apart from that —as a good time: a kind, forgiving, charitable, pleasant time: the only time I know of, in the long calendar of the year, when men and women seem by one consent to open their shut-up hearts freely, and to think of people below them as if they really were fellow-passengers to the grave, and not another race of creatures bound on other journeys. And therefore, uncle, though it has never put a scrap of gold or silver in my pocket, I believe that it *has* done me good, and *will* do me good; and I say, God bless it!"

The clerk in the tank involuntarily applauded: becoming immediately sensible of the impropriety, he poked the fire, and extinguished the last frail spark for ever.

"Let me hear another sound from *you*" said Scrooge, "and you'll keep your Christmas by losing your situation. You're quite a powerful speaker, sir," he added, turning to his nephew. "I wonder you don't go into Parliament."

"Don't be angry, uncle. Come! Dine with us to-morrow."

Scrooge said that he would see him—yes, indeed he did. He went the whole length of the expression, and said that he would see him in that extremity first.

"But why?" cried Scrooge's nephew. "Why?"

"Why did you get married?" said Scrooge.

"Because I fell in love."

"Because you fell in love!" growled Scrooge, as if that were the only one thing in the world more ridiculous than a merry Christmas. "Good afternoon!"

"Nay, uncle, but you never came to see me before that happened. Why give it as a reason for not coming now?"

"Good afternoon," said Scrooge.

"I want nothing from you; I ask nothing of you; why cannot we be friends?"

"Good afternoon," said Scrooge.

"I am sorry, with all my heart, to find you so resolute.

We have never had any quarrel, to which I have been a party. But I have made the trial in homage to Christmas, and I'll keep my Christmas humour to the last. So A Merry Christmas, uncle!"

"Good afternoon!" said Scrooge.

"And A Happy New Year!"

"Good afternoon!" said Scrooge.

His nephew left the room without an angry word, notwithstanding. He stopped at the outer door to bestow the greetings of the season on the clerk, who, cold as he was, was warmer than Scrooge; for he returned them cordially.

"There's another fellow," muttered Scrooge; who overheard him: "my clerk, with fifteen shillings a-week, and a wife and family, talking about a merry Christmas. I'll retire to Bedlam."

This lunatic, in letting Scrooge's nephew out, had let two other people in. They were portly gentlemen, pleasant to behold, and now stood, with their hats off, in Scrooge's office. They had books and papers in their hands, and bowed to him.

"Scrooge and Marley's, I believe,' said one of the gentlemen, referring to his list. "Have I the pleasure of addressing Mr. Scrooge, or Mr. Marley?"

"Mr. Marley has been dead these seven years," Scrooge replied. "He died seven years ago, this very night."

"We have no doubt his liberality is well represented by his surviving partner," said the gentleman, presenting his credentials.

It certainly was; for they had been two kindred spirits. At the ominous word "liberality," Scrooge frowned, and shook his head, and handed the credentials back.

"At this festive season of the year, Mr. Scrooge," said the gentleman, taking up a pen, "it is more than usually desirable that we should make some slight provision for the poor and destitute, who suffer greatly at the present time. Many thousands are in want of common necessaries; hundreds of thousands are in want of common comforts, sir."

"Are there no prisons?" asked Scrooge.

"Plenty of prisons," said the gentleman, laying down the pen again.

"And the Union workhouses⁴?" demanded Scrooge. "Are they still in operation?"

"They are. Still," returned the gentleman, "I wish I could say they were not."

"The Treadmill and the Poor Law are in full vigour, then?" said Scrooge.

"Both very busy, sir."

"Oh! I was afraid, from what you said at first, that something had occurred to stop them in their useful course," said Scrooge. "I'm very glad to hear it."

"Under the impression that they scarcely furnish Christian cheer of mind or body to the multitude," returned the gentleman, "a few of us are endeavouring to raise a fund to buy the Poor some meat and drink, and means of warmth. We choose this time because it is a time, of all others, when Want is keenly felt, and Abundance rejoices. What shall I put you down for?"

"Nothing!" Scrooge replied.

"You wish to be anonymous?"

"I wish to be left alone," said Scrooge. "Since you ask me what I wish, gentlemen, that is my answer. I don't make merry myself at Christmas, and I can't afford to make idle people merry. I help to support the establishments I have mentioned: they cost enough: and those who are badly off must go there."

"Many can't go there; and many would rather die."

"If they would rather die," said Scrooge, "they had better do it, and decrease the surplus population.⁵ Besides—excuse me—I don't know that."

"But you might know it," observed the gentleman.

"It's not my business," Scrooge returned. "It's enough for a man to understand his own business, and not to interfere with other people's. Mine occupies me constantly. Good afternoon, gentlemen!"

Seeing clearly that it would be useless to pursue their point, the gentlemen withdrew. Scrooge resumed his labours with an improved opinion of himself, and in a more facetious temper than was usual with him.

Meanwhile the fog and darkness thickened so, that people ran about with flaring links, proffering their services to go before horses in carriages, and conduct them on their way. The ancient tower of a church, whose gruff old bell was always peeping slily down at Scrooge out of a gothic window in the wall, became invisible, and struck the hours and quarters in the clouds, with tremulous vibrations afterwards, as if its teeth were chattering in its frozen head up there. The cold became intense. In the main street, at the corner of the court, some labourers were repairing the gas-pipes, and had lighted a great fire in a brazier, round which a party of ragged men and boys were gathered: warming their hands and winking their eyes before the blaze in rapture. The water-plug being left in solitude, its overflowings sullenly congealed, and turned to misanthropic ice. The brightness of the shops where holly sprigs and berries crackled in the lamp-heat of the windows, made pale faces ruddy as they passed. Poulterers' and grocers' trades became a splendid joke: a glorious pageant, with which it was next to impossible to believe that such dull principles as bargain and sale had anything to do. The Lord Mayor, in the stronghold of the mighty Mansion House, gave orders to his fifty cooks and butlers to keep Christmas as a Lord Mayor's household should; and even the little tailor, whom he had fined five shillings on the previous Monday for being drunk and blood-thirsty in the streets, stirred up to-morrow's pudding in his garret, while his lean wife and the baby sallied out to buy the beef.

Foggier yet, and colder! Piercing, searching, biting cold. If the good Saint Dunstan had but nipped the Evil Spirit's nose with a touch of such weather as that, instead of using his familiar weapons, then indeed he would have roared to lusty purpose[6]. The owner of one scant young nose, gnawed and mumbled by the hungry cold as bones are gnawed by dogs, stooped down at Scrooge's keyhole to regale him with a Christmas carol: but at the first sound of—

"God bless you merry gentleman!
May nothing you dismay!"

Scrooge seized the ruler with such energy of action, that the singer fled in terror, leaving the keyhole to the fog and even more congenial frost.

At length the hour of shutting up the counting-house arrived. With an ill-will Scrooge dismounted from his stool, and tacitly admitted the fact to the expectant clerk in the Tank, who instantly snuffed his candle out, and put on his hat.

"You'll want all day to-morrow, I suppose?" said Scrooge.

"If quite convenient, sir."

"It's not convenient," said Scrooge, "and it's not fair. If I was to stop half-a-crown for it, you'd think yourself ill used, I'll be bound?"

The clerk smiled faintly.

"And yet," said Scrooge, "you don't think *me* ill used, when I pay a day's wages for no work."

The clerk observed that it was only once a year.

"A poor excuse for picking a man's pocket every twenty-fifth of December!" said Scrooge, buttoning his great-coat to the chin. "But I suppose you must have the whole day. Be here all the earlier next morning!"[7]

The clerk promised that he would; and Scrooge walked out with a growl. The office was closed in a twinkling, and the clerk, with the long ends of his white comforter dangling below his waist (for he boasted no great-coat), went down a slide on Cornhill, at the end of a lane of boys, twenty times, in honour of its being Christmas-eve, and then ran home to Camden Town as hard as he could pelt, to play at blindman's-buff.

Scrooge took his melancholy dinner in his usual melancholy tavern; and having read all the newspapers, and beguiled the rest of the evening with his banker's-book, went home to bed. He lived in chambers which had once belonged to his deceased partner. They were a gloomy suite of rooms, in a lowering pile of building up a yard, where it had so little business to be, that one could scarcely help fancying it must have run there when it was a young house, playing at hide-and-seek with other houses, and have forgotten the way out again. It was old enough now, and dreary enough, for nobody lived in it but Scrooge, the other rooms being all let out as offices. The yard was so dark that even Scrooge, who knew its every stone, was fain to grope with his hands. The fog and frost so hung about the black old gateway of the house, that it seemed as if the Genius of the Weather sat in mournful meditation on the threshold.

Now, it is a fact, that there was nothing at all particular about the knocker on the door, except that it was very large. It is also a fact, that Scrooge had seen it night and morning during his whole residence in that place; also that Scrooge had as little of what is called fancy about him as any man in the City of London, even including—which is a bold word—the corporation, aldermen, and livery. Let it also be borne in mind that Scrooge had not bestowed one thought on Marley, since his last mention of his seven-years' dead partner that afternoon. And then let any man explain to me, if he can, how it happened that Scrooge, having his key in the lock of the door, saw in the knocker, without its undergoing any intermediate process of change: not a knocker, but Marley's face.

Marley's face. It was not in impenetrable shadow as the other objects in the yard were, but had a dismal light about it, like a bad lobster in a dark cellar. It was not angry or ferocious, but looked at Scrooge as Marley used to look: with ghostly spectacles turned up upon its ghostly forehead. The hair was curiously stirred, as if by breath or hot-air; and though the eyes were wide open, they were perfectly motion-less. That, and its livid colour, made it horrible; but its horror seemed to be, in spite of the face and beyond its control, rather than a part of its own expression.

As Scrooge looked fixedly at this phenomenon, it was a knocker again.

To say that he was not startled, or that his blood was not conscious of a terrible sensation to which it had been a stranger from infancy, would be untrue. But he put his hand upon the key he had relinquished, turned it sturdily, walked in, and lighted his candle.

He *did* pause, with a moment's irresolution, before he shut the door; and he *did* look cautiously behind it first, as if he half-expected to be terrified with the sight of Marley's pigtail sticking out into the hall. But there was nothing on the back of the door, except the screws and nuts that held the knocker on; so he said "Pooh, pooh!" and closed it with a bang.

The sound resounded through the house like thunder. Every room above, and every cask in the wine-merchant's cellars below, appeared to have a separate peal of echoes of its own. Scrooge was not a man to be frightened by echoes. He fastened the door, and walked across the hall, and up the stairs: slowly too: trimming his candle as he went.

You may talk vaguely about driving a coach-and-six up a good old flight of stairs, or through a bad young Act of Parliament; but I mean to say you might have got a hearse up that staircase, and taken it broadwise, with the splinter-bar towards the wall, and the door towards the balustrades: and done it easy. There was plenty of width for that, and room to spare; which is perhaps the reason why Scrooge thought he saw a locomotive hearse going on before him in the gloom. Half a dozen gas-lamps out of the street wouldn't have lighted the entry too well, so you may suppose that it was pretty dark with Scrooge's dip.[8]

Up Scrooge went, not caring a button for that: darkness is cheap, and Scrooge liked it. But before he shut his heavy door, he walked through his rooms to see that all was right.

He had just enough recollection of the face to desire to do that.

Sitting room, bed-room, lumber-room. All as they should be. Nobody under the table, nobody under the sofa; a small fire in the grate; spoon and basin ready; and the little sauce-pan of gruel (Scrooge had a cold in his head) upon the hob. Nobody under the bed; nobody in the closet; nobody in his dressing-gown, which was hanging up in a suspicious atti-tude against the wall. Lumber-room as usual. Old fire-guard, old shoes, two fish-baskets, washing-stand on three legs, and a poker.

Quite satisfied, he closed his door, and locked himself in; double-locked himself in, which was not his custom. Thus secured against surprise, he took off his cravat; put on his dressing-gown and slippers, and his night-cap; and sat down before the fire to take his gruel.

It was a very low fire indeed; nothing on such a bitter night. He was obliged to sit close to it, and brood over it, before he could extract the least sensation of warmth from such a handful of fuel. The fireplace was an old one, built by some Dutch merchant long ago, and paved all round with quaint Dutch tiles, designed to illustrate the Scriptures. There were Cains and Abels; Pharaoh's daughters, Queens of Sheba, Angelic messengers descending through the air on clouds like feather-beds, Abrahams, Belshazzars, Apostles putting off to sea in butter-boats, hundreds of figures to attract his thoughts; and yet that face of Marley, seven years dead, came like the ancient Prophet's rod[9], and swallowed up the whole. If each smooth tile had been a blank at first, with power to shape some picture on its surface from the disjointed fragments of his thoughts, there would have been a copy of old Marley's head on every one.

"Humbug!" said Scrooge; and walked across the room.

After several turns, he sat down again. As he threw his head back in the chair, his glance happened to rest upon a bell, a disused bell, that hung in the room, and communicated for some purpose now forgotten with a chamber in the highest story of the building. It was with great astonishment, and with a strange, inexplicable dread, that as he looked, he saw this bell begin to swing. It swung so softly in the outset that it scarcely made a sound; but soon it rang out loudly, and so did every bell in the house.

This might have lasted half a minute, or a minute, but it seemed an hour. The bells ceased as they had begun, together. They were succeeded by a clanking noise, deep down below; as if some person were dragging a heavy chain over the casks in the wine-merchant's cellar. Scrooge then remembered to have heard that ghosts in haunted houses were described as dragging chains.

The cellar-door flew open with a booming sound, and then he heard the noise much louder, on the floors below; then coming up the stairs; then coming straight towards his door.

"It's humbug still!" said Scrooge. "I won't believe it."

His colour changed though, when, without a pause, it came on through the heavy door, and passed into the room before his eyes. Upon its coming in, the dying flame leaped up, as though it cried "I know him! Marley's Ghost!" and fell again.

The same face: the very same. Marley in his pig-tail, usual waistcoat, tights, and boots; the tassels on the latter bristling, like his pigtail, and his coat-skirts, and the hair upon his head. The chain he drew was clasped about his middle. It was long, and wound about him like a tail; and it was made (for Scrooge observed it closely) of cash-boxes, keys, padlocks, ledgers, deeds, and heavy purses wrought in steel. His body was transparent: so that Scrooge, observing him, and looking through his waistcoat, could see the two buttons on his coat behind.

Scrooge had often heard it said that Marley had no bowels, but he had never believed it until now.

No, nor did he believe it even now. Though he looked the phantom through and through, and saw it standing before him; though he felt the chilling influence of its death-cold

John Leech

eyes; and marked the very texture of the folded kerchief bound about its head and chin, which wrapper he had not observed before: he was still incredulous, and fought against his senses.

"How now!" said Scrooge, caustic and cold as ever. "What do you want with me?"

"Much!"—Marley's voice, no doubt about it.

"Who are you?'

"Ask me who I *was*."

"Who *were* you then?" said Scrooge, raising his voice. "You're particular—for a shade." He was going to say "*to* a shade," but substituted this, as more appropriate.

"In life I was your partner, Jacob Marley."

"Can you—can you sit down?" asked Scrooge, looking doubtfully at him.

"I can."

"Do it then."

Scrooge asked the question, because he didn't know whether a ghost so transparent might find himself in a condition to take a chair; and felt that in the event of its being impossible, it might involve the necessity of an embarrassing explanation. But the ghost sat down on the opposite side of the fireplace, as if he were quite used to it.

"You don't believe in me," observed the Ghost.

"I don't," said Scrooge.

"What evidence would you have of my reality, beyond that of your senses?"

"I don't know," said Scrooge.

"Why do you doubt your senses?"

"Because," said Scrooge, "a little thing affects them. A slight disorder of the stomach makes them cheats. You may be an undigested bit of beef, a blot of mustard, a crumb of cheese, a fragment of an underdone potato. There's more of gravy than of grave about you, whatever you are!"

Scrooge was not much in the habit of cracking jokes, nor did he feel, in his heart, by any means waggish then. The truth is, that he tried to be smart, as a means of distracting his own attention, and keeping down his terror; for the spectre's voice disturbed the very marrow in his bones.

To sit, staring at those fixed, glazed eyes, in silence for a moment, would play, Scrooge felt, the very deuce with him. There was something very awful, too, in the spectre's being provided with an infernal atmosphere of its own. Scrooge could not feel it himself, but this was clearly the case; for though the Ghost sat perfectly motionless, its hair, and skirts, and tassels, were still agitated as by the hot vapour from an oven.

"You see this toothpick?" said Scrooge, returning quickly to the charge, for the reason just assigned; and wishing, though it were only for a second, to divert the vision's stony gaze from himself.

"I do," replied the Ghost.

"You are not looking at it," said Scrooge.

"But I see it," said the Ghost, "notwithstanding."

"Well!" returned Scrooge. "I have but to swallow this, and be for the rest of my days persecuted by a legion of goblins, all of my own creation. Humbug, I tell you— humbug!"

At this, the spirit raised a frightful cry, and shook its chain with such a dismal and appalling noise, that Scrooge held on tight to his chair, to save himself from falling in a swoon. But how much greater was his horror, when the phantom taking off the bandage round its head, as if it were too warm to wear in-doors, its lower jaw dropped down upon its breast!

Scrooge fell upon his knees, and clasped his hands before his face.

"Mercy!" he said. "Dreadful apparition, why do you trouble me?"

"Man of the worldly mind!" replied the Ghost, "do you believe in me or not?"

"I do," said Scrooge. "I must. But why do spirits walk the earth, and why do they come to me?"

"It is required of every man," the Ghost returned, "that

the spirit within him should walk abroad among his fellow-men, and travel far and wide; and if that spirit goes not forth in life, it is condemned to do so after death. It is doomed to wander through the world—oh, woe is me!—and witness what it cannot share, but might have shared on earth, and turned to happiness!"

Again the spectre raised a cry, and shook its chain and wrung its shadowy hands.

"You are fettered," said Scrooge, trembling. "Tell me why?"

"I wear the chain I forged in life," replied the Ghost. "I made it link by link, and yard by yard; I girded it on of my own free will, and of my own free will I wore it. Is its pattern strange to *you*?"

Scrooge trembled more and more.

"Or would you know," pursued the Ghost, "the weight and length of the strong coil you bear yourself? It was full as heavy and as long as this, seven Christmas Eves ago. You have laboured on it, since. It is a ponderous chain!"

Scrooge glanced about him on the floor, in the expectation of finding himself surrounded by some fifty or sixty fathoms of iron cable: but he could see nothing.

"Jacob," he said, imploringly. "Old Jacob Marley, tell me more. Speak comfort to me, Jacob."

"I have none to give," the Ghost replied. "It comes from other regions, Ebenezer Scrooge, and is conveyed by other ministers, to other kinds of men. Nor can I tell you what I would. A very little more is all permitted to me. I cannot rest, I cannot stay, I cannot linger anywhere. My spirit never walked beyond our counting-house—mark me!—in life my spirit never roved beyond the narrow limits of our money-changing hole; and weary journeys lie before me!"

It was a habit with Scrooge, whenever he became thoughtful, to put his hands in his breeches pockets. Pondering on what the Ghost had said, he did so now, but without lifting up his eyes, or getting off his knees.

"You must have been very slow about it, Jacob," Scrooge

observed, in a business-like manner, though with humility and deference.

"Slow!" the Ghost repeated.

"Seven years dead," mused Scrooge. "And travelling all the time?"

"The whole time," said the Ghost. "No rest, no peace. Incessant torture of remorse."

"You travel fast?" said Scrooge.

"On the wings of the wind," replied the Ghost.

"You might have got over a great quantity of ground in seven years," said Scrooge.

The Ghost, on hearing this, set up another cry, and clanked its chain so hideously in the dead silence of the night, that the Ward[10] would have been justified in indicting it for a nuisance.

"Oh! captive, bound, and double-ironed," cried the phantom, "not to know, that ages of incessant labour by immortal creatures, for this earth must pass into eternity before the good of which it is susceptible is all developed. Not to know that any Christian spirit working kindly in its little sphere, whatever it may be, will find its mortal life too short for its vast means of usefulness. Not to know that no space of regret can make amends for one life's opportunity misused! Yet such was I! Oh! such was I!"

"But you were always a good man of business, Jacob," faultered Scrooge, who now began to apply this to himself.

"Business!" cried the Ghost, wringing its hands again. "Mankind was my business. The common welfare was my business; charity, mercy, forbearance, and benevolence, were, all, my business. The dealings of my trade were but a drop of water in the comprehensive ocean of my business!"

It held up its chain at arm's length, as if that were the cause of all its unavailing grief, and flung it heavily upon the ground again.

"At this time of the rolling year," the spectre said, "I suffer most. Why did I walk through crowds of fellow-beings with my eyes turned down, and never raise them to that blessed Star which led the Wise Men to a poor abode? Were there no poor homes to which its light would have conducted *me!*"

Scrooge was very much dismayed to hear the spectre going on at this rate, and began to quake exceedingly.

"Hear me!" cried the Ghost. "My time is nearly gone."

"I will," said Scrooge. "But don't be hard upon me! Don't be flowery, Jacob! Pray!"

"How it is that I appear before you in a shape that you can see, I may not tell. I have sat invisible beside you many and many a day."

It was not an agreeable idea. Scrooge shivered, and wiped the perspiration from his brow.

"That is no light part of my penance," pursued the Ghost. "I am here to-night to warn you, that you have yet a chance and hope of escaping my fate. A chance and hope of my procuring, Ebenezer."

"You were always a good friend to me," said Scrooge. "Thank'ee!"

"You will be haunted," resumed the Ghost, "by Three Spirits."

Scrooge's countenance fell almost as low as the Ghost's had done.

"Is that the chance and hope you mentioned, Jacob?" he demanded, in a faultering voice.

"It is."

"I—I think I'd rather not," said Scrooge.

"Without their visits," said the Ghost, "you cannot hope to shun the path I tread. Expect the first to-morrow, when the bell tolls one."

"Couldn't I take 'em all at once, and have it over, Jacob?" hinted Scrooge.

"Expect the second on the next night at the same hour. The third upon the next night when the last stroke of twelve has ceased to vibrate. Look to see me no more; and look that, for your own sake, you remember what has passed between us!"

When it had said these words, the spectre took its wrapper from the table, and bound it round its head, as before. Scrooge knew this, by the smart sound its teeth made, when the jaws were brought together by the bandage. He ventured to raise his eyes again, and found his supernatural visitor confronting him in an erect attitude, with its chain wound over and about its arm.

The apparition walked backward from him; and at every step it took, the window raised itself a little, so that when the spectre reached it, it was wide open. It beckoned Scrooge to approach, which he did. When they were within two paces of each other, Marley's Ghost held up its hand, warning him to come no nearer. Scrooge stopped.

Not so much in obedience, as in surprise and fear: for on the raising of the hand, he became sensible of confused noises in the air; incoherent sounds of lamentation and regret; wailings inexpressibly sorrowful and self-accusatory. The spectre, after listening for a moment, joined in the mournful dirge; and floated out upon the bleak, dark night.

Scrooge followed to the window: desperate in his curiosity. He looked out.

The air filled with phantoms, wandering hither and thither in restless haste, and moaning as they went. Every one of them wore chains like Marley's Ghost; some few (they might be guilty governments) were linked together; none were free. Many had been personally known to Scrooge in their lives. He had been quite familiar with one old ghost, in a white waistcoat, with a monstrous iron safe attached to its ankle, who cried piteously at being unable to assist a wretched woman with an infant, whom it saw below, upon a door-step. The misery with them all was, clearly, that they sought to interfere, for good, in human matters, and had lost the power for ever.

Whether these creatures faded into mist, or mist enshrouded them, he could not tell. But they and their spirit voices faded together; and the night became as it had been when he walked home.

Scrooge closed the window, and examined the door by which the Ghost had entered. It was double-locked, as he had locked it with his own hands, and the bolts were undisturbed. He tried to say "Humbug!" but stopped at the first syllable. And being, from the emotion he had undergone, or the fatigues of the day, or his glimpse of the Invisible World, or the dull conversation of the Ghost, or the lateness of the hour, much in need of repose; went straight to bed, without undressing, and fell asleep upon the instant.

STAVE TWO

THE FIRST OF THE THREE SPIRITS

WHEN Scrooge awoke, it was so dark, that looking out of bed, he could scarcely distinguish the transparent window from the opaque walls of his chamber. He was endeavouring to pierce the darkness with his ferret eyes, when the chimes of a neighbouring church struck the four quarters. So he listened for the hour.

To his great astonishment the heavy bell went on from six to seven, and from seven to eight, and regularly up to twelve; then stopped. Twelve! It was past two when he went to bed. The clock was wrong. An icicle must have got into the works. Twelve!

He touched the spring of his repeater, to correct this most preposterous clock. Its rapid little pulse beat twelve; and stopped.

"Why, it isn't possible," said Scrooge, "that I can have slept through a whole day and far into another night. It isn't possible that anything has happened to the sun, and this is twelve at noon!"

The idea being an alarming one, he scrambled out of bed, and groped his way to the window. He was obliged to rub the frost off with the sleeve of his dressing-gown before he could see anything; and could see very little then. All he could make out was, that it was still very foggy and extremely cold, and that there was no noise of people running to and fro, and making a great stir, as there unquestionably would have been if night had beaten off bright day, and taken possession of the world. This was a great relief, because "three days after sight of this First of Exchange pay to Mr. Ebenezer Scrooge or his order," and so forth, would have become a mere United States' security[11] if there were no days to count by.

Scrooge went to bed again, and thought, and thought, and thought it over and over and over, and could make nothing of it. The more he thought, the more perplexed he was; and the more he endeavoured not to think, the more he thought. Marley's Ghost bothered him exceedingly. Every time he resolved within himself, after mature inquiry, that it was all a dream, his mind flew back again, like a strong spring released, to its first position, and presented the same problem to be worked all through, "Was it a dream or not?"

Scrooge lay in this state until the chimes had gone three quarters more, when he remembered, on a sudden, that the Ghost had warned him of a visitation when the bell tolled one. He resolved to lie awake until the hour was passed; and, considering that he could no more go to sleep than go to Heaven, this was perhaps the wisest resolution in his power.

The quarter was so long, that he was more than once convinced he must have sunk into a doze unconsciously, and missed the clock. At length it broke upon his listening ear.

"Ding, dong!"

"A quarter past," said Scrooge, counting.

"Ding, dong!"

"Half past!" said Scrooge.

"Ding, dong!"

"A quarter to it," said Scrooge.

"Ding, dong!"

"The hour itself," said Scrooge, triumphantly, "and nothing else!"

He spoke before the hour bell sounded, which it now did with a deep, dull, hollow, melancholy ONE. Light flashed up in the room upon the instant, and the curtains of his bed were drawn.

The curtains of his bed were drawn aside, I tell you, by a hand. Not the curtains at his feet, nor the curtains at his back, but those to which his face was addressed. The curtains of his bed were drawn aside; and Scrooge, starting up into a half-recumbent attitude, found himself face to face with the unearthly visitor who drew them: as close to it as I am now to you, and I am standing in the spirit at your elbow.

It was a strange figure—like a child: yet not so like a child as like an old man, viewed through some supernatural medium, which gave him the appearance of having receded from the view, and being diminished to a child's proportions. Its hair, which hung about its neck and down its back, was white as if with age; and yet the face had not a wrinkle in it, and the tenderest bloom was on the skin. The arms were very long and muscular; the hands the same, as if its hold were of uncommon strength. Its legs and feet, most delicately formed, were, like those upper members, bare. It wore a tunic of the purest white; and round its waist was bound a lustrous belt, the sheen of which was beautiful. It held a branch of fresh green holly in its hand; and, in singular contradiction of that wintry emblem, had its dress trimmed with summer flowers. But the strangest thing about it was, that from the crown of its head there sprung a bright clear jet of light, by which all this was visible; and which was doubtless the occasion of its using, in its duller moments, a great extinguisher for a cap, which it now held under its arm.

Even this, though, when Scrooge looked at it with increasing steadiness, was *not* its strangest quality. For as its belt sparkled and glittered now in one part and now in another, and what was light one instant, at another time was dark, so the figure itself fluctuated in its distinctness: being now a thing with one arm, now with one leg, now with twenty legs, now a pair of legs without a head, now a head without a body: of which dissolving parts, no outline would be visible in the dense gloom wherein they melted away. And in the very wonder of this, it would be itself again; distinct and clear as ever.

"Are you the Spirit, sir, whose coming was foretold to me?" asked Scrooge.

"I am!"

The voice was soft and gentle. Singularly low, as if instead of being so close beside him, it were at a distance.

"Who, and what are you?" Scrooge demanded.

"I am the Ghost of Christmas Past."

"Long Past?" inquired Scrooge: observant of its dwarfish stature.

"No. Your past."

Perhaps, Scrooge could not have told anybody why, if anybody could have asked him; but he had a special desire to see the Spirit in his cap; and begged him to be covered.

"What!" exclaimed the Ghost, "would you so soon put out, with worldly hands, the light I give? Is it not enough that you are one of those whose passions made this cap, and force me through whole trains of years to wear it low upon my brow!"

Scrooge reverently disclaimed all intention to offend, or any knowledge of having wilfully "bonneted" the Spirit at any period of his life. He then made bold to inquire what business brought him there.

"Your welfare!" said the Ghost.

Scrooge expressed himself much obliged, but could not help thinking that a night of unbroken rest would have been more conducive to that end. The Spirit must have heard him thinking for it said immediately:

"Your reclamation, then. Take heed!"

It put out its strong hand as it spoke, and clasped him gently by the arm.

"Rise! and walk with me!"

It would have been in vain for Scrooge to plead that the weather and the hour were not adapted to pedestrian purposes; that bed was warm, and the thermometer a long way below freezing; that he was clad but lightly in his slippers, dressing-gown, and nightcap; and that he had a cold upon him at that time. The grasp, though gentle as a woman's hand, was not to be resisted. He rose: but finding that the Spirit made towards the window, clasped its robe in supplication.

"I am a mortal," Scrooge remonstrated, "and liable to fall."

"Bear but a touch of my hand *there*," said the Spirit, laying it upon his heart, "and you shall be upheld in more than this!"

As the words were spoken, they passed through the wall, and stood upon an open country road, with fields on either hand. The city had entirely vanished. Not a vestige of it was to be seen. The darkness and the mist had vanished with it, for it was a clear, cold, winter day, with snow upon the ground.

"Good Heaven!" said Scrooge, clasping his hands together, as he looked about him. "I was bred in this place. I was a boy here!"

The Spirit gazed upon him mildly. Its gentle touch, though it had been light and instantaneous, appeared still present to the old man's sense of feeling. He was conscious of a thousand odours floating in the air, each one connected with a thousand thoughts, and hopes, and joys, and cares long, long, forgotten!

"Your lip is trembling," said the Ghost. "And what is that upon your cheek?"

Scrooge muttered, with an unusual catching in his voice, that it was a pimple; and begged the Ghost to lead him where he would.

"You recollect the way?" inquired the Spirit.

"Remember it!" cried Scrooge with fervour—"I could walk it blindfold."

"Strange to have forgotten it for so many years!" observed the Ghost. "Let us go on."

They walked along the road; Scrooge recognising every gate, and post, and tree; until a little market-town appeared in the distance, with its bridge, its church, and winding river. Some shaggy ponies now were seen trotting towards them with boys upon their backs, who called to other boys in country gigs and carts, driven by farmers. All these boys were in great spirits, and shouted to each other, until the broad fields were so full of merry music, that the crisp air laughed to hear it.

"These are but shadows of the things that have been," said the Ghost. "They have no consciousness of us."

The jocund travellers came on; and as they came, Scrooge knew and named them every one. Why was he rejoiced beyond all bounds to see them! Why did his cold eye glisten, and his heart leap up as they went past! Why was he filled with gladness when he heard them give each other Merry Christmas, as they parted at cross-roads and bye-ways, for their several homes! What was merry Christmas to Scrooge? Out upon merry Christmas! What good had it ever done to him?

"The school is not quite deserted," said the Ghost. "A solitary child, neglected by his friends, is left there still."

Scrooge said he knew it. And he sobbed.

They left the high-road, by a well remembered lane, and soon approached a mansion of dull red brick, with a little weathercock-surmounted cupola on the roof, and a bell hanging in it. It was a large house, but one of broken fortunes; for the spacious offices were little used, their walls were damp and mossy, their windows broken, and their gates decayed. Fowls clucked and strutted in the stables; and the coach-houses and sheds were over-run with grass. Nor was it more retentive of its ancient state, within; for entering the dreary hall, and glancing through the open doors of many rooms, they found them poorly furnished, cold, and vast. There was an earthy savour in the air, a chilly bareness in the place, which associated itself somehow with too much getting up by candle-light, and not too much to eat.

They went, the Ghost and Scrooge, across the hall, to a door at the back of the house. It opened before them, and disclosed a long, bare, melancholy room, made barer still by lines of plain deal forms and desks. At one of these a lonely boy was reading near a feeble fire; and Scrooge sat down upon a form, and wept to see his poor forgotten self as he had used to be.

Not a latent echo in the house, not a squeak and scuffle from the mice behind the panelling, not a drip from the half-thawed water-spout in the dull yard behind, not a sigh among the leafless boughs of one despondent poplar, not the idle swinging of an empty store-house door, no, not a clicking in the fire, but fell upon the heart of Scrooge[12] with a softening influence, and gave a freer passage to his tears.

The Spirit touched him on the arm, and pointed to his younger self, intent upon his reading. Suddenly a man, in foreign garments: wonderfully real and distinct to look at: stood outside the window, with an axe stuck in his belt, and leading an ass laden with wood by the bridle.

"Why, it's Ali Baba!" Scrooge exclaimed in ecstasy. "It's dear old honest Ali Baba! Yes, yes, I know! One Christmas time, when yonder solitary child was left here all alone, he *did* come, for the first time, just like that. Poor boy! And Valentine," said Scrooge, "and his wild brother, Orson[13]; there they go! And what's his name, who was put down in his drawers, asleep, at the Gate of Damascus; don't you see him! And the Sultan's Groom turned upside-down by the Genii; there he is upon his head! Serve him right. I'm glad of it. What business had *he* to be married to the Princess!"[14]

To hear Scrooge expending all the earnestness of his nature on such subjects, in a most extraordinary voice between laughing and crying; and to see his heightened and excited face; would have been a surprise to his business friends in the city, indeed.

"There's the Parrot!" cried Scrooge. "Green body and yellow tail, with a thing like a lettuce growing out of the top of his head; there he is! Poor Robin Crusoe, he called him, when he came home again after sailing round the island. 'Poor Robin Crusoe, where have you been, Robin Crusoe?' The man thought he was dreaming, but he wasn't. It was the Parrot, you know. There goes Friday, running for his life to the little creek![15] Halloa! Hoop! Halloa!"

Then, with a rapidity of transition very foreign to his usual character, he said, in pity for his former self, "Poor boy!" and cried again.

"I wish," Scrooge muttered, putting his hand in his pocket, and looking about him, after drying his eyes with his cuff: "but it's too late now."

"What is the matter?" asked the Spirit.

"Nothing," said Scrooge. "Nothing. There was a boy singing a Christmas Carol at my door last night. I should like to have given him something: that's all."

The Ghost smiled thoughtfully, and waved its hand: saying as it did so, "Let us see another Christmas!"

Scrooge's former self grew larger at the words, and the room became a little darker and more dirty. The panels shrunk, the windows cracked; fragments of plaster fell out of the ceiling, and the naked laths were shown instead; but how all this was brought about, Scrooge knew no more than you do. He only knew that it was quite correct; that everything had happened so; that there he was, alone again, when all the other boys had gone home for the jolly holidays.

He was not reading now, but walking up and down despairingly. Scrooge looked at the Ghost, and with a mournful shaking of his head, glanced anxiously towards the door.

It opened; and a little girl, much younger than the boy, came darting in, and putting her arms about his neck, and often kissing him, addressed him as her "Dear, dear brother."

"I have come to bring you home, dear brother!" said the child, clapping her tiny hands, and bending down to laugh. "To bring you home, home, home!"

"Home, little Fan?" returned the boy.

"Yes!" said the child, brimful of glee. "Home, for good and all. Home, for ever and ever. Father is so much kinder than he used to be, that home's like Heaven! He spoke so gently to me one dear night when I was going to bed, that I was not afraid to ask him once more if you might come home; and he said Yes, you should; and sent me in a coach to bring you. And you're to be a man!" said the child, opening her eyes, "and are never to come back here; but first, we're to be together all the Christmas long, and have the merriest time in all the world."

"You are quite a woman, little Fan!" exclaimed the boy.

She clapped her hands and laughed, and tried to touch his head; but being too little, laughed again, and stood on tiptoe to embrace him. Then she began to drag him, in her childish eagerness, towards the door; and he, nothing loth to go, accompanied her.

A terrible voice in the hall cried, "Bring down Master Scrooge's box, there!" and in the hall appeared the school-master himself, who glared on Master Scrooge with a ferocious condescension, and threw him into a dreadful state of mind by shaking hands with him. He then conveyed him and his sister into the veriest old well of a shivering best-parlour that ever was seen, where the maps upon the wall, and the celestial and terrestrial globes in the windows were waxy with cold. Here he produced a decanter of curiously light wine, and a block of curiously heavy cake, and administered instalments of those dainties to the young people: at the same time, sending out a meagre servant to offer a glass of "something" to the postboy, who answered that he thanked the gentleman, but if it was the same tap as he had tasted before, he had rather not. Master Scrooge's trunk being by this time tied on to the top of the chaise, the children bade the schoolmaster good-bye right willingly; and getting into it, drove gaily down the garden-sweep: the quick wheels dashing the hoar-frost and snow from off the dark leaves of the evergreens like spray.

"Always a delicate creature, whom a breath might have withered," said the Ghost. "But she had a large heart!"

"So she had," cried Scrooge. "You're right. I'll not gainsay it, Spirit. God forbid!"

"She died a woman," said the Ghost, "and had, as I think, children."

"One child," Scrooge returned.

"True," said the Ghost. "Your nephew!"

Scrooge seemed uneasy in his mind; and answered briefly, "Yes."

Although they had but that moment left the school behind them, they were now in the busy thoroughfares of a city, where shadowy passengers passed and repassed; where shadowy carts and coaches battled for the way, and all the strife and tumult of a real city were. It was made plain enough, by the dressing of the shops, that here too it was Christmas time again; but it was evening, and the streets were lighted up.

The Ghost stopped at a certain warehouse door, and asked Scrooge if he knew it.

"Know it!" said Scrooge. "Was I apprenticed here?"

They went in. At sight of an old gentleman in a Welch wig[16], sitting behind such a high desk, that if he had been two inches taller he must have knocked his head against the ceiling, Scrooge cried in great excitement:

"Why, it's old Fezziwig! Bless his heart; it's Fezziwig alive again!"

Old Fezziwig laid down his pen, and looked up at the clock, which pointed to the hour of seven. He rubbed his hands; adjusted his capacious waistcoat; laughed all over himself, from his shoes to his organ of benevolence[17]; and called out in a comfortable, oily, rich, fat, jovial voice:

"Yo ho, there! Ebenezer! Dick!"

Scrooge's former self, now grown a young man, came briskly in, accompanied by his fellow-'prentice.

"Dick Wilkins, to be sure!" said Scrooge to the Ghost. "Bless me, yes. There he is. He was very much attached to me, was Dick. Poor Dick! Dear, dear!"

"Yo ho, my boys!" said Fezziwig. "No more work to-night. Christmas Eve, Dick. Christmas, Ebenezer! Let's have the shutters up," cried old Fezziwig, with a sharp clap of his hands, "before a man can say, Jack Robinson!"

You wouldn't believe how those two fellows went at it!

They charged into the street with the shutters—one, two, three—had 'em up in their places—four, five, six—barred 'em and pinned 'em—seven, eight, nine—and came back before you could have got to twelve, panting like race-horses.

"Hilli-ho!" cried old Fezziwig, skipping down from the high desk, with wonderful agility. "Clear away, my lads, and let's have lots of room here! Hilli-ho, Dick! Chirrup, Ebenezer!"

Clear away! There was nothing they wouldn't have cleared away, or couldn't have cleared away, with old Fezziwig looking on. It was done in a minute. Every movable was packed off, as if it were dismissed from public life for ever-more; the floor was swept and watered, the lamps were trimmed, fuel was heaped upon the fire; and the warehouse was as snug, and warm, and dry, and bright a ball-room, as you would desire to see upon a winter's night.

In came a fiddler with a music-book, and went up to the lofty desk, and made an orchestra of it, and tuned like fifty stomach-aches. In came Mrs. Fezziwig, one vast sub-stantial smile. In came the three Miss Fezziwigs, beaming and lovable. In came the six young followers whose hearts they broke. In came all the young men and women employed in the business. In came the housemaid, with her cousin, the baker. In came the cook, with her brother's particular friend, the milkman. In came the boy from over the way, who was suspected of not having board enough from his master; trying to hide himself behind the girl from next door but one, who was proved to have had her ears pulled by her Mistress. In they all came, one after another; some shyly, some boldly, some gracefully, some awkwardly, some pushing, some pulling; in they all came, anyhow and every-how. Away they all went, twenty couple at once, hands half round and back again the other way; down the middle and up again; round and round in various stages of affectionate grouping; old top couple always turning up in the wrong place; new top couple starting off again, as soon as they got there; all top couples at last, and not a bottom one to help them. When this result was brought about, old Fezziwig, clapping his hands to stop the dance, cried out, "Well done!" and the fiddler plunged his hot face into a pot of porter, especially provided for that purpose. But scorning rest upon his reappearance, he instantly began again, though there were no dancers yet, as if the other fiddler had been carried home, exhausted, on a shutter; and he were a bran-new man resolved to beat him out of sight, or perish.

There were more dances, and there were forfeits, and more dances, and there was cake, and there was negus, and there was a great piece of Cold Roast, and there was a great piece of Cold Boiled, and there were mince-pies, and plenty of beer. But the great effect of the evening came after the Roast and Boiled, when the fiddler (an artful dog, mind! The sort of man who knew his business better than you or I could have told it him!) struck up "Sir Roger de Coverley." Then old Fezziwig stood out to dance with Mrs. Fezziwig. Top couple, too; with a good stiff piece of work cut out for them; three or four and twenty pair of partners; people who were not to be trifled with; people who *would* dance, and had no notion of walking.

But if they had been twice as many: ah, four times: old Fezziwig would have been a match for them, and so would Mrs. Fezziwig. As to *her*, she was worthy to be his partner in every sense of the term. If that's not high praise, tell me higher, and I'll use it. A positive light appeared to issue from Fezziwig's calves. They shone in every part of the dance like moons. You couldn't have predicted, at any given time, what would become of 'em next. And when old Fezziwig and Mrs. Fezziwig had gone all through the dance; advance and retire, hold hands with your partner; bow and curtsey; corkscrew; thread-the-needle, and back again to your place; Fezziwig "cut"[18]—cut so deftly, that he appeared to wink with his legs, and came upon his feet again without a stagger.

When the clock struck eleven, this domestic ball broke up. Mr. and Mrs. Fezziwig took their stations, one on either side the door, and shaking hands with every person individually as he or she went out, wished him or her a Merry Christmas. When everybody had retired but the two 'prentices, they did the same to them; and thus the cheerful voices died away, and the lads were left to their beds; which were under a counter in the back-shop.

During the whole of this time, Scrooge had acted like a man out of his wits. His heart and soul were in the scene, and with his former self. He corroborated everything, remembered everything, enjoyed everything, and underwent the strangest agitation. It was not until now, when the bright faces of his former self and Dick were turned from them, that he remembered the Ghost, and became conscious that it was looking full upon him, while the light upon its head burnt very clear.

"A small matter," said the Ghost, "to make these silly folks so full of gratitude."

"Small!" echoed Scrooge.

The Spirit signed to him to listen to the two apprentices, who were pouring out their hearts in praise of Fezziwig: and when he had done so, said,

"Why! Is it not? He has spent but a few pounds of your mortal money: three or four, perhaps. Is that so much that he deserves this praise?"

"It isn't that," said Scrooge, heated by the remark, and speaking unconsciously like his former, not his latter, self. "It isn't that, Spirit. He has the power to render us happy or unhappy; to make our service light or burdensome; a pleasure or a toil. Say that his power lies in words and looks; in things so slight and insignificant that it is impossible to add and count 'em up: what then? The happiness he gives, is quite as great as if it cost a fortune."

He felt the Spirit's glance, and stopped.

"What is the matter?" asked the Ghost.

"Nothing particular," said Scrooge.

"Something, I think?" the Ghost insisted.

"No," said Scrooge, "No. I should like to be able to say a word or two to my clerk just now! That's all."

His former self turned down the lamps as he gave utterance to the wish; and Scrooge and the Ghost again stood side by side in the open air.

"My time grows short," observed the Spirit. "Quick!"

This was not addressed to Scrooge, or to any one whom he could see, but it produced an immediate effect. For again Scrooge saw himself. He was older now; a man in the prime of life. His face had not the harsh and rigid lines of later years; but it had begun to wear the signs of care and avarice. There was an eager, greedy, restless motion in the eye, which showed the passion that had taken root, and where the shadow of the growing tree would fall.

He was not alone, but sat by the side of a fair young girl in a mourning-dress: in whose eyes there were tears, which sparkled in the light that shone out of the Ghost of Christmas Past.

"It matters little," she said, softly. "To you, very little. Another idol has displaced me; and if it can cheer and comfort you in time to come, as I would have tried to do, I have no just cause to grieve."

"What Idol has displaced you?" he rejoined.

"A golden one."

"This is the even-handed dealing of the world!" he said. "There is nothing on which it is so hard as poverty; and there is nothing it professes to condemn with such severity as the pursuit of wealth!"

"You fear the world too much," she answered, gently. "All your other hopes have merged into the hope of being beyond the chance of its sordid reproach. I have seen your nobler aspirations fall off one by one, until the master-passion, Gain, engrosses you. Have I not?"

"What then?" he retorted. "Even if I have grown so much wiser, what then? I am not changed towards you."

She shook her head.

"Am I?"

"Our contract is an old one. It was made when we were both poor and content to be so, until, in good season, we could improve our worldly fortune by our patient industry. You *are* changed. When it was made, you were another man."

"I was a boy," he said impatiently.

"Your own feeling tells you that you were not what you are," she returned. "I am. That which promised happiness when we were one in heart, is fraught with misery now that we are two. How often and how keenly I have thought of this, I will not say. It is enough that I *have* thought of it, and can release you."

"Have I ever sought release?"

"In words. No. Never."

"In what, then?"

"In a changed nature; in an altered spirit; in another atmosphere of life; another Hope as its great end. In everything that made my love of any worth or value in your sight. If this had never been between us," said the girl, looking mildly, but with steadiness, upon him; "tell me, would you seek me out and try to win me now? Ah, no!"

He seemed to yield to the justice of this supposition, in spite of himself. But he said, with a struggle, "You think not."

"I would gladly think otherwise if I could," she answered, "Heaven knows! When *I* have learned a Truth like this, I know how strong and irresistible it must be. But if you were free to-day, to-morrow, yesterday, can even I believe that you would choose a dowerless girl—you who, in your very confidence with her, weigh everything by Gain: or, choosing her, if for a moment you were false enough to your one guiding principle to do so, do I not know that your repentance and regret would surely follow? I do; and I release you. With a full heart, for the love of him you once were."

He was about to speak; but with her head turned from him, she resumed.

"You may—the memory of what is past half makes me hope you will—have pain in this. A very, very brief time, and you will dismiss the recollection of it, gladly, as an unprofitable dream, from which it happened well that you awoke. May you be happy in the life you have chosen!"

She left him; and they parted.

"Spirit!" said Scrooge, "show me no more! Conduct me home. Why do you delight to torture me?'

"One shadow more!" exclaimed the Ghost.

"No more!" cried Scrooge. "No more. I don't wish to see it. Show me no more!"

But the relentless Ghost pinioned him in both his arms, and forced him to observe what happened next.

They were in another scene and place: a room, not very large or handsome, but full of comfort. Near to the winter fire sat a beautiful young girl, so like the last that Scrooge believed it was the same, until he saw *her*, now a comely matron, sitting opposite her daughter. The noise in this room was perfectly tumultuous, for there were more children there, than Scrooge in his agitated state of mind could count; and, unlike the celebrated herd in the poem[19], they were not forty children conducting themselves like one, but every child was conducting itself like forty. The consequences were uproarious beyond belief; but no one seemed to care; on the contrary, the mother and daughter laughed heartily, and enjoyed it very much; and the latter, soon beginning to mingle in the sports, got pillaged by the young brigands most ruthlessly. What would I not have given to be one of them! Though I never could have been so rude, no, no! I wouldn't for the wealth of all the world have crushed that braided hair, and torn it down; and for the precious little shoe, I wouldn't have plucked it off, God bless my soul! to save my life. As to measuring her waist in sport, as they did, bold young brood, I couldn't have done it; I should have expected my arm to have grown round it for a punishment, and never come straight again. And yet I should have dearly liked, I own, to have touched her lips; to have questioned her, that she might have opened them; to have looked upon the lashes of her downcast eyes, and never raised a blush; to have let loose waves of hair, an inch of which would be a keepsake beyond price: in short, I should have liked, I do confess, to have had the lightest licence of a child, and yet been man enough to know its value.

But now a knocking at the door was heard, and such a rush immediately ensued that she with laughing face and plundered dress was borne towards it the centre of a flushed and boisterous group, just in time to greet the father, who came home attended by a man laden with Christmas toys and presents. Then the shouting and the struggling, and the onslaught that was made on the defenceless porter! The scaling him with chairs for ladders, to dive into his pockets, despoil him of brown-paper parcels, hold on tight by his cravat, hug him round the neck, pommel his back, and kick his legs in irrepressible affection! The shouts of wonder and delight with which the development of every package was received! The terrible announcement that the baby had been taken in the act of putting a doll's frying-pan into his mouth, and was more than suspected of having swallowed a fictitious turkey, glued on a wooden platter! The immense relief of finding this a false alarm! The joy, and gratitude, and ecstasy! They are all indescribable alike. It is enough that by degrees the children and their emotions got out of the parlour and by one stair at a time, up to the top of the house; where they went to bed, and so subsided.

And now Scrooge looked on more attentively than ever, when the master of the house, having his daughter leaning fondly on him, sat down with her and her mother at his own fireside; and when he thought that such another creature, quite as graceful and as full of promise, might have called him father, and been a spring-time in the haggard winter of his life, his sight grew very dim indeed.

"Belle," said the husband, turning to his wife with a smile, "I saw an old friend of yours this afternoon."

"Who was it?"

"Guess!"

"How can I? Tut, don't I know," she added in the same breath, laughing as he laughed. "Mr. Scrooge."

"Mr. Scrooge it was. I passed his office window; and as it was not shut up, and he had a candle inside, I could scarcely help seeing him. His partner lies upon the point of death, I hear; and there he sat alone. Quite alone in the world, I do believe."

"Spirit!" said Scrooge in a broken voice, "remove me from this place."

"I told you these were shadows of the things that have been," said the Ghost. "That they are what they are, do not blame me!"

"Remove me!" Scrooge exclaimed. "I cannot bear it!"

He turned upon the Ghost, and seeing that it looked upon him with a face, in which in some strange way there were fragments of all the faces it had shown him, wrestled with it.

"Leave me! Take me back. Haunt me no longer!"

In the struggle, if that can be called a struggle in which the Ghost with no visible resistance on its own part was undisturbed by any effort of its adversary, Scrooge observed that its light was burning high and bright; and dimly connecting that with its influence over him, he seized the extinguisher-cap, and by a sudden action pressed it down upon its head.

The Spirit dropped beneath it, so that the extinguisher covered its whole form; but though Scrooge pressed it down with all his force, he could not hide the light: which streamed from under it, in a unbroken flood upon the ground.

He was conscious of being exhausted, and overcome by an irresistible drowsiness; and, further, of being in his own bedroom. He gave the cap a parting squeeze, in which his hand relaxed; and had barely time to reel to bed, before he sank into a heavy sleep.

STAVE THREE
THE SECOND OF THE THREE SPIRITS

Awaking in the middle of a prodigiously tough snore, and sitting up in bed to get his thoughts together, Scrooge had no occasion to be told that the bell was again upon the stroke of One. He felt that he was restored to consciousness in the right nick of time, for the especial purpose of holding a conference with the second messenger despatched to him through Jacob Marley's intervention. But, finding that he turned uncomfortably cold when he began to wonder which of his curtains this new spectre would draw back, he put them every one aside with his own hands; and lying down again, established a sharp look-out all round the bed. For he wished to challenge the Spirit on the moment of its appearance, and did not wish to be taken by surprise and made nervous.

Gentlemen of the free-and-easy sort, who plume themselves on being acquainted with a move or two, and being usually equal to the time-of-day, express the wide range of their capacity for adventure by observing that they are good for anything from pitch-and-toss to manslaughter; between which opposite extremes, no doubt, there lies a tolerably wide and comprehensive range of subjects. Without venturing for Scrooge quite as hardily as this, I don't mind calling on you to believe that he was ready for a good broad field of strange appearances, and that nothing between a baby and a rhinoceros would have astonished him very much.

Now, being prepared for almost anything, he was not by any means prepared for nothing; and, consequently, when the Bell struck One, and no shape appeared, he was taken with a violent fit of trembling. Five minutes, ten minutes, a quarter of an hour went by, yet nothing came. All this time, he lay upon his bed, the very core and centre of a blaze of ruddy light, which streamed upon it when the clock proclaimed the hour; and which being only light, was more alarming than a dozen ghosts, as he was powerless to make out what it meant, or would be at; and was sometimes apprehensive that he might be at that very moment an interesting case of spontaneous combustion[20], without having the consolation of knowing it. At last, however, he began to think—as you or I would have thought at first; for it is always the person not in the predicament who knows what ought to have been done in it, and would unquestionably have done it too—at last, I say, he began to think that the source and secret of this ghostly light might be in the adjoining room: from whence, on further tracing it, it seemed to shine. This idea taking full possession of his mind, he got up softly and shuffled in his slippers to the door.

The moment Scrooge's hand was on the lock, a strange voice called him by his name, and bade him enter. He obeyed.

It was his own room. There was no doubt about that. But it had undergone a surprising transformation. The walls and ceiling were so hung with living green, that it looked a perfect grove, from every part of which, bright gleaming berries glistened. The crisp leaves of holly, mistletoe, and ivy reflected back the light, as if so many little mirrors had been scattered there; and such a mighty blaze went roaring up the chimney, as that dull petrification of a hearth had never known in Scrooge's time, or Marley's, or for many and many a winter season gone. Heaped up on the floor, to form a kind of throne, were turkeys, geese, game, poultry, brawn, great joints of meat, sucking-pigs, long wreaths of sausages, mince-pies, plum-puddings, barrels of oysters, red-hot chestnuts, cherry-cheeked apples, juicy oranges, luscious pears, immense twelfth-cakes[21], and seething bowls of punch, that made the chamber dim with their delicious steam. In easy state upon this couch, there sat a jolly Giant, glorious to see; who bore a glowing torch, in shape not unlike Plenty's horn, and held it up, high up, to shed its light on Scrooge, as he came peeping round the door.

"Come in!" exclaimed the Ghost. "Come in! and know me better, man!"

Scrooge entered timidly, and hung his head before this Spirit. He was not the dogged Scrooge he had been; and though the Spirit's eyes were clear and kind, he did not like to meet them.

"I am the Ghost of Christmas Present," said the Spirit. "Look upon me!"

Scrooge reverently did so. It was clothed in one simple deep green robe, or mantle, bordered with white fur. This garment hung so loosely on the figure, that its capacious breast was bare, as if disdaining to be warded or concealed by any artifice. Its feet, observable beneath the ample folds of the garment, were also bare; and on its head it wore no other covering than a holly wreath, set here and there with shining icicles. Its dark brown curls were long and free: free as its genial face, its sparkling eye, its open hand, its cheery voice, its unconstrained demeanour, and its joyful air. Girded round its middle was an antique scabbard; but no sword was in it, and the ancient sheath was eaten up with rust.

"You have never seen the like of me before!" exclaimed the Spirit.

"Never," Scrooge made answer to it.

"Have never walked forth with the younger members of my family; meaning (for I am very young) my elder brothers born in these later years?" pursued the Phantom.

"I don't think I have," said Scrooge. "I am afraid I have not. Have you had many brothers, Spirit?"

"More than eighteen hundred," said the Ghost.

"A tremendous family to provide for!" muttered Scrooge. The Ghost of Christmas Present rose.

"Spirit," said Scrooge submissively, "conduct me where you will. I went forth last night on compulsion, and I learnt a lesson which is working now. To-night, if you have aught to teach me, let me profit by it."

"Touch my robe!"

J Leech

Scrooge did as he was told, and held it fast.

Holly, mistletoe, red berries, ivy, turkeys, geese, game, poultry, brawn, meat, pigs, sausages, oysters, pies, puddings, fruit, and punch, all vanished instantly. So did the room, the fire, the ruddy glow, the hour of night, and they stood in the city streets on Christmas morning, where (for the weather was severe) the people made a rough, but brisk and not unpleasant kind of music, in scraping the snow from the pavement in front of their dwellings, and from the tops of their houses: whence it was mad delight to the boys to see it come plumping down into the road below, and splitting into artificial little snow-storms.

The house fronts looked black enough, and the windows blacker, contrasting with the smooth white sheet of snow upon the roofs, and with the dirtier snow upon the ground; which last deposit had been ploughed up in deep furrows by the heavy wheels of carts and waggons; furrows that crossed and re-crossed each other hundreds of times where the great streets branched off, and made intricate channels, hard to trace, in the thick yellow mud and icy water. The sky was gloomy, and the shortest streets were choked up with a dingy mist, half thawed, half frozen, whose heavier particles descended in a shower of sooty atoms, as if all the chimneys in Great Britain had, by one consent, caught fire, and were blazing away to their dear hearts' content. There was nothing very cheerful in the climate or the town, and yet was there an air of cheerfulness abroad that the clearest summer air and brightest summer sun might have endeavoured to diffuse in vain.

For the people who were shovelling away on the housetops were jovial and full of glee; calling out to one another from the parapets, and now and then exchanging a facetious snow-ball—better-natured missile far than many a wordy jest— laughing heartily if it went right, and not less heartily if it went wrong. The poulterers' shops were still half open, and the fruiterers' were radiant in their glory. There were great round, pot-bellied baskets of chestnuts, shaped like the waistcoats of jolly old gentlemen, lolling at the doors, and tumbling out into the street in their apoplectic opulence. There were ruddy, brown-faced, broad-girthed Spanish Onions, shining in the fatness of their growth like Spanish Friars; and winking from their shelves in wanton slyness at the girls as they went by, and glanced demurely at the hung-up mistletoe. There were pears and apples, clustered high in blooming pyramids; there were bunches of grapes, made in the shopkeepers' benevolence to dangle from conspicuous hooks, that people's mouths might water gratis as they passed; there were piles of filberts, mossy and brown, recalling, in their fragrance, ancient walks among the woods, and pleasant shufflings ankle deep through withered leaves; there were Norfolk Biffins²², squab and swarthy, setting off the yellow of the oranges and lemons, and, in the great compactness of their juicy persons, urgently entreating and beseeching to be carried home in paper bags and eaten after dinner. The very gold and silver fish, set forth among these choice fruits in a bowl, though members of a dull and stagnant-blooded race, appeared to know that there was something going on; and, to a fish, went gasping round and round their little world in slow and passionless excitement.

The Grocers'! oh the Grocers'! nearly closed, with perhaps two shutters down, or one; but through those gaps such glimpses! It was not alone that the scales descending on the counter made a merry sound, or that the twine and roller parted company so briskly, or that the canisters were rattled up and down like juggling tricks, or even that the blended scents of tea and coffee were so grateful to the nose, or even that the raisins were so plentiful and rare, the almonds so extremely white, the sticks of cinnamon so long and straight, the other spices so delicious, the candied fruits so caked and spotted with molten sugar as to make the coldest lookers-on feel faint and subsequently bilious. Nor was it that the figs were moist and pulpy, or that the French plums blushed in modest tartness from their highly-decorated boxes, or that everything was good to eat and in its Christmas dress: but the customers were all so hurried and so eager in the hopeful promise of the day, that they tumbled up against each other at the door, clashing their wicker baskets wildly, and left their purchases upon the counter, and came running back to fetch them, and committed hundreds of the like mistakes in the best humour possible; while the Grocer and his people were so frank and fresh that the polished hearts with which they fastened their aprons behind might have been their own, worn outside for general inspection, and for Christmas daws to peck at[23] if they chose.

But soon the steeples called good people all, to church and chapel, and away they came, flocking through the streets in their best clothes, and with their gayest faces. And at the same time there emerged from scores of bye streets, lanes, and nameless turnings, innumerable people, carrying their dinners to the bakers' shops.[24] The sight of these poor revellers appeared to interest the Spirit very much, for he stood with Scrooge beside him in a baker's doorway, and taking off the covers as their bearers passed, sprinkled incense on their dinners from his torch. And it was a very uncommon kind of torch, for once or twice when there were angry words between some dinner-carriers who had jostled each other, he shed a few drops of water on them from it, and their good humour was restored directly. For they said, it was a shame to quarrel upon Christmas Day. And so it was! God love it, so it was!

In time the bells ceased, and the bakers' were shut up; and yet there was a genial shadowing forth of all these dinners and the progress of their cooking, in the thawed blotch of wet above each baker's oven; where the pavement smoked as if its stones were cooking too.

"Is there a peculiar flavour in what you sprinkle from your torch?" asked Scrooge.

"There is. My own."

"Would it apply to any kind of dinner on this day?" asked Scrooge.

"To any kindly given. To a poor one most."

"Why to a poor one most?" asked Scrooge.

"Because it needs it most."

"Spirit," said Scrooge, after a moment's thought, "I wonder you, of all the beings in the many worlds about us, should desire to cramp these people's opportunities of innocent enjoyment."

"I!" cried the Spirit.

"You would deprive them of their means of dining every seventh day, often the only day on which they can be said to dine at all," said Scrooge. "Wouldn't you?"

"I!" cried the Spirit.

"You seek to close these places on the Seventh Day[25]?" said Scrooge. "And it comes to the same thing."

"*I* seek!" exclaimed the Spirit.

"Forgive me if I am wrong. It has been done in your name, or at least in that of your family," said Scrooge.

"There are some upon this earth of yours," returned the Spirit, "who lay claim to know us, and who do their deeds of passion, pride, ill-will, hatred, envy, bigotry, and selfishness in our name, who are as strange to us and all our kith and kin, as if they had never lived. Remember that, and charge their doings on themselves, not us."

Scrooge promised that he would; and they went on, invisible, as they had been before, into the suburbs of the town. It was a remarkable quality of the Ghost (which Scrooge had observed at the baker's) that notwithstanding his gigantic size, he could accommodate himself to any place with ease; and that he stood beneath a low roof quite as gracefully and like a supernatural creature, as it was possible he could have done in any lofty hall.

And perhaps it was the pleasure the good Spirit had in showing off this power of his, or else it was his own kind, generous, hearty nature, and his sympathy with all poor men, that led him straight to Scrooge's clerk's; for there he went, and took Scrooge with him, holding to his robe; and on the threshold of the door the Spirit smiled, and stopped to bless Bob Cratchit's dwelling with the sprinkling of his torch. Think of that! Bob had but fifteen "Bob" a-week himself; he pocketed on Saturdays but fifteen copies of his Christian name; and yet the Ghost of Christmas Present blessed his four-roomed house!

Then up rose Mrs. Cratchit, Cratchit's wife, dressed out but poorly in a twice-turned gown, but brave in ribbons, which are cheap and make a goodly show for sixpence; and she laid the cloth, assisted by Belinda Cratchit, second of her daughters, also brave in ribbons; while Master Peter Cratchit plunged a fork into the saucepan of potatoes, and getting the corners of his monstrous shirt-collar (Bob's private property, conferred upon his son and heir in honour of the day) into his mouth, rejoiced to find himself so gallantly attired, and yearned to show his linen in the fashionable Parks. And now two smaller Cratchits, boy and girl, came tearing in, screaming that outside the baker's they had smelt the goose, and known it for their own; and basking in luxurious thoughts of sage and onion, these young Cratchits danced about the table, and exalted Master Peter Cratchit to the skies, while he (not proud, although his collars nearly choked him) blew the fire, until the slow potatoes bubbling up, knocked loudly at the saucepan-lid to be let out and peeled.

"What has ever got your precious father then," said Mrs. Cratchit. "And your brother, Tiny Tim; and Martha warn't as late last Christmas Day by half-an-hour!"

"Here's Martha, mother!" said a girl, appearing as she spoke.

"Here's Martha, mother!" cried the two young Cratchits. "Hurrah! There's *such* a goose, Martha!"

"Why, bless your heart alive, my dear, how late you are!" said Mrs. Cratchit, kissing her a dozen times, and taking off her shawl and bonnet for her, with officious zeal.

"We'd a deal of work to finish up last night," replied the girl, "and had to clear away this morning, mother!"

"Well! Never mind so long as you are come," said Mrs.

Cratchit. "Sit ye down before the fire, my dear, and have a warm, Lord bless ye!"

"No no! There's father coming," cried the two young Cratchits, who were everywhere at once. "Hide Martha, hide!"

So Martha hid herself, and in came little Bob, the father, with at least three feet of comforter exclusive of the fringe, hanging down before him; and his thread-bare clothes darned up and brushed, to look seasonable; and Tiny Tim upon his shoulder. Alas for Tiny Tim, he bore a little crutch, and had his limbs supported by an iron frame!

"Why, where's our Martha?" cried Bob Cratchit looking round.

"Not coming," said Mrs. Cratchit.

"Not coming!" said Bob, with a sudden declension in his high spirits; for he had been Tim's blood horse all the way from church, and had come home rampant. "Not coming upon Christmas Day!"

Martha didn't like to see him disappointed, if it were only in joke; so she came out prematurely from behind the closet door, and ran into his arms, while the two young Cratchits hustled Tiny Tim, and bore him off into the wash-house, that he might hear the pudding singing in the copper.

"And how did little Tim behave?" asked Mrs. Cratchit, when she had rallied Bob on his credulity and Bob had hugged his daughter to his heart's content.

"As good as gold," said Bob, "and better. Somehow he gets thoughtful sitting by himself so much, and thinks the strangest things you ever heard. He told me, coming home, that he hoped the people saw him in the church, because he was a cripple, and it might be pleasant to them to remember upon Christmas Day, who made lame beggars walk and blind men see."

Bob's voice was tremulous when he told them this, and trembled more when he said that Tiny Tim was growing strong and hearty.

His active little crutch was heard upon the floor, and back

came Tiny Tim before another word was spoken, escorted by his brother and sister to his stool before the fire; and while Bob, turning up his cuffs—as if, poor fellow, they were capable of being made more shabby—compounded some hot mixture in a jug with gin and lemons, and stirred it round and round and put it on the hob to simmer; Master Peter, and the two ubiquitous young Cratchits went to fetch the goose, with which they soon returned in high processsion.

Such a bustle ensued that you might have thought a goose the rarest of all birds; a feathered phenomenon, to which a black swan was a matter of course; and in truth it was something very like it in that house. Mrs. Cratchit made the gravy (ready beforehand in a little saucepan) hissing hot; Master Peter mashed the potatoes with incredible vigour; Miss Belinda sweetened up the apple-sauce; Martha dusted the hot plates; Bob took Tiny Tim beside him in a tiny corner at the table; the two young Cratchits set chairs for everybody, not forgetting themselves, and mounting guard upon their posts, crammed spoons into their mouths, lest they should shriek for goose before their turn came to be helped. At last the dishes were set on, and grace was said. It was succeeded by a breathless pause, as Mrs. Cratchit, looking slowly all along the carving-knife, prepared to plunge it in the breast; but when she did, and when the long expected gush of stuffing issued forth, one murmur of delight arose all round the board, and even Tiny Tim, excited by the two young Cratchits, beat on the table with the handle of his knife, and feebly cried Hurrah!

There never was such a goose. Bob said he didn't believe there ever was such a goose cooked. Its tenderness and flavour, size and cheapness, were the themes of universal admiration. Eked out by the apple-sauce and mashed potatoes, it was a sufficient dinner for the whole family; indeed, as Mrs. Cratchit said with great delight (surveying one small atom of a bone upon the dish), they hadn't ate it all at last! Yet every one had had enough, and the youngest

Cratchits in particular, were steeped in sage and onion to the eyebrows! But now, the plates being changed by Miss Belinda, Mrs. Cratchit left the room alone—too nervous to bear witnesses—to take the pudding up, and bring it in.

Suppose it should not be done enough! Suppose it should break in turning out! Suppose somebody should have got over the wall of the back-yard, and stolen it, while they were merry with the goose: a supposition at which the two young Cratchits became livid! All sorts of horrors were supposed.

Hallo! A great deal of steam! The pudding was out of the copper. A smell like a washing-day! That was the cloth. A smell like an eating-house, and a pastry cook's next door to each other, with a laundress's next door to that! That was the pudding. In half a minute Mrs. Cratchit entered: flushed, but smiling proudly: with the pudding, like a speckled cannon-ball, so hard and firm, blazing in half of half-a-quartern of ignited brandy, and bedight with Christmas holly stuck into the top.

Oh, a wonderful pudding! Bob Cratchit said, and calmly too, that he regarded it as the greatest success achieved by Mrs. Cratchit since their marriage. Mrs. Cratchit said that now the weight was off her mind, she would confess she had had her doubts about the quantity of flour. Everybody had something to say about it, but nobody said or thought it was at all a small pudding for a large family. It would have been flat heresy to do so. Any Cratchit would have blushed to hint at such a thing.

At last the dinner was all done, the cloth was cleared, the hearth swept, and the fire made up. The compound in the jug being tasted, and considered perfect, apples and oranges were put upon the table, and a shovel-full of chestnuts on the fire. Then all the Cratchit family drew round the hearth, in what Bob Cratchit called a circle, meaning half a one; and at Bob Cratchit's elbow stood the family display of glass; two tumblers, and a custard-cup without a handle.

These held the hot stuff from the jug, however, as well as golden goblets would have done; and Bob served it out with beaming looks, while the chestnuts on the fire sputtered and crackled noisily. Then Bob proposed:

"A Merry Christmas to us all, my dears. God bless us!"
Which all the family re-echoed.

"God bless us every one!" said Tiny Tim, the last of all.

He sat very close to his father's side, upon his little stool. Bob held his withered little hand in his, as if he loved the child, and wished to keep him by his side, and dreaded that he might be taken from him.

"Spirit," said Scrooge, with an interest he had never felt before, "tell me if Tiny Tim will live."

"I see a vacant seat," replied the Ghost, "in the poor chimney corner, and a crutch without an owner, carefully preserved. If these shadows remain unaltered by the Future, the child will die."

"No, no," said Scrooge. "Oh no, kind Spirit! say he will be spared."

"If these shadows remain unaltered by the Future, none other of my race," returned the Ghost, "will find him here. What then? If he be like to die, he had better do it, and decrease the surplus population."

Scrooge hung his head to hear his own words quoted by the Spirit, and was overcome with penitence and grief.

"Man," said the Ghost, "if man you be in heart, not adamant, forbear that wicked cant until you have discovered What the surplus is, and Where it is. Will you decide what men shall live, what men shall die? It may be, that in the sight of Heaven, you are more worthless and less fit to live than millions like this poor man's child. Oh God! to hear the Insect on the leaf pronouncing on the too much life among his hungry brothers in the dust!"

Scrooge bent before the Ghost's rebuke, and trembling cast his eyes upon the ground. But he raised them speedily, on hearing his own name.

"Mr. Scrooge!" said Bob; "I'll give you Mr. Scrooge, the Founder of the Feast!"

"The Founder of the Feast indeed!" cried Mrs. Cratchit,

reddening. "I wish I had him here. I'd give him a piece of my mind to feast upon, and I hope he'd have a good appetite for it."

"My dear," said Bob, "the children; Christmas Day."

"It should be Christmas Day, I am sure," said she, "on which one drinks the health of such an odious, stingy, hard, unfeeling man as Mr. Scrooge. You know he is, Robert! Nobody knows it better than you do, poor fellow!"

"My dear," was Bob's mild answer, "Christmas Day."

"I'll drink his health for your sake and the Day's," said Mrs. Cratchit, "not for his. Long life to him! A merry Christmas and a happy new year!—he'll be very merry and very happy, I have no doubt!"

The children drank the toast after her. It was the first of their proceedings which had no heartiness in it. Tiny Tim drank it last of all, but he didn't care twopence for it. Scrooge was the Ogre of the family. The mention of his name cast a dark shadow on the party, which was not dispelled for full five minutes.

After it had passed away, they were ten times merrier than before, from the mere relief of Scrooge the Baleful being done with. Bob Cratchit told them how he had a situation in his eye for Master Peter, which would bring in, if obtained, full five-and-sixpence weekly. The two young Cratchits laughed tremendously at the idea of Peter's being a man of business; and Peter himself looked thoughtfully at the fire from between his collars, as if he were deliberating what particular investments he should favour when he came into the receipt of that bewildering income. Martha, who was a poor apprentice at a milliner's, then told them what kind of work she had to do, and how many hours she worked at a stretch, and how she meant to lie a-bed to-morrow morning for a good long rest; to-morrow being a holiday she passed at home. Also how she had seen a countess and a lord some days before, and how the lord "was much about as tall as Peter"; at which Peter pulled up his collars so high that you couldn't have seen his head if you had been there. All this time the chestnuts and the jug went round and round; and bye and bye they had a song, about a lost child travelling in the snow, from Tiny Tim; who had a plaintive little voice, and sang it very well indeed.

There was nothing of high mark in this. They were not a handsome family; they were not well dressed; their shoes were far from being water-proof; their clothes were scanty; and Peter might have known, and very likely did, the inside of a pawnbroker's. But they were happy, grateful, pleased with one another, and contented with the time; and when they faded, and looked happier yet in the bright sprinklings of the Spirit's torch at parting, Scrooge had his eye upon them, and especially on Tiny Tim, until the last.

By this time it was getting dark, and snowing pretty heavily; and as Scrooge and the Spirit went along the streets, the brightness of the roaring fires in kitchens, parlours, and all sorts of rooms, was wonderful. Here, the flickering of the blaze showed preparations for a cosy dinner, with hot plates baking through and through before the fire, and deep red curtains, ready to be drawn, to shut out cold and darkness. There, all the children of the house were running out into the snow to meet their married sisters, brothers, cousins, uncles, aunts, and be the first to greet them. Here, again, were shadows on the window-blind of guests assembling; and there a group of handsome girls, all hooded and fur-booted, and all chattering at once, tripped lightly off to some near neighbour's house; where, woe upon the single man who saw them enter—artful witches: well they knew it —in a glow!

But if you had judged from the numbers of people on their way to friendly gatherings, you might have thought that no one was at home to give them welcome when they got there, instead of every house expecting company, and piling up its fires half-chimney high. Blessings on it, how the Ghost exulted! How it bared its breadth of breast, and opened its capacious palm, and floated on, outpouring, with a generous hand, its bright and harmless mirth on everything within its reach! The very lamplighter, who ran on before dotting the dusky street with specks of light, and who was dressed to spend the evening somewhere, laughed out loudly as the Spirit passed: though little kenned the lamplighter that he had any company but Christmas!

And now, without a word of warning from the Ghost, they stood upon a bleak and desert moor, where monstrous masses of rude stone were cast about, as though it were the burial-place of giants; and water spread itself wheresoever it listed—or would have done so, but for the frost that held it prisoner; and nothing grew but moss and furze, and coarse, rank grass. Down in the west the setting sun had left a streak of fiery red, which glared upon the desolation for an instant, like a sullen eye, and frowning lower, lower, lower yet, was lost in the thick gloom of darkest night.

"What place is this?" asked Scrooge.

"A place where Miners live, who labour in the bowels of the earth," returned the Spirit. "But they know me. See!"

A light shone from the window of a hut, and swiftly they advanced towards it. Passing through the wall of mud and stone, they found a cheerful company assembled round a glowing fire. An old, old man and woman, with their children and their children's children, and another generation beyond that, all decked out gaily in their holiday attire. The old man, in a voice that seldom rose above the howling of the wind upon the barren waste, was singing them a Christmas song; it had been a very old song when he was a boy; and from time to time they all joined in the chorus. So surely as they raised their voices, the old man got quite blithe and loud; and so surely as they stopped, his vigour sang again.

The Spirit did not tarry here, but bade Scrooge hold his robe, and passing on above the moor, sped whither? Not to sea? To sea. To Scrooge's horror, looking back, he saw the last of the land, a frightful range of rocks, behind them; and his ears were deafened by the thundering of water, as it rolled, and roared, and raged among the dreadful caverns it had worn, and fiercely tried to undermine the earth.

Built upon a dismal reef of sunken rocks, some league or so from shore, on which the waters chafed and dashed, the wild year through, there stood a solitary lighthouse. Great heaps of sea-weed clung to its base, and storm-birds—born of the wind one might suppose, as sea-weed of the water—rose and fell about it, like the waves they skimmed.

But even here, two men who watched the light had made a fire, that through the loophole in the thick stone wall shed out a ray of brightness on the awful sea. Joining their horny hands over the rough table at which they sat, they wished each other Merry Christmas in their can of grog; and one of them: the elder, too, with his face all damaged and scarred with hard weather, as the figure-head of an old ship might be: struck up a sturdy song that was like a Gale in itself.

Again the Ghost sped on, above the black and heaving sea —on, on—until, being far away, as he told Scrooge, from any shore, they lighted on a ship. They stood beside the helmsman at the wheel, the look-out in the bow, the officers who had the watch; dark, ghostly figures in their several stations; but every man among them hummed a Christmas tune, or had a Christmas thought, or spoke below his breath to his companion of some bygone Christmas Day, with homeward hopes belonging to it. And every man on board, waking or sleeping, good or bad, had had a kinder word for another on that day than on any day in the year; and had shared to some extent in its festivities; and had remembered those he cared for at a distance, and had known that they delighted to remember him.

It was a great surprise to Scrooge, while listening to the moaning of the wind, and thinking what a solemn thing it was to move on through the lonely darkness over an unknown abyss, whose depths were secrets as profound as Death: it was a great surprise to Scrooge, while thus engaged, to hear a hearty laugh. It was a much greater surprise to Scrooge to recognise it as his own nephew's, and to find himself in a bright, dry, gleaming room, with the Spirit standing smiling by his side, and looking at that same nephew with approving affability!

"Ha, ha!" laughed Scrooge's nephew. "Ha, ha, ha!"

If you should happen, by any unlikely chance, to know a man more blest in a laugh than Scrooge's nephew, all I can say is, I should like to know him too. Introduce him to me, and I'll cultivate his acquaintance.

It is a fair, even-handed, noble adjustment of things, that while there is infection in disease and sorrow, there is nothing in the world so irresistibly contagious as laughter and good-humour. When Scrooge's nephew laughed in this way: holding his sides, rolling his head, and twisting his face into the most extravagant contortions: Scrooge's niece, by marriage, laughed as heartily as he. And their assembled friends being not a bit behindhand, roared out, lustily.

"Ha, ha! Ha, ha, ha, ha!"

"He said that Christmas was a humbug, as I live!" cried Scrooge's nephew. "He believed it too!"

"More shame for him, Fred!" said Scrooge's niece, indignantly. Bless those women; they never do anything by halves. They are always in earnest.

She was very pretty: exceedingly pretty. With a dimpled, surprised-looking, capital face; a ripe little mouth, that seemed made to be kissed—as no doubt it was; all kinds of good little dots about her chin, that melted into one another when she laughed; and the sunniest pair of eyes you ever saw in any little creature's head. Altogether she was what you would have called provoking, you know; but satisfactory too. Oh, perfectly satisfactory!

"He's a comical old fellow," said Scrooge's nephew, "that's the truth: and not so pleasant as he might be. However, his offences carry their own punishment, and I have nothing to say against him."

"I'm sure he is very rich, Fred," hinted Scrooge's niece. "At least you always tell *me* so."

"What of that, my dear!" said Scrooge's nephew. "His wealth is of no use to him. He don't do any good with it.

He don't make himself comfortable with it. He hasn't the satisfaction of thinking—ha, ha, ha!—that he is ever going to benefit Us with it."

"I have no patience with him," observed Scrooge's niece. Scrooge's niece's sisters, and all the other ladies, expressed the same opinion.

"Oh, I have!" said Scrooge's nephew. "I am sorry for him; I couldn't be angry with him if I tried. Who suffers by his ill whims! Himself, always. Here, he takes it into his head to dislike us, and he won't come and dine with us. What's the consequence? He don't lose much of a dinner.'

"Indeed, I think he loses a very good dinner," interrupted Scrooge's niece. Everybody else said the same, and they must be allowed to have been competent judges, because they had just had dinner; and, with the dessert upon the table, were clustered round the fire, by lamplight.

"Well! I'm very glad to hear it," said Scrooge's nephew, "because I haven't great faith in these young housekeepers. What do *you* say, Topper?"

Topper had clearly got his eye upon one of Scrooge's niece's sisters, for he answered that a bachelor was a wretched outcast, who had no right to express an opinion on the subject. Whereat Scrooge's niece's sister—the plump one with the lace tucker: not the one with the roses—blushed.

"Do go on, Fred," said Scrooge's niece, clapping her hands. "He never finishes what he begins to say! He is such a ridiculous fellow!"

Scrooge's nephew revelled in another laugh, and as it was impossible to keep the infection off; though the plump sister tried hard to do it with aromatic vinegar; his example was unanimously followed.

"I was going to say," said Scrooge's nephew, "that the consequence of his taking a dislike to us, and not making merry with us, is, as I think, that he loses some pleasant moments, which could do him no harm. I am sure he loses pleasanter companions than he can find in his own thoughts, either in his mouldy old office, or his dusty chambers. I mean to give him the same chance every year, whether he likes it or not, for I pity him. He may rail at Christmas till he dies, but he can't help thinking better of it—I defy him— if he finds me going there, in good temper, year after year, and saying Uncle Scrooge, how are you? If it only puts him in the vein to leave his poor clerk fifty pounds, *that's* something; and I think I shook him, yesterday."

It was their turn to laugh now, at the notion of his shaking Scrooge. But being thoroughly good-natured, and not much caring what they laughed at, so that they laughed at any rate, he encouraged them in their merriment, and passed the bottle, joyously.

After tea, they had some music. For they were a musical family, and knew what they were about, when they sung a Glee or Catch, I can assure you: especially Topper, who could growl away in the bass like a good one, and never swell the large veins in his forehead, or get red in the face over it. Scrooge's niece played well upon the harp; and played among other tunes a simple little air (a mere nothing: you might learn to whistle it in two minutes), which had been familiar to the child who fetched Scrooge from the boarding-school, as he had been reminded by the Ghost of Christmas Past. When this strain of music sounded, all the things that Ghost had shown him, came upon his mind; he softened more and more; and thought that if he could have listened to it often, years ago, he might have cultivated the kindnesses of life for his own happiness with his own hands, without resorting to the sexton's spade that buried Jacob Marley.

But they didn't devote the whole evening to music. After a while they played at forfeits; for it is good to be children sometimes, and never better than at Christmas, when its mighty Founder was a child himself. Stop! There was first a game at blind-man's buff. Of course there was. And I no more believe Topper was really blind than I believe he had eyes in his boots. My opinion is, that it was a done thing between him and Scrooge's nephew; and that the Ghost of Christmas Present knew it. The way he went after that plump sister in the lace tucker, was an outrage on the credulity of human nature. Knocking down the fire-irons, tumbling over the chairs, bumping against the piano, smothering himself among the curtains, wherever she went, there went he. He always knew where the plump sister was. He wouldn't catch anybody else. If you had fallen up against him, as some of them did, and stood there; he would have made a feint of endeavouring to seize you, which would have been an affront to your understanding; and would instantly have sidled off in the direction of the plump sister. She often cried out that it wasn't fair; and it really was not. But when at last, he caught her; when, in spite of all her silken rustlings, and her rapid flutterings past him, he got her into a corner whence there was no escape; then his conduct was the most execrable. For his pretending not to know her; his pretending that it was necessary to touch her head-dress, and further to assure himself of her identity by pressing a certain ring upon her finger, and a certain chain about her neck; was vile, monstrous! No doubt she told him her opinion of it, when, another blind-man being in office, they were so very confidential together, behind the curtains.

Scrooge's niece was not one of the blind-man's buff party, but was made comfortable with a large chair and a footstool, in a snug corner, where the Ghost and Scrooge were close behind her. But she joined in the forfeits, and loved her love to admiration with all the letters of the alphabet. Likewise at the game of How, When, and Where, she was very great, and to the secret joy of Scrooge's nephew, beat her sisters hollow: though they were sharp girls too, as Topper could have told you. There might have been twenty people there, young and old, but they all played, and so did Scrooge; for wholly forgetting in the interest he had in what was going on, that his voice made no sound in their ears, he sometimes came out with his guess quite loud, and very often guessed quite right, too; for the sharpest needle, best Whitechapel, warranted not to cut in the eye, was not sharper than Scrooge: blunt as he took it in his head to be.

The Ghost was greatly pleased to find him in this mood, and looked upon him with such favour that he begged like a boy to be allowed to stay until the guests departed. But this the Spirit said could not be done.

"Here's a new game," said Scrooge. "One half hour, Spirit, only one!"

It was a Game called Yes and No, where Scrooge's nephew had to think of something, and the rest must find out what; he only answering to their questions yes or no as the case was. The brisk fire of questioning to which he was exposed, elicited from him that he was thinking of an animal, a live animal, rather a disagreeable animal, a savage animal, an animal that growled and grunted sometimes, and talked sometimes, and lived in London, and walked about the streets, and wasn't made a show of, and wasn't led by any-body, and didn't live in a menagerie, and was never killed in a market, and was not a horse, or an ass, or a cow, or a bull, or a tiger, or a dog, or a pig, or a cat, or a bear. At every fresh question that was put to him, this nephew burst into a fresh roar of laughter; and was so inexpressibly tickled, that he was obliged to get up off the sofa and stamp. At last the plump sister, falling into a similar state, cried out:

"I have found it out! I know what it is, Fred! I know what it is!"

"What is it?" cried Fred.

"It's your Uncle Scro-o-o-o-oge!"

Which it certainly was. Admiration was the universal sentiment, though some objected that the reply to "Is it a bear?" ought to have been "Yes;" inasmuch as an answer in the negative was sufficient to have diverted their thoughts from Mr. Scrooge, supposing they had ever had any tendency that way.

"He has given us plenty of merriment, I am sure," said Fred, "and it would be ungrateful not to drink his health.

Here is a glass of mulled wine ready to our hand at the moment; and I say 'Uncle Scrooge!'"

"Well! Uncle Scrooge!" they cried.

"A Merry Christmas and a Happy New Year to the old man, whatever he is!" said Scrooge's nephew. "He wouldn't take it from me, but may he have it, nevertheless. Uncle Scrooge!"

Uncle Scrooge had imperceptibly become so gay and light of heart, that he would have pledged the unconscious company in return, and thanked them in an inaudible speech, if the Ghost had given him time. But the whole scene passed off in the breath of the last word spoken by his nephew; and he and the Spirit were again upon their travels.

Much they saw, and far they went, and many homes they visited, but always with a happy end. The Spirit stood beside sick beds, and they were cheerful; on foreign lands, and they were close at home; by struggling men, and they were patient in their greater hope; by poverty, and it was rich. In alms-house, hospital, and jail, in misery's every refuge, where vain man in his little brief authority[26] had not made fast the door, and barred the Spirit out, he left his blessing, and taught Scrooge his precepts.

It was a long night, if it were only a night; but Scrooge had his doubts of this, because the Christmas Holidays appeared to be condensed into the space of time they passed together. It was strange, too, that while Scrooge remained unaltered in his outward form, the Ghost grew older, clearly older. Scrooge had observed this change, but never spoke of it, until they left a children's Twelfth Night party, when, looking at the Spirit as they stood together in an open place, he noticed that its hair was gray.

"Are spirits' lives so short?" asked Scrooge.

"My life upon this globe, is very brief," replied the Ghost. "It ends to-night."

"To-night!" cried Scrooge.

"To-night at midnight. Hark! The time is drawing near."

The chimes were ringing the three quarters past eleven at that moment.

"Forgive me if I am not justified in what I ask," said Scrooge, looking intently at the Spirit's robe, "but I see something strange, and not belonging to yourself, protruding from your skirts. Is it a foot or a claw!"

"It might be a claw, for the flesh there is upon it," was the Spirit's sorrowful reply. "Look here."

From the foldings of its robe, it brought two children; wretched, abject, frightful, hideous, miserable. They knelt down at its feet, and clung upon the outside of its garment.

"Oh, Man! look here. Look, look, down here!" exclaimed the Ghost.

They were a boy and girl. Yellow, meagre, ragged, scowling, wolfish; but prostrate, too, in their humility. Where graceful youth should have filled their features out, and touched them with its freshest tints, a stale and shrivelled hand, like that of age, had pinched, and twisted them, and pulled them into shreds. Where angels might have sat enthroned, devils lurked, and glared out menacing. No change, no degradation, no perversion of humanity, in any grade, through all the mysteries of wonderful creation, has monsters half so horrible and dread.

Scrooge started back, appalled. Having them shown to him in this way, he tried to say they were fine children, but the words choked themselves, rather than be parties to a lie of such enormous magnitude.

"Spirit! are they yours?" Scrooge could say no more.

"They are Man's," said the Spirit, looking down upon them. "And they cling to me, appealing from their fathers. This boy is Ignorance. This girl is Want. Beware them both, and all of their degree, but most of all beware this boy, for on his brow I see that written which is Doom, unless the writing be erased. Deny it!" cried the Spirit, stretching out its hand towards the city. "Slander those who tell it ye! Admit it for your factious purposes, and make it worse. And bide the end!"

"Have they no refuge or resource?" cried Scrooge.

"Are there no prisons?" said the Spirit, turning on him for the last time with his own words. "Are there no work-houses?"

The bell struck twelve.

Scrooge looked about him for the Ghost, and saw it not. As the last stroke ceased to vibrate, he remembered the prediction of old Jacob Marley, and lifting up his eyes, beheld a solemn Phantom, draped and hooded, coming, like a mist along the ground, towards him.

STAVE FOUR
THE LAST OF THE SPIRITS

THE Phantom slowly, gravely, silently, approached. When it came near him, Scrooge bent down upon his knee; for in the very air through which this Spirit moved it seemed to scatter gloom and mystery.

It was shrouded in a deep black garment, which concealed its head, its face, its form, and left nothing of it visible save one outstretched hand. But for this it would have been difficult to detach its figure from the night, and separate it from the darkness by which it was surrounded.

He felt that it was tall and stately when it came beside him, and that its mysterious presence filled him with a solemn dread. He knew no more, for the Spirit neither spoke nor moved.

"I am in the presence of the Ghost of Christmas Yet To Come?" said Scrooge.

The Spirit answered not, but pointed onward with its hand.

"You are about to show me shadows of the things that have not happened, but will happen in the time before us," Scrooge pursued. "Is that so, Spirit?"

The upper portion of the garment was contracted for an instant in its folds, as if the Spirit had inclined its head. That was the only answer he received.

Although well used to ghostly company by this time, Scrooge feared the silent shape so much that his legs trembled beneath him, and he found that he could hardly stand when he prepared to follow it. The Spirit paused a moment, as observing his condition, and giving him time to recover.

But Scrooge was all the worse for this. It thrilled him with a vague uncertain horror, to know that behind the dusky shroud, there were ghostly eyes intently fixed upon him, while he, though he stretched his own to the utmost, could see nothing but a spectral hand and one great heap of black.

"Ghost of the Future!" he exclaimed, "I fear you more than any Spectre I have seen. But as I know your purpose is to do me good, and as I hope to live to be another man from what I was, I am prepared to bear you company, and do it with a thankful heart. Will you not speak to me?"

It gave him no reply. The hand was pointed straight before them.

"Lead on!" said Scrooge. "Lead on! The night is waning fast, and it is precious time to me, I know. Lead on, Spirit!"

The Phantom moved away as it had come towards him. Scrooge followed in the shadow of its dress, which bore him up, he thought, and carried him along.

They scarcely seemed to enter the city; for the city rather seemed to spring up about them, and encompass them of its own act. But there they were, in the heart of it; on 'Change, amongst the merchants; who hurried up and down, and chinked the money in their pockets, and conversed in groups, and looked at their watches, and trifled thoughtfully with their great gold seals; and so forth, as Scrooge had seen them often.

The Spirit stopped beside one little knot of business men. Observing that the hand was pointed to them, Scrooge advanced to listen to their talk.

"No," said a great fat man with a monstrous chin, "I don't know much about it, either way. I only know he's dead."

"When did he die?" inquired another.

"Last night, I believe."

"Why, what was the matter with him?" asked a third, taking a vast quantity of snuff out of a very large snuff-box. "I thought he'd never die."

"God knows," said the first, with a yawn.

"What has he done with his money?" asked a red-faced gentleman with a pendulous excrescence on the end of his nose, that shook like the gills of a turkey-cock.

"I haven't heard," said the man with the large chin, yawning again. "Left it to his Company, perhaps. He hasn't left it to *me*. That's all I know."

This pleasantry was received with a general laugh.

"It's likely to be a very cheap funeral," said the same speaker; "for upon my life I don't know of anybody to go to it. Suppose we make up a party and volunteer?"

"I don't mind going if a lunch is provided," observed the gentleman with the excrescence on his nose. "But I must be fed, if I make one."

Another laugh.

"Well, I am the most disinterested among you, after all," said the first speaker, "for I never wear black gloves, and I never eat lunch. But I'll offer to go, if anybody else will. When I come to think of it, I'm not at all sure that I wasn't his most particular friend; for we used to stop and speak whenever we met. Bye, bye!"

Speakers and listeners strolled away, and mixed with other groups. Scrooge knew the men, and looked towards the Spirit for an explanation.

The Phantom glided on into a street. Its finger pointed to two persons meeting. Scrooge listened again, thinking that the explanation might lie here.

He knew these men, also, perfectly. They were men of business: very wealthy, and of great importance. He had made a point always of standing well in their esteem: in a business point of view, that is; strictly in a business point of view.

"How are you?" said one.

"How are you?" returned the other.

"Well!" said the first. "Old Scratch[27] has got his own at last, hey?"

"So I am told," returned the second. "Cold, isn't it?"

"Seasonable for Christmas time. You're not a skaiter, I suppose?"

"No. No. Something else to think of. Good morning!"

Not another word. That was their meeting, their conversation, and their parting.

Scrooge was at first inclined to be surprised that the Spirit should attach importance to conversations apparently so trivial; but feeling assured that they must have some hidden purpose, he set himself to consider what it was likely to be. They could scarcely be supposed to have any bearing on the death of Jacob, his old partner, for that was Past, and this Ghost's province was the Future. Nor could he think of any one immediately connected with himself, to whom he could apply them. But nothing doubting that to whomsoever they applied they had some latent moral for his own improvement, he resolved to treasure up every word he heard, and everything he saw; and especially to observe the shadow of himself when it appeared. For he had an expectation that the conduct of his future self would give him the clue he missed, and would render the solution of these riddles easy.

He looked about in that very place for his own image; but another man stood in his accustomed corner, and though the clock pointed to his usual time of day for being there, he saw no likeness of himself among the multitudes that poured in through the Porch. It gave him little surprise, however; for he had been revolving in his mind a change of life, and thought and hoped he saw his new-born resolutions carried out in this.

Quiet and dark, beside him stood the Phantom, with its outstretched hand. When he roused himself from his thoughtful quest, he fancied from the turn of the hand, and its situation in reference to himself, that the Unseen Eyes were looking at him keenly. It made him shudder, and feel very cold.

They left the busy scene, and went into an obscure part of the town, where Scrooge had never penetrated before although he recognised its situation, and its bad repute. The ways were foul and narrow; the shops and houses wretched; the people half-naked, drunken, slipshod, ugly. Alleys and archways, like so many cesspools, disgorged their offences of smell, and dirt, and life, upon the straggling streets; and the whole quarter reeked with crime, with filth, and misery.

Far in this den of infamous resort, there was a low-browed, beetling shop, below a pent-house roof, where iron, old rags, bottles, bones, and greasy offal, were bought. Upon the floor within, were piled up heaps of rusty keys, nails, chains, hinges, files, scales, weights, and refuse iron of all kinds. Secrets that few would like to scrutinise were bred and hidden in mountains of unseemly rags, masses of corrupted fat, and sepulchres of bones. Sitting in among the wares he dealt in, by a charcoal-stove, made of old bricks, was a gray-haired rascal, nearly seventy years of age; who had screened himself from the cold air without, by a frousy curtaining of miscellaneous tatters, hung upon a line; and smoked his pipe in all the luxury of calm retirement.

Scrooge and the Phantom came into the presence of this man, just as a woman with a heavy bundle slunk into the shop. But she had scarcely entered, when another woman, similarly laden, came in too; and she was closely followed by a man in faded black, who was no less startled by the sight of them, than they had been upon the recognition of each other. After a short period of blank astonishment, in which the old man with the pipe had joined them, they all three burst into a laugh.

"Let the charwoman alone to be the first!" cried she who had entered first. "Let the laundress alone to be the second; and let the undertaker's man alone to be the third. Look here, old Joe, here's a chance! If we haven't all three met here without meaning it."

"You couldn't have met in a better place," said old Joe, removing his pipe from his mouth. "Come into the parlour. You were made free of it long ago, you know; and the other two an't strangers. Stop till I shut the door of the shop. Ah! How it skreeks! There an't such a rusty bit of metal in the place as its own hinges, I believe; and I'm sure there's no such old bones here, as mine. Ha, ha! We're all suitable to our calling, we're well matched. Come into the parlour. Come into the parlour."

The parlour was the space behind the screen of rags. The old man raked the fire together with an old stair-rod, and having trimmed his smoky lamp (for it was night), with the stem of his pipe, put it in his mouth again.

While he did this, the woman who had already spoken threw her bundle on the floor and sat down in a flaunting manner on a stool; crossing her elbows on her knees, and looking with a bold defiance at the other two.

"What odds then! What odds, Mrs. Dilber?" said the woman. "Every person has a right to take care of themselves. *He* always did!"

"That's true, indeed!" said the laundress. "No man more so."

"Why then, don't stand staring as if you was afraid, woman; who's the wiser? We're not going to pick holes in each other's coats, I suppose?"

"No, indeed!" said Mrs. Dilber and the man together. "We should hope not."

"Very well, then!" cried the woman. "That's enough. Who's the worse for the loss of a few things like these? Not a dead man, I suppose."

"No, indeed," said Mrs. Dilber, laughing.

"If he wanted to keep 'em after he was dead, a wicked old screw," pursued the woman, "why wasn't he natural in his lifetime? If he had been, he'd have had somebody to look after him when he was struck with Death, instead of lying gasping out his last there, alone by himself."

"It's the truest word that ever was spoke," said Mrs. Dilber. "It's a judgment on him."

"I wish it was a little heavier one," replied the woman; "and it should have been, you may depend upon it, if I could have laid my hands on anything else. Open that bundle, old Joe, and let me know the value of it. Speak out plain. I'm not afraid to be the first, nor afraid for them to see it. We knew pretty well that we were helping ourselves, before we met here, I believe. It's no sin. Open the bundle, Joe."

But the gallantry of her friends would not allow of this; and the man in faded black, mounting the breach first, produced *his* plunder. It was not extensive. A seal or two, a pencil-case, a pair of sleeve-buttons, and a brooch of no great value, were all. They were severally examined and appraised by old Joe, who chalked the sums he was disposed to give for each, upon the wall, and added them up into a total when he found there was nothing more to come.

"That's your account," said Joe, "and I wouldn't give another sixpence, if I was to be boiled for not doing it. Who's next?"

Mrs. Dilber was next. Sheets and towels, a little wearing apparel, two old-fashioned silver teaspoons, a pair of sugar-tongs, and a few boots. Her account was stated on the wall in the same manner.

"I always give too much to ladies. It's a weakness of mine, and that's the way I ruin myself," said old Joe. "That's your account. If you asked me for another penny, and made it an open question, I'd repent of being so liberal and knock off half-a-crown."

"And now undo *my* bundle, Joe," said the first woman.

Joe went down on his knees for the greater convenience of opening it, and having unfastened a great many knots, dragged out a large and heavy roll of some dark stuff.

"What do you call this?" said Joe. "Bed-curtains!"

"Ah!" returned the woman, laughing and leaning forward on her crossed arms. "Bed-curtains!"

"You don't mean to say you took 'em down, rings and all, with him lying there?" said Joe.

"Yes I do," replied the woman. "Why not?"

"You were born to make your fortune," said Joe, "and you'll certainly do it."

"I certainly shan't hold my hand, when I get anything in it by reaching it out, for the sake of such a man as He was,

I promise you, Joe," returned the woman coolly. "Don't drop that oil upon the blankets, now."

"His blankets?" asked Joe.

"Whose else's do you think?" replied the woman. "He isn't likely to take cold without 'em, I dare say."

"I hope he didn't die of anything catching? Eh?" said old Joe, stopping in his work, and looking up.

"Don't you be afraid of that," returned the woman. "I an't so fond of his company that I'd loiter about him for such things, if he did. Ah! you may look through that shirt till your eyes ache; but you won't find a hole in it, nor a threadbare place. It's the best he had, and a fine one too. They'd have wasted it, if it hadn't been for me."

"What do you call wasting of it?" asked old Joe.

"Putting it on him to be buried in, to be sure," replied the woman with a laugh. "Somebody was fool enough to do it, but I took it off again. If calico an't good enough for such a purpose, it isn't good enough for anything. It's quite as becoming to the body. He can't look uglier than he did in that one."

Scrooge listened to this dialogue in horror. As they sat grouped about their spoil, in the scanty light afforded by the old man's lamp, he viewed them with a detestation and disgust, which could hardly have been greater, though they had been obscene demons, marketing the corpse itself.

"He, ha!" laughed the same woman, when old Joe, producing a flannel bag with money in it, told out their several gains upon the ground. "This is the end of it, you see! He frightened every one away from him when he was alive, to profit us when he was dead! Ha, ha, ha!"

"Spirit!" said Scrooge, shuddering from head to foot. "I see, I see. The case of this unhappy man might be my own. My life tends that way, now. Merciful Heaven, what is this!"

He recoiled in terror, for the scene had changed, and now he almost touched a bed: a bare, uncurtained bed: on which, beneath a ragged sheet, there lay a something covered up, which, though it was dumb, announced itself in awful language.

The room was very dark, too dark to be observed with any accuracy, though Scrooge glanced round it in obedience to a secret impulse, anxious to know what kind of room it was. A pale light, rising in the outer air, fell straight upon the bed; and on it, plundered and bereft, unwatched, unwept, uncared for, was the body of this man.

Scrooge glanced towards the Phantom. Its steady hand was pointed to the head. The cover was so carelessly adjusted that the slightest raising of it, the motion of a finger upon Scrooge's part, would have disclosed the face. He thought of it, felt how easy it would be to do, and longed to do it; but had no more power to withdraw the veil than to dismiss the spectre at his side.

Oh cold, cold, rigid, dreadful Death, set up thine altar here, and dress it with such terrors as thou hast at thy command: for this is thy dominion! But of the loved, revered, and honoured head, thou canst not turn one hair to thy dread purposes, or make one feature odious. It is not that the hand is heavy and will fall down when released; it is not that the heart and pulse are still; but that the hand WAS open, generous, and true; the heart brave, warm, and tender; and the pulse a man's. Strike, Shadow, strike! And see his good deeds springing from the wound, to sow the world with life immortal!

No voice pronounced these words in Scrooge's ears, and yet he heard them when he looked upon the bed. He thought, if this man could be raised up now, what would be his foremost thoughts? Avarice, hard dealing, griping cares? They have brought him to a rich end, truly!

He lay, in the dark empty house, with not a man, a woman, or a child, to say that he was kind to me in this or that, and for the memory of one kind word I will be kind to him. A cat was tearing at the door, and there was a sound of gnawing rats beneath the hearth-stone. What *they* wanted in the room of death, and why they were so restless and disturbed, Scrooge did not dare to think.

"Spirit!" he said, "this is a fearful place. In leaving it, I shall not leave its lesson, trust me. Let us go!"

Still the Ghost pointed with an unmoved finger to the head.

"I understand you," Scrooge returned, "and I would do it, if I could. But I have not the power, Spirit. I have not the power."

Again it seemed to look upon him.

"If there is any person in the town, who feels emotion caused by this man's death," said Scrooge quite agonised, "show that person to me, Spirit, I beseech you!"

The Phantom spread its dark robe before him for a moment, like a wing; and withdrawing it, revealed a room by daylight, where a mother and her children were.

She was expecting some one, and with anxious eagerness; for she walked up and down the room; started at every sound; looked out from the window; glanced at the clock; tried, but in vain, to work with her needle; and could hardly bear the voices of the children in their play.

At length the long-expected knock was heard. She hurried to the door, and met her husband; a man whose face was care-worn and depressed, though he was young. There was a remarkable expression in it now; a kind of serious delight of which he felt ashamed, and which he struggled to repress.

He sat down to the dinner that had been hoarding for him by the fire; and when she asked him faintly what news (which was not until after a long silence), he appeared embarrassed how to answer.

"Is it good," she said, "or bad?"—to help him.

"Bad," he answered.

"We are quite ruined?"

"No. There is hope yet, Caroline."

"If *he* relents," she said, amazed, "there is! Nothing is past hope, if such a miracle has happened."

"He is past relenting," said her husband. "He is dead."

She was a mild and patient creature if her face spoke truth; but she was thankful in her soul to hear it, and she said so, with clasped hands. She prayed forgiveness the next moment, and was sorry; but the first was the emotion of her heart.

"What the half-drunken woman whom I told you of last night, said to me, when I tried to see him and obtain a week's delay; and what I thought was a mere excuse to avoid me; turns out to have been quite true. He was not only very ill, but dying, then."

"To whom will our debt be transferred?"

"I don't know. But before that time we shall be ready with the money; and even though we were not, it would be bad fortune indeed to find so merciless a creditor in his successor. We may sleep to-night with light hearts, Caroline!"

Yes. Soften it as they would, their hearts were lighter. The children's faces, hushed and clustered round to hear what they so little understood, were brighter; and it was a happier house for this man's death! The only emotion that the Ghost could show him, caused by the event, was one of pleasure.

"Let me see some tenderness connected with a death," said Scrooge; "or that dark chamber, Spirit, which we left just now, will be for ever present to me."

The Ghost conducted him through several streets familiar to his feet; and as they went along, Scrooge looked here and there to find himself, but nowhere was he to be seen. They entered poor Bob Cratchit's house; the dwelling he had visited before; and found the mother and the children seated round the fire.

Quiet. Very quiet. The noisy little Cratchits were as still as statues in one corner, and sat looking up at Peter, who had a book before him. The mother and her daughters were engaged in sewing. But surely they were very quiet!

"'And He took a child, and set him in the midst of them.'"[28]

Where had Scrooge heard those words? He had not

dreamed them. The boy must have read them out, as he and the Spirit crossed the threshold. Why did he not go on?

The mother laid her work upon the table, and put her hand up to her face.

"The colour hurts my eyes," she said.

The colour? Ah, poor Tiny Tim!

"They're better now again," said Cratchit's wife. "It makes them weak by candle-light; and I wouldn't show weak eyes to your father when he comes home, for the world. It must be near his time."

"Past it rather," Peter answered, shutting up his book. "But I think he's walked a little slower than he used, these few last evenings, mother."

They were very quiet again. At last she said, and in a steady, cheerful voice, that only faultered once:

"I have known him walk with—I have known him walk with Tiny Tim upon his shoulder, very fast indeed."

"And so have I," cried Peter. "Often."

"And so have I!" exclaimed another. So had all.

"But he was very light to carry," she resumed, intent upon her work, "and his father loved him so, that it was no trouble—no trouble. And there is your father at the door!"

She hurried out to meet him; and little Bob in his comforter —he had need of it, poor fellow—came in. His tea was ready for him on the hob, and they all tried who should help him to it most. Then the two young Cratchits got upon his knees and laid, each child a little cheek, against his face, as if they said, "Don't mind it, father. Don't be grieved!"

Bob was very cheerful with them, and spoke pleasantly to all the family. He looked at the work upon the table, and praised the industry and speed of Mrs. Cratchit and the girls. They would be done long before Sunday, he said.

"Sunday! You went to-day then, Robert?" said his wife.

"Yes, my dear," returned Bob. "I wish you could have gone. It would have done you good to see how green a place it is. But you'll see it often. I promised him that I would walk there on a Sunday. My little, little child!" cried Bob. "My little child!"

He broke down all at once. He couldn't help it. If he could have helped it, he and his child would have been farther apart perhaps than they were.

He left the room, and went up stairs into the room above, which was lighted cheerfully, and hung with Christmas. There was a chair set close beside the child, and there were signs of some one having been there, lately. Poor Bob sat down in it, and when he had thought a little and composed himself, he kissed the little face. He was reconciled to what had happened, and went down again quite happy.

They drew about the fire, and talked; the girls and mother working still. Bob told them of the extraordinary kindness of Mr. Scrooge's nephew, whom he had scarcely seen but once, and who, meeting him in the street that day, and seeing that he looked a little—"just a little down you know" said Bob, inquired what had happened to distress him. "On which," said Bob, "for he is the pleasantest-spoken gentleman you ever heard, I told him. 'I am heartily sorry for it, Mr. Cratchit,' he said, 'and heartily sorry for your good wife.' By the bye, how he ever knew *that*, I don't know."

"Knew what, my dear."

"Why, that you were a good wife," replied Bob.

"Everybody knows that!" said Peter.

"Very well observed, my boy!" cried Bob. "I hope they do. 'Heartily sorry,' he said, 'for your good wife. If I can be of any service to you in any way,' he said, giving me his card, 'that's where I live. Pray come to me.' Now, it wasn't," cried Bob, "for the sake of anything he might be able to do for us, so much as for his kind way, that this was quite delightful. It really seemed as if he had known our Tiny Tim, and felt with us."

"I'm sure he's a good soul!" said Mrs. Cratchit.

"You would be surer of it, my dear," returned Bob, "if you saw and spoke to him. I shouldn't be at all surprised, mark what I say, if he got Peter a better situation."

"Only hear that, Peter," said Mrs. Cratchit.

"And then," cried one of the girls, "Peter will be keeping company with some one, and setting up for himself."

"Get along with you!" retorted Peter, grinning.

"It's just as likely as not," said Bob, "one of these days; though there's plenty of time for that, my dear. But however and whenever we part from one another, I am sure we shall none of us forget poor Tiny Tim—shall we—or this first parting that there was among us?"

"Never, father!" cried they all.

"And I know," said Bob, "I know, my dears, that when we recollect how patient and how mild he was; although he was a little, little child; we shall not quarrel easily among ourselves, and forget poor Tiny Tim in doing it."

"No, never, father!" they all cried again.

"I am very happy," said little Bob, "I am very happy!"

Mrs. Cratchit kissed him, his daughters kissed him, the two young Cratchits kissed him, and Peter and himself shook hands. Spirit of Tiny Tim, thy childish essence was from God!

"Spectre," said Scrooge, "something informs me that our parting moment is at hand. I know it, but I know not how. Tell me what man that was whom we saw lying dead?"

The Ghost of Christmas Yet To Come conveyed him, as before—though at a different time, he thought: indeed, there seemed no order in these latter visions, save that they were in the Future—into the resorts of business men, but showed him not himself. Indeed, the Spirit did not stay for anything, but went straight on, as to the end just now desired, until besought by Scrooge to tarry for a moment.

"This court," said Scrooge, "through which we hurry now, is where my place of occupation is, and has been for a length of time. I see the house. Let me behold what I shall be, in days to come."

The Spirit stopped; the hand was pointed elsewhere.

"The house is yonder," Scrooge exclaimed. "Why do you point away?"

The inexorable finger underwent no change.

Scrooge hastened to the window of his office, and looked in. It was an office still, but not his. The furniture was not the same, and the figure in the chair was not himself. The Phantom pointed as before.

He joined it once again, and wondering why and whither he had gone, accompanied it until they reached an iron gate. He paused to look round before entering.

A churchyard. Here, then, the wretched man whose name he had now to learn, lay underneath the ground. It was a worthy place. Walled in by houses; overrun by grass and weeds, the growth of vegetation's death, not life; choked up with too much burying; fat with repleted appetite. A worthy place!

The Spirit stood among the graves, and pointed down to One. He advanced towards it trembling. The Phantom was exactly as it had been, but he dreaded that he saw new meaning in its solemn shape.

"Before I draw nearer to that stone to which you point," said Scrooge, "answer me one question. Are these the shadows of the things that Will be, or are they shadows of things that May be, only?"

Still the Ghost pointed downward to the grave by which it stood.

"Men's courses will foreshadow certain ends, to which, if persevered in, they must lead," said Scrooge. "But if the courses be departed from, the ends will change. Say it is thus with what you show me!"

The Spirit was immovable as ever.

Scrooge crept towards it, trembling as he went; and following the finger, read upon the stone of the neglected grave his own name, EBENEZER SCROOGE.

"Am *I* that man who lay upon the bed?" he cried, upon his knees.

The finger pointed from the grave to him, and back again.

"No, Spirit! Oh, no, no!"

The finger still was there.

"Spirit!" he cried, tight clutching at its robe, "hear me! I am not the man I was. I will not be the man I must have been but for this intercourse. Why show me this, if I am past all hope?"

For the first time the hand appeared to shake.

"Good Spirit," he pursued, as down upon the ground he fell before it: "Your nature intercedes for me, and pities me. Assure me that I yet may change these shadows you have shown me, by an altered life!"

The kind hand trembled.

"I will honour Christmas in my heart, and try to keep it all the year. I will live in the Past, Present, and the Future. The Spirits of all Three shall strive within me. I will not shut out the lessons that they teach. Oh, tell me I may sponge away the writing on this stone!"

In his agony, he caught the spectral hand. It sought to free itself, but he was strong in his entreaty, and detained it. The Spirit, stronger yet, repulsed him.

Holding up his hands in a last prayer to have his fate reversed, he saw an alteration in the Phantom's hood and dress. It shrunk, collapsed, and dwindled down into a bed-post.

STAVE FIVE
THE END OF IT

———

YES! and the bedpost was his own. The bed was his own, the room was his own. Best and happiest of all, the Time before him was his own, to make amends in!

"I will live in the Past, the Present, and the Future!" Scrooge repeated, as he scrambled out of bed. "The Spirits of all Three shall strive within me. Oh Jacob Marley! Heaven, and the Christmas Time be praised for this! I say it on my knees, old Jacob; on my knees!"

He was so fluttered and so glowing with his good intentions, that his broken voice would scarcely answer to his call. He had been sobbing violently in his conflict with the Spirit, and his face was wet with tears.

"They are not torn down," cried Scrooge, folding one of his bed-curtains in his arms, "they are not torn down, rings and all. They are here: I am here: the shadows of the things that would have been, may be dispelled. They will be. I know they will!"

His hands were busy with his garments all this time: turning them inside out, putting them on upside down, tearing them, mislaying them, making them parties to every kind of extravagance.

"I don't know what to do!" cried Scrooge, laughing and crying in the same breath; and making a perfect Laocoön[29] of himself with his stockings. "I am as light as a feather, I am as happy as an angel, I am as merry as a school-boy. I am as giddy as a drunken man. A merry Christmas to everybody! A happy New Year to all the world! Hallo here! Whoop! Hallo!"

He had frisked into the sitting-room, and was now standing there: perfectly winded.

"There's the saucepan that the gruel was in!" cried

Scrooge, starting off again, and frisking round the fire-place. "There's the door, by which the Ghost of Jacob Marley entered! There's the corner where the Ghost of Christmas Present, sat! There's the window where I saw the wandering Spirits! It's all right, it's all true, it all happened. Ha ha ha!"

Really, for a man who had been out of practice for so many years, it was a splendid laugh, a most illustrious laugh. The father of a long, long line of brilliant laughs!

"I don't know what day of the month it is!" said Scrooge. "I don't know how long I've been among the Spirits. I don't know anything. I'm quite a baby. Never mind. I don't care. I'd rather be a baby. Hallo! Whoop! Hallo here!"

He was checked in his transports by the churches ringing out the lustiest peals he had ever heard. Clash, clang, hammer, ding, dong, bell. Bell, dong, ding, hammer, clang, clash! Oh, glorious, glorious!

Running to the window, he opened it, and put out his head. No fog, no mist; clear, bright, jovial, stirring, cold; cold, piping for the blood to dance to; Golden sunlight; Heavenly sky; sweet fresh air; merry bells. Oh, glorious. Glorious!

"What's to-day?" cried Scrooge, calling downward to a boy in Sunday clothes, who perhaps had loitered in to look about him.

"Eh?" returned the boy, with all his might of wonder.

"What's to-day, my fine fellow?" said Scrooge.

"To-day!" replied the boy. "Why, CHRISTMAS DAY."

"It's Christmas Day!" said Scrooge to himself. "I haven't missed it. The Spirits have done it all in one night. They can do anything they like. Of course they can. Of course they can. Hallo, my fine fellow!"

"Hallo!" returned the boy.

"Do you know the Poulterer's, in the next street but one, at the corner?" Scrooge inquired.

"I should hope I did," replied the lad.

"An intelligent boy!" said Scrooge. "A remarkable boy!

Do you know whether they've sold the prize Turkey that was hanging up there? Not the little prize Turkey: the big one?"

"What, the one as big as me?" returned the boy.

"What a delightful boy!" said Scrooge. "It's a pleasure to talk to him. Yes, my buck!"

"It's hanging there now," replied the boy.

"Is it?" said Scrooge. "Go and buy it."

"Walk-ER!" exclaimed the boy[30].

"No, no," said Scrooge, "I am in earnest. Go and buy it, and tell 'em to bring it here, that I may give them the direction where to take it. Come back with the man, and I'll give you a shilling. Come back with him in less than five minutes, and I'll give you half-a-crown!"

The boy was off like a shot. He must have had a steady hand at a trigger who could have got a shot off half so fast.

"I'll send it to Bob Cratchit's!" whispered Scrooge, rubbing his hands, and splitting with a laugh. "He shan't know who sends it. It's twice the size of Tiny Tim. Joe Miller[31] never made such a joke as sending it to Bob's will be!"

The hand in which he wrote the address was not a steady one, but write it he did, somehow, and went down stairs to open the street door, ready for the coming of the poulterer's man. As he stood there, waiting his arrival, the knocker caught his eye.

"I shall love it, as long as I live!" cried Scrooge, patting it with his hand. "I scarcely ever looked at it before. What an honest expression it has in its face! It's a wonderful knocker! —Here's the Turkey. Hallo! Whoop! How are you! Merry Christmas!"

It *was* a Turkey! He never could have stood upon his legs, that bird. He would have snapped 'em short off in a minute, like sticks of sealing-wax.

"Why, it's impossible to carry that to Camden Town," said Scrooge. "You must have a cab."

The chuckle with which he said this, and the chuckle

with which he paid for the Turkey, and the chuckle with which he paid for the cab, and the chuckle with which he recompensed the boy, were only to be exceeded by the chuckle with which he sat down breathless in his chair again, and chuckled till he cried.

Shaving was not an easy task, for his hand continued to shake very much; and shaving requires attention, even when you don't dance while you are at it. But if he had cut the end of his nose off, he would have put a piece of sticking-plaister over it, and been quite satisfied.

He dressed himself "all in his best," and at last got out into the streets. The people were by this time pouring forth, as he had seen them with the Ghost of Christmas Present; and walking with his hands behind him, Scrooge regarded every one with a delighted smile. He looked so irresistibly pleasant, in a word, that three or four good-humoured fellows said, "Good morning, sir! A merry Christmas to you!" And Scrooge said often afterwards, that of all the blithe sounds he had ever heard, those were the blithest in his ears.

He had not gone far, when coming on towards him he beheld the portly gentleman, who had walked into his counting-house the day before and said, "Scrooge and Marley's, I believe?" It sent a pang across his heart to think how this old gentleman would look upon him when they met; but he knew what path lay straight before him, and he took it.

"My dear sir," said Scrooge, quickening his pace, and taking the old gentleman by both his hands. "How do you do? I hope you succeeded yesterday. It was very kind of you. A merry Christmas to you, sir!"

"Mr. Scrooge?"

"Yes," said Scrooge. "That is my name, and I fear it may not be pleasant to you. Allow me to ask your pardon. And will you have the goodness"—here Scrooge whispered in his ear.

"Lord bless me!" cried the gentleman, as if his breath were gone. "My dear Mr. Scrooge, are you serious?"

"If you please," said Scrooge. "Not a farthing less. A great many back-payments are included in it, I assure you. Will you do me that favour?"

"My dear sir," said the other, shaking hands with him. "I don't know what to say to such munifi—"

"Don't say anything, please," retorted Scrooge. "Come and see me. Will you come and see me?"

"I will!" cried the old gentleman. And it was clear he meant to do it.

"Thank'ee," said Scrooge. "I am much obliged to you. I thank you fifty times. Bless you!"

He went to church, and walked about the streets, and watched the people hurrying to and fro, and patted children on the head, and questioned beggars, and looked down into the kitchens of houses, and up to the windows; and found that everything could yield him pleasure. He had never dreamed that any walk—that anything—could give him so much happiness. In the afternoon, he turned his steps towards his nephew's house.

He passed the door a dozen times, before he had the courage to go up and knock. But he made a dash, and did it:

"Is your master at home, my dear?" said Scrooge to the girl. Nice girl! Very.

"Yes, sir."

"Where is he, my love?" said Scrooge.

"He's in the dining-room, sir, along with mistress. I'll show you up stairs, if you please."

"Thank'ee. He knows me," said Scrooge, with his hand already on the dining-room lock. "I'll go in here, my dear."

He turned it gently, and sidled his face in, round the door. They were looking at the table (which was spread out in great array); for these young housekeepers are always nervous on such points, and like to see that everything is right.

"Fred!" said Scrooge.

Dear heart alive, how his niece by marriage started! Scrooge had forgotten, for the moment, about her sitting in the corner with the footstool, or he wouldn't have done it, on any account.

"Why bless my soul!" cried Fred, "who's that?"

"It's I. Your uncle Scrooge. I have come to dinner. Will you let me in, Fred?"

Let him in! It is a mercy he didn't shake his arm off. He was at home in five minutes. Nothing could be heartier. His niece looked just the same. So did Topper when *he* came. So did the plump sister, when *she* came. So did every one when *they* came. Wonderful party, wonderful games, wonderful unanimity, won-der-ful happiness!

But he was early at the office next morning. Oh, he was early there. If he could only be there first, and catch Bob Cratchit coming late! That was the thing he had set his heart upon.

And he did it; yes, he did! The clock struck nine. No Bob. A quarter past. No Bob. He was full eighteen minutes and a half, behind his time. Scrooge sat with his door wide open, that he might see him come into the Tank.

His hat was off, before he opened the door; his comforter too. He was on his stool in a jiffy; driving away with his pen, as if he were trying to overtake nine o'clock.

"Hallo!" growled Scrooge, in his accustomed voice as near as he could feign it. "What do you mean by coming here at this time of day?"

"I am very sorry, sir," said Bob. "I *am* behind my time."

"You are?" repeated Scrooge. "Yes. I think you are. Step this way, if you please."

"It's only once a year, sir," pleaded Bob, appearing from the Tank. "It shall not be repeated. I was making rather merry yesterday, sir."

"Now, I'll tell you what, my friend," said Scrooge, "I am not going to stand this sort of thing any longer. And therefore," he continued, leaping from his stool, and giving Bob such a dig in the waistcoat that he staggered back into the Tank again: "and therefore I am about to raise your salary!"

Bob trembled, and got a little nearer to the ruler. He had a momentary idea of knocking Scrooge down with it; holding him; and calling to the people in the court for help and a strait-waistcoat.

"A merry Christmas, Bob!" said Scrooge, with an earnestness that could not be mistaken, as he clapped him on the back. "A merrier Christmas, Bob, my good fellow, than I have given you, for many a year! I'll raise your salary, and endeavour to assist your struggling family, and we will discuss your affairs this very afternoon, over a Christmas bowl of smoking bishop[32], Bob! Make up the fires, and buy another coal-scuttle before you dot another i, Bob Cratchit!"

Scrooge was better than his word. He did it all, and infinitely more; and to Tiny Tim, who did NOT die, he was a second father. He became as good a friend, as good a master, and as good a man, as the good old city knew, or any other good old city, town, or borough, in the good old world. Some people laughed to see the alteration in him, but he let them laugh, and little heeded them; for he was wise enough to know that nothing ever happened on this globe, for good, at which some people did not have their fill of laughter in the outset; and knowing that such as these would be blind anyway, he thought it quite as well that they should wrinkle up their eyes in grins, as have the malady in less attractive forms. His own heart laughed: and that was quite enough for him.

He had no further intercourse with Spirits, but lived upon the Total Abstinence Principle, ever afterwards; and it was always said of him, that he knew how to keep Christmas well, if any man alive possessed the knowledge. May that be truly said of us, and all of us! And so, as Tiny Tim observed, God bless Us, Every One!

THE END

THE CHIMES

INTRODUCTION TO
THE CHIMES

WHEN Dickens signed an agreement with his new publishers, Bradbury and Evans, on 1 June 1844, there was, Forster tells us, 'an understanding . . . that a successor to the *Carol* would be ready for the Christmas of 1844'. By August Dickens, established with his family in a Genoese villa, wrote to Forster, 'I have begun to [think] every morning – with a business-like air, of the Christmas book' but he seems not to have got down to the actual writing until the beginning of October, after moving to a more satisfactory residence than the 'pink gaol' (as he called the first villa). For a month he shut himself up 'close and tight' over the work, sending the manuscript to Forster in instalments and writing also frequent letters to his friend outlining the proposed development of the story and describing his progress. He 'staggered on the threshold', missing the stimulation of his London environment, until the 'maddening' bells of Genoa inspired him with a title and an idea for 'working the story round': 'We have heard THE CHIMES at midnight, Master Shallow!' he wrote triumphantly to Forster and he soon was reporting that his 'steam [was] very much up' (though he sorely lacked 'a crowded street to plunge into at night'). 'I am in a regular, ferocious excitement with *The Chimes*,' he announced,

get up at seven; have a cold bath before breakfast; and blaze away, wrathful and red-hot until three o'clock or so; when I usually knock off (unless it rains) for the day . . . I am fierce to finish in a spirit bearing some affinity to those of truth and mercy, and to shame the cruel and the canting.

At last came the announcement, 'Third of November, 1844. Half-past two, afternoon. Thank God! I have finished *The Chimes*. This moment. I take up my pen again to-day, to say only that much; and to add that I have had what women call "a real good cry".'

The Chimes, with its intensely topical satire, was far more of an overt political manifesto than the *Carol*. Dickens was out to strike the heaviest blow in his power on behalf of the poor and oppressed of early Victorian England by fiercely attacking a number of prominent theories and attitudes held by the upper and middle classes which tended to see the swarming ranks of the underprivileged as at best a super- fluous nuisance and at worst 'born bad', naturally vicious and depraved (I have drawn attention, in my notes to this story, to the precise nature of some of Dickens's targets). He was very eager to see at first hand what effect the story would have on those friends like Carlyle whose opinions he cared deeply for, and he made a lightning pre-publication visit to London in December in order to read it aloud to a select group assembled in Forster's rooms. The painter Daniel Maclise was of the party and wrote to Mrs Dickens,

You will never be able to conceive the effect of this perusal. We should borrow the high language of the minor theatre and even then not do the effect justice – shrieks of laughter – there were indeed – and floods of tears as a relief to them – I do not think there was ever such a triumphant hour for Charles.[1]

The Chimes was published, under the imprint of Chapman and Hall (since Bradbury and Evans, who were primarily printers, had not yet organized proper distributive facilities) on 16 December and nearly 20,000 copies were sold within the next two or three months: 'The Chimes,' Dickens wrote happily to his old friend, Thomas Beard, in May 1845, 'have been a most sweeping success.' The book was produced in the same format and binding as the *Carol* but there were no expensive coloured illustrations this time. The black and white illustration was profuse, however, the *Carol* illustrator

1. Unpublished letter in the Pierpont Morgan Library quoted by K. J. Fielding in his *Charles Dickens: A Critical Introduction*, rev. ed. 1965, p. 108.

John Leech being joined in the work by two leading painters who were close friends of Dickens's, Maclise and Clarkson Stanfield (who had already contributed several illustrations to Dickens's *Master Humphrey's Clock*), and also the young artist Richard Doyle. No less than five dramatizations of the story appeared on the London stage during the few weeks following its publication and two of these at least (at the Adelphi and Lyceum theatres) met with great success, especially with the working-class spectators in the galleries who, it seems, took Will Fern to their hearts and applauded him to the very echo.

'I believe I have written a tremendous book . . .' Dickens confided to Thomas Mitton on 5 November 1844, 'It will make a great uproar, I have no doubt.' He proved an accurate prophet. 'Dicken's new work', commented the *Globe* on 31 December, 'is attacked and defended with a degree of ardour which scarcely any other subject is capable of inspiring.' It was, declared Thackeray's friend, the Rev. William Brookfield, 'as utter trash as was ever trodden underfoot'[2] but the young R. H. Hutton wrote to his fellow-undergraduate, Walter Bagehot, 'I think it is the finest thing Dickens has ever written'.[3] Forster himself thought highly of it and praised it at length in an anonymous review in the *Edinburgh* but another friend of Dickens's, Bulwer Lytton, wrote to Forster, that, although it was 'cleverer' than the *Carol*, 'it does not create the same agreeable feelings . . . its moral is untrue and dangerous . . . the fierce tone of menace to the rich is unreasonable and ignorant'.[4]

The reviewers differed just as sharply about the book, which was very widely noticed. By and large, the critics' reactions were governed by their political affiliations. Dickens was pandering, thundered the Tory *John Bull* (28 December 1844),

2. *Mrs Brookfield and her Circle*, C. and F. Brookfield, 1905, i, 145.
3. *Life of Walter Bagehot*, Mrs Russell Barrington, 1914, p. 147.
4. Unpublished letter among the Lytton papers at Knebworth. Quoted here by permission of Lady Hermione Cobbold.

to the low Radical doctrines of the day as regards the poor by holding up to ridicule and contempt the efforts of the higher classes to ameliorate their condition. ... All the vices, all the crimes, all the profligacy of the lower orders, are represented as the necessary consequences of the neglect of society.

The Chartist organ, the *Northern Star*, on the other hand, could not praise the book highly enough: 'Expressing views of man and society far more comprehensive than he has before put forth, Mr DICKENS enters the public arena, as *the champion of the poor*!' it exulted on 28 December. *The Times*, which had relentlessly attacked the New Poor Law, also praised *The Chimes* and, equally predictably, the Tory *Morning Post* damned it. There were some surprises, however. Dickens's old newspaper, the Liberal *Morning Chronicle*, strongly disapproved of the book: Dickens had betrayed his own *Carol* philosophy, it said on 17 December, and had 'gone into the very opposite extreme of ranging party against party and class against class'. On the other hand the *Economist*, which one might have expected to have been outraged by the satire on political economists in the figure of Mr Filer, declared, on 18 January, that *The Chimes* was 'one of the most remarkable books of the day, and it will mark, if not form, an epoch in the thoughts, creeds and minds of mankind'.

The Tories were not long in producing a counterblast. Early in 1845 a young lady (who was later, as Mrs Mackarness, to become a noted writer of children's books) anonymously published a little book called *Old Jolliffe: Not a Goblin Story* which attacked *The Chimes* for its unfairness to the rich. The latter, who have 'much to worry and annoy them', get tired out by the incessant demands of the poor, comments Old Jolliffe and he goes about preaching (almost in the words of Lady Bowley's verse) the virtues of contentment with one's station in life, however humble, and one's wages, however meagre, – 'Suppose you do only get a penny for your work, a penny will buy a roll and that's better than nothing.' He observes some orphans whose mother, worn down by poverty, has just killed herself being taken to the workhouse' and rewards with a half-crown tip a 'decent' neighbour of the dead woman who remarks, 'I'm sure one need not die of starvation whilst there's a poor-house.'

Such egregious counter-propaganda as this can only have reassured Dickens that he had truly struck home. He must have been further reassured by *The Chimes*'s continued popularity (in 1853, for example, the librarian of Manchester public library reported that it was the most frequently issued volume in the 'Novels and Romances' department[5]) and, Forster tells us, 'There was that in it which more than repaid the suffering its writing cost him, and the enmity its opinions provoked; and in his own heart it had a cherished corner to the last.'

5. *History of Local Government in Manchester*, A. Redford, 1940, 2, 225.

ILLUSTRATIONS TO
THE CHIMES

The Spirits of the Bells.

THE CHIMES

GOBLIN STORY

OF SOME BELLS THAT RANG AN OLD YEAR OUT AND A NEW YEAR IN

Charles Dickens

18 45

Maclise, R.A. del.

E.P. Becker, sc.

Facsimile title page from first edition of The Chimes

THE CHIMES:

A Goblin Story

OF

SOME BELLS THAT RANG AN OLD YEAR OUT
AND A NEW YEAR IN.

———•———

BY CHARLES DICKENS.

LONDON:
CHAPMAN AND HALL, 186, STRAND.

MDCCCXLV.

FIRST QUARTER.

HERE are not many people —and as it is desirable that a story-teller and a story-reader should establish a mutual understanding as soon as possible, I beg it to be noticed that I confine this observation neither to young people nor to little people, but extend it to all conditions of people: little and big, young and old: yet growing up, or already growing down again—there are not, I say, many people who would care to sleep in a church. I don't mean at sermon-time in warm weather (when the thing has actually been done, once or twice), but in the night, and alone. A great multitude of persons will be violently astonished, I know, by this position, in the broad bold Day. But it applies to Night. It must be argued by night. And I will undertake to maintain it successfully on any gusty winter's night appointed for the purpose, with any one opponent chosen from the rest, who will meet me singly in an old churchyard, before an old church door; and will previously empower me to lock him in, if needful to his satisfaction, until morning.

For the night-wind has a dismal trick of wandering round and round a building of that sort, and moaning as it goes; and of trying, with its unseen hand, the windows and the doors; and seeking out some crevices by which to enter. And when it has got in; as one not finding what it seeks, whatever that may be, it wails and howls to issue forth again: and not content with stalking through the aisles, and gliding round and round the pillars, and tempting the deep organ, soars up to the roof, and strives to rend the rafters: then flings itself despairingly upon the stones below, and passes, muttering, into the vaults. Anon, it comes up stealthily, and creeps along the walls: seeming to read, in whispers, the Inscriptions sacred to the Dead. At some of these, it breaks out shrilly, as with laughter; and at others, moans and cries as if it were lamenting. It has a ghostly sound too, lingering within the altar; where it seems to chaunt, in its wild way, of Wrong and Murder done, and false Gods worshipped, in defiance of the Tables of the Law, which look so fair and smooth, but are so flawed and broken. Ugh! Heaven preserve us, sitting snugly round the fire! It has an awful voice, that wind at Midnight, singing in a church!

But high up in the steeple! There the foul blast roars and whistles! High up in the steeple, where it is free to come and go through many an airy arch and loophole, and to twist and twine itself about the giddy stair, and twirl the groaning weathercock, and make the very tower shake and shiver! High up in the steeple, where the belfry is; and iron rails are ragged with rust; and sheets of lead and copper, shrivelled by the changing weather, crackle and heave beneath the unaccustomed tread; and birds stuff shabby nests into corners of old oaken joists and beams; and dust grows old and grey; and speckled spiders, indolent and fat with long security, swing idly to and fro in the vibration of the bells, and never loose their hold upon their thread-spun castles in the air, or climb up sailor-like in quick alarm, or drop upon the ground and ply a score of nimble legs to save a life! High up in the steeple of an old church, far above the light and murmur of the town and far below the flying clouds that shadow it, is the wild and dreary place at night: and high up in the steeple of an old church[1], dwelt the Chimes I tell of.

They were old chimes, trust me. Centuries ago, these Bells had been baptized by bishops: so many centuries ago, that the register of their baptism was lost long, long before the memory of man: and no one knew their names. They had had their Godfathers and Godmothers, these Bells (for my own part, by the way, I would rather incur the responsibility of being Godfather to a Bell than a Boy): and had had their silver mugs no doubt, besides. But Time had mowed down their sponsors, and Henry the Eighth had melted down their mugs: and they now hung, nameless and mugless, in the church tower.

Not speechless, though. Far from it. They had clear, loud, lusty, sounding voices, had these Bells; and far and wide they might be heard upon the wind. Much too sturdy Chimes were they, to be dependent on the pleasure of the wind, moreover; for, fighting gallantly against it when it took an adverse whim, they would pour their cheerful notes into a listening ear right royally; and bent on being heard, on stormy nights, by some poor mother watching a sick child, or some lone wife whose husband was at sea, they had been sometimes known to beat a blustering Nor'-Wester; aye, "all to fits," as Toby Veck said;—for though they chose to call him Trotty Veck, his name was Toby, and nobody could make it anything else either (except Tobias) without a special act of parliament; he having been as lawfully christened in his day as the Bells had been in theirs, though with not quite so much of solemnity or public rejoicing.

For my part, I confess myself of Toby Veck's belief, for I am sure he had opportunities enough of forming a correct one. And whatever Toby Veck said, I say. And I take my stand by Toby Veck, although he *did* stand all day long (and weary work it was) just outside the church-door. In fact he was a ticket-porter², Toby Veck, and waited there for jobs.

And a breezy, goose-skinned, blue-nosed, red-eyed, stony-toed, tooth-chattering place it was, to wait in, in the winter-time, as Toby Veck well knew. The wind came tearing round the corner—especially the east wind—as if it had sallied forth, express, from the confines of the earth, to have a blow at Toby. And oftentimes it seemed to come upon him sooner than it had expected, for bouncing round the corner, and passing Toby, it would suddenly wheel round again, as if it cried "Why, here he is!" Incontinently his little white apron would be caught up over his head like a naughty boy's garments, and his feeble little cane would be seen to wrestle and struggle unavailingly in his hand, and his legs would undergo tremendous agitation, and Toby himself all aslant, and facing now in this direction, now in that, would be so banged and buffeted, and touzled, and worried, and hustled, and lifted off his feet, as to render it a state of things but one degree removed from a positive miracle, that he wasn't carried up bodily into the air as a colony of frogs or snails or other portable creatures sometimes are, and rained down again, to the great astonishment of the natives, on some strange corner of the world where ticket-porters are un-known.

But, windy weather, in spite of its using him so roughly, was, after all, a sort of holiday for Toby. That's the fact. He didn't seem to wait so long for a sixpence in the wind, as at other times; for the having to fight with that boisterous element took off his attention, and quite freshened him up, when he was getting hungry and low-spirited. A hard frost too, or a fall of snow, was an Event; and it seemed to do him good, somehow or other—it would have been hard to say in what respect though, Toby! So wind and frost and snow, and perhaps a good stiff storm of hail, were Toby Veck's red-letter days.

Wet weather was the worst: the cold, damp, clammy wet, that wrapped him up like a moist great-coat: the only kind of great-coat Toby owned, or could have added to his comfort by dispensing with. Wet days, when the rain came slowly, thickly, obstinately down; when the street's throat, like his own, was choked with mist; when smoking umbrellas passed and repassed, spinning round and round like so many tee-totums, as they knocked against each other on the crowded footway, throwing off a little whirlpool of uncomfortable sprinklings; when gutters brawled and waterspouts were full and noisy; when the wet from the projecting stones and ledges of the church fell drip, drip, drip, on Toby, making the wisp of straw on which he stood mere mud in no time; those were the days that tried him. Then indeed, you might see Toby looking anxiously out from his shelter in an angle of the church wall—such a meagre shelter that in summer time it never cast a shadow thicker than a good-sized walking stick upon the sunny pavement—with a disconsolate and lengthened face. But coming out, a minute afterwards, to warm himself by exercise: and trotting up and down some dozen times: he would brighten even then, and go back more brightly to his niche.

They called him Trotty from his pace, which meant speed if it didn't make it. He could have Walked faster perhaps; most likely; but rob him of his trot, and Toby would have taken to his bed and died. It bespattered him with mud in dirty weather; it cost him a world of trouble; he could have walked with infinitely greater ease; but that was one reason for his clinging to it so tenaciously. A weak, small, spare old man, he was a very Hercules, this Toby, in his good intentions. He loved to earn his money. He delighted to believe— Toby was very poor, and couldn't well afford to part with a delight—that he was worth his salt. With a shilling or an eighteenpenny message or small parcel in hand, his courage, always high, rose higher. As he trotted on, he would call out to fast Postmen ahead of him, to get out of the way; devoutly believing that in the natural course of things he must inevitably overtake and run them down; and he had perfect faith—not often tested—in his being able to carry anything that man could lift.

Thus, even when he came out of his nook to warm himself on a wet day, Toby trotted. Making, with his leaky shoes, a crooked line of slushy footprints in the mire; and blowing on his chilly hands and rubbing them against each other, poorly defended from the searching cold by thread-bare mufflers of grey worsted, with a private apartment only for the thumb, and a common room or tap for the rest of the fingers; Toby, with his knees bent and his cane beneath his arm, still trotted. Falling out into the road to look up at the belfry when the Chimes resounded, Toby trotted still.

He made this last excursion several times a day, for they were company to him; and when he heard their voices, he had an interest in glancing at their lodging-place, and think-ing how they were moved, and what hammers beat upon them. Perhaps he was the more curious about these Bells, because there were points of resemblance between themselves and him. They hung there, in all weathers: with the wind and rain driving in upon them: facing only the outsides of all those houses; never getting any nearer to the blazing fires that gleamed and shone upon the windows, or came puffing out of the chimney tops; and incapable of participation in any of the good things that were constantly being handed, through the street doors and the area railings, to prodigious cooks. Faces came and went at many windows: sometimes pretty faces, youthful faces, pleasant faces: sometimes the reverse: but Toby knew no more (though he often speculated on these trifles, standing idle in the streets) whence they came, or where they went, or whether, when the lips moved, one kind word was said of him in all the year, than did the Chimes themselves.

Toby was not a casuist—that he knew of, at least—and I don't mean to say that when he began to take to the Bells, and to knit up his first rough acquaintance with them into something of a closer and more delicate woof, he passed through these considerations one by one, or held any formal review or great field-day in his thoughts. But what I mean to say, and do say is, that as the functions of Toby's body, his digestive organs for example, did of their own cunning, and by a great many operations of which he was altogether ignorant, and the knowledge of which would have astonished him very much, arrive at a certain end; so his mental faculties, without his privity or concurrence, set all these wheels and springs in motion, with a thousand others, when they worked to bring about his liking for the Bells.

And though I had said his love, I would not have recalled the word, though it would scarcely have expressed his complicated feeling. For, being but a simple man, he invested them with a strange and solemn character. They were so mysterious, often heard and never seen; so high up, so far off, so full of such a deep strong melody, that he regarded them with a species of awe; and sometimes when he looked up at the dark arched windows in the tower, he half expected to be beckoned to by something which was not a Bell, and yet was what he heard so often sounding in the Chimes. For all this, Toby scouted with indignation a certain flying rumour that the Chimes were haunted, as implying the possibility of their being connected with any Evil thing. In short, they were very often in his ears, and very often in his thoughts, but always in his good opinion; and he very often got such a crick in his neck by staring with his mouth wide open, at the steeple where they hung, that he was fain to take an extra trot or two, afterwards, to cure it.

The very thing he was in the act of doing one cold day, when the last drowsy sound of Twelve o'clock, just struck, was humming like a melodious monster of a Bee, and not by any means a busy bee, all through the steeple.

"Dinner-time eh!" said Toby, trotting up and down before the church. "Ah!"

Toby's nose was very red, and his eyelids were very red, and he winked very much, and his shoulders were very near his ears, and his legs were very stiff; and altogether he was evidently a long way upon the frosty side of cool.

"Dinner-time, eh!" repeated Toby, using his right-hand muffler like an infantine boxing-glove, and punishing his chest for being cold. "Ah-h-h-h!"

He took a silent trot, after that, for a minute or two.

"There's nothing," said Toby, breaking forth afresh,—but here he stopped short in his trot, and with a face of great interest and some alarm, felt his nose carefully all the way up. It was but a little way: not being much of a nose: and he had soon finished.

"I thought it was gone," said Toby, trotting off again. "It's all right, however. I am sure I couldn't blame it if it was to go. It has a precious hard service of it in the bitter weather, and precious little to look forward to: for I don't take snuff myself. It's a good deal tried, poor creetur, at the best of times; for when it *does* get hold of a pleasant whiff or so (which an't too often), it's generally from somebody else's dinner, a-coming home from the baker's."

The reflection reminded him of that other reflection, which he had left unfinished.

"There's nothing," said Toby, "more regular in its coming round than dinner-time, and nothing less regular in its coming round than dinner. That's the great difference between 'em. It's took me a long time to find it out. I wonder whether it would be worth any gentleman's while, now, to buy that obserwation for the Papers; or the Parliament!"

Toby was only joking, for he gravely shook his head in self-depreciation.

"Why! Lord!" said Toby. "The Papers is full of obserwations as it is; and so's the Parliament. Here's last week's paper, now;" taking a very dirty one from his pocket, and holding it from him at arm's length; "full of obserwations! Full of obserwations! I like to know the news as well as any man," said Toby, slowly; folding it a little smaller, and putting it in his pocket again; "but it almost goes against the grain with me to read a paper now. It frightens me, almost. I don't know what we poor people are coming to. Lord send we may be coming to something better in the New Year nigh upon us!"

"Why, father, father!" said a pleasant voice, hard by.

But Toby, not hearing it, continued to trot backwards and forwards: musing as he went, and talking to himself.

"It seems as if we can't go right, or do right, or be righted," said Toby. "I hadn't much schooling, myself, when I was young; and I can't make out whether we have any business on the face of the earth, or not. Sometimes I think we must have a little; and sometimes I think we must be intruding. I get so puzzled sometimes that I am not even able to make up my mind whether there is any good at all in us, or whether we are born bad. We seem to do dreadful things; we seem to give a deal of trouble; we are always being complained of and guarded against. One way or another, we fill the papers. Talk of a New Year!" said Toby, mournfully. "I can bear up as well as another man at most times; better than a good many, for I am as strong as a lion, and all men an't; but supposing it should really be that we have no right to a New Year—supposing we really *are* intruding——"

"Why, father, father!" said the pleasant voice again.

Toby heard it this time; started; stopped; and shortening his sight, which had been directed a long way off as seeking for enlightenment in the very heart of the approaching year, found himself face to face with his own child, and looking close into her eyes.

Bright eyes they were. Eyes that would bear a world of looking in, before their depth was fathomed. Dark eyes, that reflected back the eyes which searched them; not flashingly, or at the owner's will, but with a clear, calm, honest, patient radiance, claiming kindred with that light which Heaven called into being. Eyes that were beautiful and true, and beaming with Hope. With Hope so young and fresh; with Hope so buoyant, vigorous, and bright, despite the twenty years of work and poverty on which they had looked; that they became a voice to Trotty Veck, and said: "I think we have some business here—a little!"

Trotty kissed the lips belonging to the eyes, and squeezed the blooming face between his hands.

"Why, Pet," said Trotty. "What's to-do? I didn't expect you to-day, Meg."

"Neither did I expect to come, father," cried the girl,

nodding her head and smiling as she spoke. "But here I am! And not alone; not alone!"

"Why you don't mean to say," observed Trotty, looking curiously at a covered basket which she carried in her hand, "that you——"

"Smell it, father dear," said Meg. "Only smell it!"

Trotty was going to lift up the cover at once, in a great hurry, when she gaily interposed her hand.

"No, no, no," said Meg, with the glee of a child. "Lengthen it out a little. Let me just lift up the corner; just the lit-tle ti-ny cor-ner, you know," said Meg, suiting the action to the word with the utmost gentleness, and speaking very softly, as if she were afraid of being overheard by something inside the basket; "there. Now. What's that?"

Toby took the shortest possible sniff at the edge of the basket, and cried out in a rapture:

"Why, it's hot!"

"It's burning hot!" cried Meg. "Ha, ha, ha! It's scalding hot!"

"Ha, ha, ha!" roared Toby, with a sort of kick. "It's scalding hot!"

"But what is it, father?" said Meg. "Come! You haven't guessed what it is. And you must guess what it is. I can't think of taking it out, till you guess what it is. Don't be in such a hurry! Wait a minute! A little bit more of the cover. Now guess!"

Meg was in a perfect fright lest he should guess right too soon; shrinking away, as she held the basket towards him; curling up her pretty shoulders; stopping her ear with her hand, as if by so doing she could keep the right word out of Toby's lips; and laughing softly the whole time.

Meanwhile Toby, putting a hand on each knee, bent down his nose to the basket, and took a long inspiration at the lid; the grin upon his withered face expanding in the process, as if he were inhaling laughing gas.

"Ah! It's very nice," said Toby. "It an't—I suppose it an't Polonies?"

"No, no, no!" cried Meg, delighted. "Nothing like Polonies!"

"No," said Toby, after another sniff. "It's—it's mellower than Polonies. It's very nice. It improves every moment. It's too decided for Trotters. An't it?"

Meg was in an ecstasy. He could *not* have gone wider of the mark than Trotters—except Polonies.

"Liver?" said Toby, communing with himself. "No. There's a mildness about it that don't answer to liver. Pettitoes?³ No. It an't faint enough for pettitoes. It wants the stringiness of Cocks' heads. And I know it an't sausages. I'll tell you what it is. It's chitterlings!"

"No, it an't!" cried Meg, in a burst of delight. "No, it an't!"

"Why, what am I a thinking of!" said Toby, suddenly recovering a position as near the perpendicular as it was possible for him to assume. "I shall forget my own name next. It's tripe!"

Tripe it was; and Meg, in high joy, protested he should say, in half a minute more, it was the best tripe ever stewed.

"And so," said Meg, busying herself exultingly with the basket, "I'll lay the cloth at once, father; for I have brought the tripe in a basin, and tied the basin up in a pocket handkerchief; and if I like to be proud for once, and spread that for a cloth, and call it a cloth, there's no law to prevent me; is there, father?"

"Not that I know of, my dear," said Toby. "But they're always a bringing up some new law or other."

"And according to what I was reading you in the paper the other day, father; what the Judge said, you know; we poor people are supposed to know them all. Ha, ha! What a mistake! My goodness me, how clever they think us!"

"Yes, my dear," said Trotty; "and they'd be very fond of any one of us that *did* know 'em all. He'd grow fat upon the work he'd get, that man, and be popular with the gentlefolks in his neighbourhood. Very much so!"

"He'd eat his dinner with an appetite, whoever he was, if it smelt like this," said Meg cheerfully. "Make haste, for there's a hot potatoe besides, and half a pint of fresh-drawn beer in a bottle. Where will you dine, father? On the Post, or on the Steps? Dear, dear, how grand we are. Two places to choose from!"

"The steps to-day, my Pet," said Trotty. "Steps in dry weather. Post in wet. There's a greater conveniency in the steps at all times, because of the sitting down; but they're rheumatic in the damp."

"Then here," said Meg, clapping her hands, after a moment's bustle; "here it is, all ready! And beautiful it looks! Come, father. Come!"

Since his discovery of the contents of the basket, Trotty had been standing looking at her—and had been speaking too—in an abstracted manner, which showed that though she was the object of his thoughts and eyes, to the exclusion even of tripe, he neither saw nor thought about her as she was at that moment, but had before him some imaginary rough sketch or drama of her future life. Roused, now, by her cheerful summons, he shook off a melancholy shake of the head which was just coming upon him, and trotted to her side. As he was stooping to sit down, the Chimes rang.

"Amen!" said Trotty, pulling off his hat and looking up towards them.

"Amen to the Bells, father?" cried Meg.

"They broke in like a grace, my dear," said Trotty, taking his seat. "They'd say a good one, I am sure, if they could. Many's the kind thing they say to me."

"The Bells do, father?" laughed Meg, as she set the basin, and a knife and fork before him. "Well!"

"Seem to, my Pet," said Trotty, falling to with great vigour. "And where's the difference? If I hear 'em, what does it matter whether they speak it or not? Why bless you, my dear," said Toby, pointing at the tower with his fork, and becoming more animated under the influence of dinner, "how often have I heard them bells say, 'Toby Veck, Toby

Veck, keep a good heart, Toby! Toby Veck, Toby Veck, keep a good heart, Toby!' A million times? More!"

"Well, I never!" cried Meg.

She had, though—over and over again. For it was Toby's constant topic.

"When things is very bad," said Trotty; "very bad indeed, I mean; almost at the worst; then it's 'Toby Veck, Toby Veck, job coming soon, Toby! Toby Veck, Toby Veck, job coming soon, Toby!' That way."

"And it comes—at last, father," said Meg, with a touch of sadness in her pleasant voice.

"Always," answered the unconscious Toby. "Never fails."

While this discourse was holding, Trotty made no pause in his attack upon the savoury meat before him, but cut and ate, and cut and drank, and cut and chewed, and dodged about, from tripe to hot potatoe, and from hot potatoe back again to tripe, with an unctuous and unflagging relish. But happening now to look all round the street—in case anybody should be beckoning from any door or window for a porter —his eyes, in coming back again, encountered Meg: sitting opposite to him, with her arms folded: and only busy in watching his progress with a smile of happiness.

"Why, Lord forgive me!" said Trotty, dropping his knife and fork. "My dove! Meg! why didn't you tell me what a beast I was?"

"Father?"

"Sitting here," said Trotty, in penitent explanation, "cramming, and stuffing, and gorging myself; and you before me there, never so much as breaking your precious fast, nor wanting to, when——"

"But I have broken it, father," interposed his daughter, laughing, "all to bits. I have had my dinner."

"Nonsense," said Trotty. "Two dinners in one day! It an't possible! You might as well tell me that two New Year's Days will come together, or that I have had a gold head all my life, and never changed it."

"I have had my dinner, father, for all that," said Meg, coming nearer to him. "And if you'll go on with yours, I'll tell you how and where; and how your dinner came to be brought; and—and something else besides."

Toby still appeared incredulous; but she looked into his face with her clear eyes, and laying her hand upon his shoulder, motioned him to go on while the meat was hot. So Trotty took up his knife and fork again, and went to work. But much more slowly than before, and shaking his head, as if he were not at all pleased with himself.

"I had my dinner, father," said Meg, after a little hesitation, "with—with Richard. His dinner-time was early; and as he brought his dinner with him when he came to see me, we—we had it together, father."

Trotty took a little beer, and smacked his lips. Then he said, "Oh!"—because she waited.

"And Richard says, father—" Meg resumed. Then stopped.

"What does Richard say, Meg?" asked Toby.

"Richard says, father—" Another stoppage.

"Richard's a long time saying it," said Toby.

"He says then, father," Meg continued, lifting up her eyes at last, and speaking in a tremble, but quite plainly; "another year is nearly gone, and where is the use of waiting on from year to year, when it is so unlikely we shall ever be better off than we are now? He says we are poor now, father, and we shall be poor then; but we are young now, and years will make us old before we know it. He says that if we wait: people in our condition: until we see our way quite clearly, the way will be a narrow one indeed—the common way—the Grave, father."

A bolder man than Trotty Veck must needs have drawn upon his boldness largely, to deny it. Trotty held his peace.

"And how hard, father, to grow old, and die, and think we might have cheered and helped each other! How hard in all our lives to love each other; and to grieve, apart, to see each other working, changing, growing old and grey. Even if I got the better of it, and forgot him (which I never could), oh father dear, how hard to have a heart so full as mine is now, and live to have it slowly drained out every drop, without the recollection of one happy moment of a woman's life, to stay behind and comfort me, and make me better!"

Trotty sat quite still. Meg dried her eyes, and said more gaily: that is to say, with here a laugh, and there a sob, and here a laugh and sob together:

"So Richard says, father; as his work was yesterday made certain for some time to come, and as I love him, and have loved him full three years—ah! longer than that, if he knew it!—will I marry him on New Year's Day; the best and happiest day, he says, in the whole year, and one that is almost sure to bring good fortune with it. It's a short notice, father—isn't it?—but I haven't my fortune to be settled, or my wedding dresses to be made, like the great ladies, father—have I? And he said so much, and said it in his way; so strong and earnest, and all the time so kind and gentle; that I said I'd come and talk to you, father. And as they paid the money for that work of mine this morning (unexpectedly, I am sure!), and as you have fared very poorly for a whole week, and as I couldn't help wishing there should be something to make this day a sort of holiday to you as well as a dear and happy day to me father, I made a little treat and brought it to surprise you."

"And see how he leaves it cooling on the step!" said another voice.

It was the voice of this same Richard, who had come upon them unobserved, and stood before the father and daughter: looking down upon them with a face as glowing as the iron on which his stout sledge-hammer daily rung[4]. A handsome, well-made, powerful youngster he was; with eyes that sparkled like the red-hot droppings from a furnace fire; black hair that curled about his swarthy temples rarely; and a smile—a smile that bore out Meg's eulogium on his style of conversation.

"See how he leaves it cooling on the step!" said Richard. "Meg don't know what he likes. Not she!"

Trotty, all action and enthusiasm, immediately reached up his hand to Richard, and was going to address him in a great hurry, when the house-door opened without any warning, and a footman very nearly put his foot in the tripe.

"Out of the vays here, will you! You must always go and be a settin on our steps, must you! You can't go and give a turn to none of the neighbours never, can't you! *Will* you clear the road, or won't you?"

Strictly speaking, the last question was irrelevant, as they had already done it.

"What's the matter, what's the matter!" said the gentleman for whom the door was opened: coming out of the house at that kind of light-heavy pace—that peculiar compromise between a walk and a jog-trot—with which a gentleman upon the smooth down-hill of life, wearing creaking boots, a watch-chain, and clean linen, *may* come out of his house: not only without any abatement of his dignity, but with an expression of having important and wealthy engagements elsewhere. "What's the matter! What's the matter!"

"You're always a being begged, and prayed, upon your bended knees you are," said the footman with great emphasis to Trotty Veck, "to let our door-steps be. Why don't you let 'em be? CAN'T you let 'em be?"

"There! That'll do, that'll do!" said the gentleman. "Halloa there! Porter!" beckoning with his head to Trotty Veck. "Come here. What's that? Your dinner?"

"Yes sir," said Trotty, leaving it behind him in a corner.

"Don't leave it there," exclaimed the gentleman. "Bring it here, bring it here. So! This is your dinner, is it?"

"Yes sir," repeated Trotty, looking, with a fixed eye and a watery mouth, at the piece of tripe he had reserved for a last delicious tit-bit; which the gentleman was now turning over and over on the end of the fork.

Two other gentlemen had come out with him. One was a low-spirited gentleman of middle age, of a meagre habit, and a disconsolate face; who kept his hands continually in the pockets of his scanty pepper-and-salt trousers, very large and dog's-eared from that custom; and was not particularly well brushed or washed.* The other, a full-sized, sleek, well-conditioned gentleman, in a blue coat with bright buttons, and a white cravat. This gentleman had a very red face, as if an undue proportion of the blood in his body were squeezed up into his head; which perhaps accounted for his having also the appearance of being rather cold about the heart.*

He who had Toby's meat upon the fork, called to the first one by the name of Filer; and they both drew near together. Mr. Filer being exceedingly short-sighted, was obliged to go so close to the remnant of Toby's dinner before he could make out what it was, that Toby's heart leaped up into his mouth. But Mr. Filer didn't eat it.

"This is a description of animal food, Alderman," said Filer, making little punches in it, with a pencil-case, "commonly known to the labouring population of this country, by the name of tripe."

The Alderman laughed, and winked; for he was a merry fellow, Alderman Cute. Oh, and a sly fellow, too! A knowing fellow. Up to everything. Not to be imposed upon. Deep in the people's hearts! He knew them, Cute did.[5] I believe you!

"But who eats tripe?" said Mr. Filer, looking round. "Tripe is without an exception the least economical, and the most wasteful article of consumption that the markets of this country can by possibility produce. The loss upon a pound of tripe has been found to be, in the boiling, seven eighths of a fifth more than the loss upon a pound of any other animal substance whatever. Tripe is more expensive, properly understood, than the hothouse pine-apple. Taking into account the number of animals slaughtered yearly within the bills of mortality[6] alone; and forming a low estimate of the quantity of tripe which the carcases of those animals, reasonably well butchered, would yield; I find that the waste on that amount of tripe, if boiled, would victual a garrison of five hundred men for five months of thirty-one days each, and a February over. The Waste, the Waste!"

* see p. xxviii and Appendix A.

Trotty stood aghast, and his legs
shook under him. He seemed to have
starved a garrison of five hundred
men with his own hand.

"Who eats tripe?" said Mr. Filer,
warmly. "Who eats tripe?"

Trotty made a miserable bow.

"You do, do you?" said Mr. Filer. "Then I'll tell you something. You snatch your tripe, my friend, out of the mouths of widows and orphans."

"I hope not, sir," said Trotty, faintly. "I'd sooner die of want!"

"Divide the amount of tripe before-mentioned, Alderman," said Mr. Filer, "by the estimated number of existing widows and orphans, and the result will be one pennyweight of tripe to each. Not a grain is left for that man. Consequently, he's a robber."[7]

Trotty was so shocked, that it gave him no concern to see the Alderman finish the tripe himself. It was a relief to get rid of it, anyhow.

*"And what do you say?" asked the Alderman, jocosely, of the red-faced gentleman in the blue coat. "You have heard friend Filer. What do *you* say?"

"What's it possible to say?" returned the gentleman. "What *is* to be said? Who can take any interest in a fellow like this," meaning Trotty; "in such degenerate times as these? Look at him! What an object! The good old times, the grand old times, the great old times! *Those* were the times for a bold peasantry, and all that sort of thing. Those were the times for every sort of thing, in fact. There's nothing now-a-days. Ah!" sighed the red-faced gentleman. "The good old times, the good old times!"[8]

The gentleman didn't specify what particular times he alluded to; nor did he say whether he objected to the present times, from a disinterested consciousness that they had done nothing very remarkable in producing himself.

"The good old times, the good old times," repeated the gentleman. "What times they were! They were the only times. It's of no use talking about any other times, or discussing what the people are in these times. You don't call these, times, do you? I don't. Look into Strutt's Costumes,[9] and see what a Porter used to be, in any of the good old English reigns."

"He hadn't, in his very best circumstances, a shirt to his

back, or a stocking to his foot; and there was scarcely a vegetable in all England for him to put into his mouth," said Mr. Filer. "I can prove it, by tables."

But still the red-faced gentleman extolled the good old times, the grand old times, the great old times. No matter what anybody else said, he still went turning round and round in one set form of words concerning them; as a poor squirrel turns and turns in its revolving cage; touching the mechanism, and trick of which, it has probably quite as distinct perceptions, as ever this red-faced gentleman had of his deceased Millennium.

It is possible that poor Trotty's faith in these very vague Old Times* was not entirely destroyed, for he felt vague enough, at that moment. One thing, however, was plain to him, in the midst of his distress; to wit, that however these gentlemen might differ in details, his misgivings of that morning, and of many other mornings, were well founded. "No, no. We can't go right or do right," thought Trotty in despair. "There is no good in us. We are born bad!"

But Trotty had a father's heart within him; which had somehow got into his breast in spite of this decree; and he could not bear that Meg, in the blush of her brief joy, should have her fortune read by these wise gentlemen. "God help her," thought poor Trotty. "She will know it soon enough."

He anxiously signed, therefore, to the young smith, to take her away. But he was so busy, talking to her softly at a little distance, that he only became conscious of this desire, simultaneously with Alderman Cute. Now, the Alderman had not yet had his say, but *he* was a philosopher, too—practical, though! Oh, very practical—and, as he had no idea of losing any portion of his audience, he cried "Stop!"

"Now, you know," said the Alderman, addressing his two friends, with a self-complacent smile upon his face, which was habitual to him, "I am a plain man, and a practical man; and I go to work in a plain practical way. That's my way. There is not the least mystery or difficulty in dealing with this sort of people if you only understand 'em, and can talk to 'em in their own manner. Now, you Porter! Don't you ever tell me, or anybody else my friend, that you haven't always enough to eat, and of the best; because I know better. I have tasted your tripe, you know, and you can't 'chaff' me. You understand what 'chaff' means, eh? That's the right word, isn't it? Ha, ha, ha! Lord bless you," said the Alderman, turning to his friends again, "it's the easiest thing on earth to deal with this sort of people, if you only understand 'em."

Famous man for the common people, Alderman Cute! Never out of temper with them! Easy, affable, joking, knowing gentleman!

"You see, my friend," pursued the Alderman, "there's a great deal of nonsense talked about Want—'hard up,' you know: that's the phrase isn't it? ha! ha! ha!—and I intend to Put it Down. There's a certain amount of cant in vogue about Starvation, and I mean to Put it Down. That's all! Lord bless you," said the Alderman, turning to his friends again, "you may Put Down anything among this sort of people, if you only know the way to set about it."

Trotty took Meg's hand and drew it through his arm. He didn't seem to know what he was doing though.

"Your daughter, eh?" said the Alderman, chucking her familiarly under the chin.

Always affable with the working classes, Alderman Cute! Knew what pleased them! Not a bit of pride!

"Where's her mother?" asked that worthy gentleman.

"Dead," said Toby. "Her mother got up linen; and was called to Heaven when She was born."

"Not to get up linen *there*, I suppose," remarked the Alderman pleasantly.

Toby might or might not have been able to separate his wife in Heaven from her old pursuits. But query: If Mrs. Alderman Cute had gone to Heaven, would Mr. Alderman Cute have pictured her as holding any state or station there?

"And you're making love to her, are you?" said Cute to the young smith.

"Yes," returned Richard quickly, for he was nettled by the question. "And we are going to be married on New Year's Day."

"What do you mean!" cried Filer sharply. "Married!"

"Why, yes, we're thinking of it, Master," said Richard. "We're rather in a hurry you see, in case it should be Put Down first."

"Ah!" cried Filer, with a groan. "Put *that* down, indeed, Alderman, and you'll do something. Married! Married!! The ignorance of the first principles of political economy on the part of these people; their improvidence; their wickedness; is, by Heavens! enough to—Now look at that couple, will you!"

Well! They were worth looking at. And marriage seemed as reasonable and fair a deed as they need have in contemplation.

"A man may live to be as old as Methusaleh," said Mr. Filer, "and may labour all his life for the benefit of such people as those; and may heap up facts on figures, facts on figures, facts on figures, mountains high and dry; and he can no more hope to persuade 'em that they have no right or business to be married[10], than he can hope to persuade 'em that they have no earthly right or business to be born. And *that* we know they haven't. We reduced it to a mathematical certainty long ago."**

Alderman Cute was mightily diverted, and laid his right forefinger on the side of his nose, as much as to say to both his friends, "Observe me, will you? Keep your eye on the practical man!"—and called Meg to him.

"Come here, my girl!" said Alderman Cute.

The young blood of her lover had been mounting, wrathfully, within the last few minutes; and he was indisposed to let her come. But setting a constraint upon himself, he came forward with a stride as Meg approached, and stood beside her. Trotty kept her hand within his arm still, but looked from face to face as wildly as a sleeper in a dream.

"Now I'm going to give you a word or two of good

advice, my girl," said the Alderman, in his nice easy way. "It's my place to give advice, you know, because I'm a Justice. You know I'm a Justice, don't you?"

Meg timidly said, "Yes." But everybody knew Alderman Cute was a Justice! O dear, so active a Justice always! Who such a mote of brightness in the public eye, as Cute!

"You are going to be married, you say," pursued the Alderman. "Very unbecoming and indelicate in one of your sex! But never mind that. After you are married, you'll quarrel with your husband, and come to be a distressed wife. You may think not: but you will, because I tell you so. Now I give you fair warning, that I have made up my mind to Put distressed wives Down. So don't be brought before me. You'll have children—boys. Those boys will grow up bad of course, and run wild in the streets, without shoes and stockings. Mind, my young friend! I'll convict 'em summarily, every one, for I am determined to Put boys without shoes and stockings, Down. Perhaps your husband will die young (most likely) and leave you with a baby. Then you'll be turned out of doors, and wander up and down the streets. Now don't wander near me, my dear, for I am resolved to Put all wandering mothers Down. All young mothers, of all sorts and kinds, it's my determination to Put Down. Don't think to plead illness as an excuse with me; or babies as an excuse with me; for all sick persons and young children (I hope you know the church-service[11], but I'm afraid not) I am determined to Put Down. And if you attempt, desperately, and ungratefully, and impiously, and fraudulently attempt, to drown yourself, or hang yourself, I'll have no pity on you, for I have made up my mind to Put all suicide Down. If there is one thing," said the Alderman, with his self-satisfied smile, "on which I can be said to have made up my mind more than on another, it is to Put suicide Down.[12] So don't try it on. That's the phrase, isn't it? Ha, ha! now we understand each other."

Toby knew not whether to be agonised or glad to see that

Meg had turned a deadly white, and dropped her lover's hand.

"And as for you, you dull dog," said the Alderman, turning with even increased cheerfulness and urbanity to the young smith, "what are you thinking of being married for? What do you want to be married for, you silly fellow! If I was a fine, young, strapping chap like you, I should be ashamed of being milksop enough to pin myself to a woman's apron-strings! Why, she'll be an old woman before you're a middle-aged man! And a pretty figure you'll cut then, with a draggle-tailed wife and a crowd of squalling children crying after you wherever you go!"

Oh, he knew how to banter the common people, Alderman Cute!

"There! Go along with you," said the Alderman, "and repent. Don't make such a fool of yourself as to get married on New Year's Day. You'll think very differently of it long before next New Year's Day: a trim young fellow like you, with all the girls looking after you. There! Go along with you!"

They went along. Not arm in arm, or hand in hand, or interchanging bright glances: but she in tears, he gloomy and down-looking. Were these the hearts that had so lately made old Toby's leap up from its faintness? No, no. The Alderman (a blessing on his head!) had Put *them* Down.

"As you happen to be here," said the Alderman to Toby, "you shall carry a letter for me. Can you be quick? You're an old man."

Toby, who had been looking after Meg, quite stupidly, made shift to murmur out that he was very quick, and very strong.

"How old are you?" inquired the Alderman.

"I'm over sixty, Sir," said Toby.

"Oh! This man's a great deal past the average age, you know," cried Mr. Filer, breaking in as if his patience would bear some trying, but this really was carrying matters a little too far.

"I feel I'm intruding, Sir," said Toby. "I—I misdoubted it this morning. Oh dear me!"

The Alderman cut him short by giving him the letter from his pocket. Toby would have got a shilling too; but Mr. Filer clearly showing that in that case he would rob a certain given number of persons of ninepence-halfpenny a-piece, he only got sixpence; and thought himself very well off to get that.

Then the Alderman gave an arm to each of his friends, and walked off in high feather; but immediately came hurrying back alone, as if he had forgotten something.

"Porter!" said the Alderman.

"Sir!" said Toby.

"Take care of that daughter of yours. She's much too handsome."

"Even her good looks are stolen from somebody or other I suppose," thought Toby, looking at the sixpence in his hand, and thinking of the tripe. "She's been and robbed five hundred ladies of a bloom a-piece, I shouldn't wonder. It's very dreadful!"

"She's much too handsome, my man," repeated the Alderman. "The chances are, that she'll come to no good, I clearly see. Observe what I say. Take care of her!" With which, he hurried off again.

"Wrong every way. Wrong every way!" said Trotty, clasping his hands. "Born bad. No business here!"

The Chimes came clashing in upon him as he said the words. Full, loud, and sounding—but with no encouragement. No, not a drop.

"The tune's changed," cried the old man, as he listened. "There's not a word of all that fancy in it. Why should there be? I have no business with the New Year nor with the old one neither. Let me die!"

Still the Bells, pealing forth their changes, made the very air spin. Put 'em down, Put 'em down! Good old Times, Good old Times! Facts and Figures, Facts and Figures! Put 'em down, Put 'em down! If they said anything they said this, till the brain of Toby reeled.

He pressed his bewildered head between his hands, as if to keep it from splitting asunder. A well-timed action, as it happened; for finding the letter in one of them, and being by that means reminded of his charge, he fell, mechanically, into his usual trot, and trotted off.

The Second Quarter.

THE letter Toby had received from Alderman Cute, was addressed to a great man in the great district of the town. The greatest district of the town, because it was commonly called The World by its inhabitants.

The letter positively seemed heavier in Toby's hand, than another letter. Not because the Alderman had sealed it with a very large coat of arms and no end of wax, but because of the weighty name on the superscription, and the ponderous amount of gold and silver with which it was associated.

"How different from us!" thought Toby, in all simplicity and earnestness, as he looked at the direction. "Divide the lively turtles in the bills of mortality, by the number of gentlefolks able to buy 'em; and whose share does he take but his own! As to snatching tripe from anybody's mouth —he'd scorn it!"

With the involuntary homage due to such an exalted character, Toby interposed a corner of his apron between the letter and his fingers.

"His children," said Trotty, and a mist rose before his eyes; "his daughters—Gentlemen may win their hearts and marry them; they may be happy wives and mothers; they may be handsome like my darling M—e—"

He couldn't finish her name. The final letter swelled in his throat, to the size of the whole alphabet.

"Never mind," thought Trotty. "I know what I mean. That's more than enough for me." And with this consolatory rumination, trotted on.

It was a hard frost, that day. The air was bracing, crisp, and clear. The wintry sun, though powerless for warmth, looked brightly down upon the ice it was too weak to melt, and set a radiant glory there. At other times, Trotty might have learned a poor man's lesson from the wintry sun; but he was past that, now.

The Year was Old that day. The patient Year had lived through the reproaches and misuses of its slanderers, and faithfully performed its work. Spring, summer, autumn, winter. It had laboured through the destined round, and now laid down its weary head to die. Shut out from hope, high impulse, active happiness, itself, but messenger of many joys to others, it made appeal in its decline to have its toiling days and patient hours remembered, and to die in peace. Trotty might have read a poor man's allegory in the fading year; but he was past that, now.

And only he? Or has the like appeal been ever made, by seventy years at once upon an English labourer's head, and made in vain!

The streets were full of motion, and the shops were decked out gaily. The New Year, like an Infant Heir to the whole world, was waited for, with welcomes, presents, and rejoicings. There were books and toys for the New Year, glittering trinkets for the New Year, dresses for the New Year, schemes of fortune for the New Year; new inventions to beguile it. Its life was parcelled out in almanacks and pocket-books; the coming of its moons, and stars, and tides, was known beforehand to the moment; all the workings of its seasons in their days and nights, were calculated with as much precision as Mr. Filer could work sums in men and women.

The New Year, the New Year. Everywhere the New Year! The Old Year was already looked upon as dead; and its effects were selling cheap like some drowned mariner's aboardship. Its patterns were Last Year's and going at a sacrifice, before its breath was gone. Its treasures were mere dirt, beside the riches of its unborn successor!

Trotty had no portion, to his thinking, in the New Year or the Old.

"Put 'em down, put 'em down! Facts and Figures, facts and figures! Good old Times, good old Times! Put 'em down, put 'em down!"—his trot went to that measure, and would fit itself to nothing else.

But even that one, melancholy as it was, brought him, in due time, to the end of his journey. To the mansion of Sir Joseph Bowley, Member of Parliament.

The door was opened by a Porter. Such a Porter! Not of Toby's order. Quite another thing. His place was the ticket though; not Toby's.

This Porter underwent some hard panting before he could speak; having breathed himself by coming incautiously out of his chair, without first taking time to think about it and compose his mind. When he had found his voice—which it took him a long time to do, for it was a long way off, and hidden under a load of meat—he said in a fat whisper,

"Who's it from?"

Toby told him.

"You're to take it in, yourself," said the Porter, pointing to a room at the end of a long passage, opening from the hall, "Everything goes straight in, on this day of the year. You're not a bit too soon, for the carriage is at the door now, and they have only come to town for a couple of hours, a' purpose."

Toby wiped his feet (which were quite dry already) with great care, and took the way pointed out to him; observing as he went that it was an awfully grand house, but hushed and covered up, as if the family were in the country. Knocking at the room door, he was told to enter from within; and doing so found himself in a spacious library, where, at a table strewn with files and papers, were a stately lady in a bonnet; and a not very stately gentleman in black who wrote from her dictation; while another, and an older, and a much statelier gentleman, whose hat and cane were on the table, walked up and down, with one hand in his breast, and looked complacently from time to time at his own picture—a full length; a very full length—hanging over the fire-place.

"What is this?" said the last-named gentleman. "Mr. Fish, will you have the goodness to attend?"

Mr. Fish begged pardon, and taking the letter from Toby, handed it, with great respect.

"From Alderman Cute, Sir Joseph."

"Is this all? Have you nothing else, Porter?" inquired Sir Joseph.

Toby replied in the negative.

"You have no bill or demand upon me; my name is Bowley, Sir Joseph Bowley; of any kind from anybody, have you?" said Sir Joseph. "If you have, present it. There is a cheque-book by the side of Mr. Fish. I allow nothing to be carried into the New Year. Every description of account is

settled in this house at the close of the old one. So that if death was to—to—"

"To cut," suggested Mr. Fish.

"To sever, Sir," returned Sir Joseph, with great asperity, "the cord of existence—my affairs would be found, I hope, in a state of preparation."

"My dear Sir Joseph!" said the lady who was greatly younger than the gentleman. "How shocking!"

"My lady Bowley," returned Sir Joseph, floundering now and then, as in the great depth of his observations, "at this season of the year we should think of—of—ourselves. We should look into our—our accounts. We should feel that every return of so eventful a period in human transactions, involves matters of deep moment between a man and his— and his banker."

Sir Joseph delivered these words as if he felt the full morality of what he was saying; and desired that even Trotty should have an opportunity of being improved by such discourse. Possibly he had this end before him in still forbearing to break the seal of the letter, and in telling Trotty to wait where he was, a minute.

"You were desiring Mr. Fish to say, my lady—" observed Sir Joseph.

"Mr. Fish has said that, I believe," returned his lady, glancing at the letter. "But, upon my word, Sir Joseph, I don't think I can let it go after all. It is so very dear."

"What is dear?" inquired Sir Joseph.

"That Charity, my love. They only allow two votes for a subscription of five pounds. Really monstrous!"

"My lady Bowley," returned Sir Joseph, "you surprise me. Is the luxury of feeling in proportion to the number of votes; or is it, to a rightly-constituted mind, in proportion to the number of applicants, and the wholesome state of mind to which their canvassing reduces them? Is there no excitement of the purest kind in having two votes to dispose of among fifty people?"

"Not to me, I acknowledge," replied the lady. "It bores

one. Besides, one can't oblige one's acquaintance. But you are the Poor Man's Friend[13], you know, Sir Joseph. You think otherwise."

"I *am* the Poor Man's Friend," observed Sir Joseph, glancing at the poor man present. "As such I may be taunted. As such I have been taunted. But I ask no other title."

"Bless him for a noble gentleman!" thought Trotty.

"I don't agree with Cute here, for instance," said Sir Joseph, holding out the letter. "I don't agree with the Filer party. I don't agree with any party. My friend the Poor Man, has no business with anything of that sort, and nothing of that sort has any business with him. My friend the Poor Man, in my district, is my business. No man or body of men has any right to interfere between my friend and me. That is the ground I take. I assume a—a paternal character towards my friend. I say, 'My good fellow, I will treat you paternally.'"

Toby listened with great gravity, and began to feel more comfortable.

"Your only business, my good fellow," pursued Sir Joseph, looking abstractedly at Toby; "your only business in life is with me. You needn't trouble yourself to think about anything. I will think for you; I know what is good for you; I am your perpetual parent. Such is the dispensation of an all-wise Providence![14] Now, the design of your creation is: not that you should swill, and guzzle, and associate your enjoyments, brutally, with food"—Toby thought remorsefully of the tripe—"but that you should feel the Dignity of Labor; go forth erect into the cheerful morning air, and—and stop there. Live hard and temperately, be respectful, exercise your self-denial, bring up your family on next to nothing, pay your rent as regularly as the clock strikes, be punctual in your dealings (I set you a good example; you will find Mr. Fish, my confidential secretary, with a cash-box before him at all times); and you may trust to me to be your Friend and Father."

"Nice children, indeed, Sir Joseph!" said the lady, with

a shudder. "Rheumatisms, and fevers, and crooked legs, and asthmas, and all kinds of horrors!"

"My lady," returned Sir Joseph, with solemnity, "not the less am I the Poor Man's Friend and Father. Not the less shall he receive encouragement at my hands. Every quarter-day he will be put in communication with Mr. Fish. Every New-Year's Day, myself and friends will drink his health. Once every year, myself and friends will address him with the deepest feeling. Once in his life, he may even perhaps receive; in public, in the presence of the gentry; a Trifle from a Friend. And when, upheld no more by these stimulants, and the Dignity of Labor, he sinks into his comfortable grave, then my lady"—here Sir Joseph blew his nose—"I will be a Friend and a Father—on the same terms—to his children."

Toby was greatly moved.

"Oh! You have a thankful family, Sir Joseph!" cried his wife.

"My lady," said Sir Joseph, quite majestically, "Ingratitude is known to be the sin of that class. I expect no other return."

"Ah! Born bad!" thought Toby. "Nothing melts us!"

"What man can do, *I* do," pursued Sir Joseph. "I do my duty as the Poor Man's Friend and Father; and I endeavour to educate his mind, by inculcating on all occasions the one great moral lesson which that class requires. That is, entire Dependence on myself. They have no business whatever with—with themselves. If wicked and designing persons tell them otherwise, and they become impatient and discontented, and are guilty of insubordinate conduct and black-hearted ingratitude; which is undoubtedly the case; I am their Friend and Father still. It is so Ordained. It is in the nature of things."

With that great sentiment, he opened the Alderman's letter; and read it.

"Very polite and attentive, I am sure!" exclaimed Sir Joseph. "My lady, the Alderman is so obliging as to remind me that he has had 'the distinguished honor'—he is very good—of meeting me at the house of our mutual friend

Deedles, the banker; and he does me the favor to inquire whether it will be agreeable to me to have Will Fern put down."

"*Most* agreeable!" replied my Lady Bowley. "The worst man among them! He has been committing a robbery, I hope?"

"Why, no," said Sir Joseph, referring to the letter. "Not quite. Very near. Not quite. He came up to London, it seems, to look for employment (trying to better himself— that's his story), and being found at night asleep in a shed, was taken into custody, and carried next morning before the Alderman. The Alderman observes (very properly) that he is determined to put this sort of thing down; and that if it will be agreeable to me to have Will Fern put down, he will be happy to begin with him."

"Let him be made an example of, by all means," returned the lady. "Last winter, when I introduced pinking and eyelet-holeing[15] among the men and boys in the village, as a nice evening employment, and had the lines,

> Oh let us love our occupations,
> Bless the squire and his relations,
> Live upon our daily rations,
> And always know our proper stations,

set to music on the new system[16], for them to sing the while; this very Fern—I see him now—touched that hat of his, and said, 'I humbly ask your pardon my lady, but *an't* I something different from a great girl?' I expected it, of course; who can expect anything but insolence and ingratitude from that class of people? That is not to the purpose, however. Sir Joseph! Make an example of him!"

"Hem!" coughed Sir Joseph. "Mr. Fish, if you'll have the goodness to attend—"

Mr. Fish immediately seized his pen, and wrote from Sir Joseph's dictation.

"Private. My dear Sir. I am very much indebted to you for your courtesy in the matter of the man William Fern, of whom, I regret to add, I can say nothing favorable. I have uniformly considered myself in the light of his Friend and Father, but have been repaid (a common case, I grieve to say) with ingratitude, and constant opposition to my plans. He is a turbulent and rebellious spirit. His character will not bear investigation. Nothing will persuade him to be happy when he might. Under these circumstances, it appears to me, I own, that when he comes before you again (as you informed me he promised to do to-morrow, pending your inquiries, and I think he may be so far relied upon), his committal for some short term as a Vagabond, would be a service to society, and would be a salutary example in a country where—for the sake of those who are, through good and evil report, the Friends and Fathers of the Poor, as well as with a view to that, generally speaking, misguided class themselves— examples are greatly needed. And I am," and so forth.

"It appears," remarked Sir Joseph when he had signed this letter, and Mr. Fish was sealing it, "as if this were Ordained: really. At the close of the year, I wind up my account and strike my balance, even with William Fern!"

Trotty, who had long ago relapsed, and was very low-spirited, stepped forward with a rueful face to take the letter.

"With my compliments and thanks," said Sir Joseph. "Stop!"

"Stop!" echoed Mr. Fish.

"You have heard, perhaps," said Sir Joseph, oracularly, "certain remarks into which I have been led respecting the solemn period of time at which we have arrived, and the duty imposed upon us of settling our affairs, and being prepared. You have observed that I don't shelter myself behind my superior standing in society, but that Mr. Fish—that gentle-man—has a cheque-book at his elbow, and is in fact here, to enable me to turn over a perfectly new leaf, and enter on the epoch before us with a clean account. Now, my friend, can you lay your hand upon your heart, and say, that you also have made preparations for a New Year?"

"I am afraid Sir," stammered Trotty, looking meekly at him, "that I am a—a—little behind-hand with the world."

"Behind-hand with the world!" repeated Sir Joseph Bowley, in a tone of terrible distinctness.

"I am afraid Sir," faltered Trotty, "that there's a matter of ten or twelve shillings owing to Mrs. Chickenstalker."

"To Mrs. Chickenstalker!" repeated Sir Joseph, in the same tone as before.

"A shop Sir," exclaimed Toby, "in the general line. Also a—a little money on account of rent. A very little Sir. It oughtn't to be owing, I know, but we have been hard put to it, indeed!"

Sir Joseph looked at his lady, and at Mr. Fish, and at Trotty, one after another, twice all round. He then made a despondent gesture with both hands at once, as if he gave the thing up altogether.

"How a man, even among this improvident and impracticable race; an old man; a man grown grey; can look a New Year in the face, with his affairs in this condition; how he can lie down on his bed at night, and get up again in the morning, and—There!" he said, turning his back on Trotty. "Take the letter. Take the letter!"

"I heartily wish it was otherwise, sir," said Trotty, anxious to excuse himself. "We have been tried very hard."

Sir Joseph still repeating "Take the letter, take the letter!" and Mr. Fish not only saying the same thing, but giving additional force to the request by motioning the bearer to the door, he had nothing for it but to make his bow and leave the house. And in the street, poor Trotty pulled his worn old hat down on his head, to hide the grief he felt at getting no hold on the New Year, anywhere.

He didn't even lift his hat to look up at the Bell tower when he came to the old church on his return. He halted there a moment, from habit: and knew that it was growing dark, and that the steeple rose above him, indistinct and faint, in the murky air. He knew, too, that the Chimes would ring immediately; and that they sounded to his fancy, at such a time, like voices in the clouds. But he only made the more haste to deliver the Alderman's letter, and get out of the way before they began; for he dreaded to hear them tagging "Friends and Fathers, Friends and Fathers," to the burden they had rung out last.

Toby discharged himself of his commission, therefore, with all possible speed, and set off trotting homeward. But what with his pace, which was at best an awkward one in the street; and what with his hat, which didn't improve it; he trotted against somebody in less than no time, and was sent staggering out into the road.

"I beg your pardon, I'm sure!" said Trotty, pulling up his hat in great confusion, and between the hat and the torn lining, fixing his head into a kind of bee-hive. "I hope I haven't hurt you."

As to hurting anybody, Toby was not such an absolute Samson, but that he was much more likely to be hurt himself: and indeed, he had flown out into the road, like a shuttlecock. He had such an opinion of his own strength, however, that he was in real concern for the other party: and said again,

"I hope I haven't hurt you?"

The man against whom he had run; a sun-browned, sinewy, country-looking man, with grizzled hair, and a rough chin; stared at him for a moment, as if he suspected him to be in jest. But satisfied of his good faith, he answered:

"No friend. You have not hurt me."

"Nor the child, I hope?" said Trotty.

"Nor the child," returned the man. "I thank you kindly."

As he said so, he glanced at a little girl he carried in his arms, asleep: and shading her face with the long end of the poor handkerchief he wore about his throat, went slowly on.

The tone in which he said "I thank you kindly," penetrated Trotty's heart. He was so jaded and foot-sore, and so soiled with travel, and looked about him so forlorn and strange, that it was a comfort to him to be able to thank any one: no matter for how little. Toby stood gazing after him as he plodded wearily away; with the child's arm clinging round his neck.

At the figure in the worn shoes—now the very shade and ghost of shoes—rough leather leggings, common frock, and broad slouched hat, Trotty stood gazing: blind to the whole street. And at the child's arm, clinging round its neck.

Before he merged into the darkness, the traveller stopped; and looking round, and seeing Trotty standing there yet, seemed undecided whether to return or go on. After doing first the one and then the other, he came back; and Trotty went half way to meet him.

"You can tell me, perhaps," said the man with a faint smile, "and if you can I am sure you will, and I'd rather ask you than another—where Alderman Cute lives."

"Close at hand," replied Toby. "I'll show you his house with pleasure."

"I was to have gone to him elsewhere to-morrow," said the man, accompanying Toby, "but I'm uneasy under suspicion, and want to clear myself, and to be free to go and seek my bread—I don't know where. So, maybe he'll forgive my going to his house to-night."

"It's impossible," cried Toby with a start, "that your name's Fern!"

"Eh!" cried the other, turning on him in astonishment.

"Fern! Will Fern!" said Trotty.

"That's my name," replied the other.

"Why then," cried Trotty, seizing him by the arm, and looking cautiously round, "for Heaven's sake don't go to him! Don't go to him! He'll put you down as sure as ever you were born. Here! come up this alley, and I'll tell you what I mean. Don't go to *him*."

His new acquaintance looked as if he thought him mad; but he bore him company nevertheless. When they were shrouded from observation, Trotty told him what he knew, and what character he had received, and all about it.

The subject of his history listened to it with a calmness that surprised him. He did not contradict or interrupt it, once. He nodded his head now and then—more in corroboration of an old and worn-out story, it appeared, than in refutation of it; and once or twice threw back his hat, and passed his freckled hand over a brow, where every furrow he had ploughed seemed to have set its image in little. But he did no more.

"It's true enough in the main," he said, "master. I could sift grain from husk here and there, but let it be as 'tis. What odds? I have gone against his plans; to my misfortun'. I can't help it; I should do the like to-morrow. As to character, them gentlefolks will search and search, and pry and pry, and have it as free from spot or speck in us, afore they'll help us to a dry good word! Well! I hope they don't lose good opinion as easy as we do, or their lives is strict indeed, and hardly worth the keeping. For myself, master, I never took with that hand"—holding it before him—"what wasn't my own; and never held it back from work, however hard, or poorly paid. Whoever can deny it, let him chop it off! But when work won't maintain me like a human creetur; when my living is so bad, that I am Hungry, out of doors and in; when I see a whole working life begin that way, go on that way, and end that way, without a chance or change; then I say to the gentlefolks 'Keep away from me! Let my cottage be. My doors is dark enough without your darkening of 'em more. Don't look for me to come up into the Park to help the show when there's a Birthday, or a fine Speechmaking, or what not. Act your Plays and Games without me, and be welcome to 'em and enjoy 'em. We've nought to do with one another. I'm best let alone!'"

Seeing that the child in his arms had opened her eyes, and was looking about her in wonder, he checked himself to say a word or two of foolish prattle in her ear, and stand her on the ground beside him. Then slowly winding one of her long tresses round and round his rough forefinger like a ring, while she hung about his dusty leg, he said to Trotty,

"I'm not a cross-grained man by natur', I believe; and easy satisfied, I'm sure. I bear no ill-will against none of 'em.

I only want to live like one of the Almighty's creeturs. I can't, I don't; and so there's a pit dug between me and them that can and do. There's others like me. You might tell 'em off by hundreds and by thousands, sooner than by ones."

Trotty knew he spoke the Truth in this, and shook his head to signify as much.

"I've got a bad name this way," said Fern; "and I'm not likely, I'm afeard, to get a better. 'Ta'n't lawful to be out of sorts, and I AM out of sorts, though God knows I'd sooner bear a cheerful spirit if I could. Well! I don't know as this Alderman could hurt *me* much by sending me to jail; but without a friend to speak a word for me, he might do it; and you see—!" pointing downward with his finger, at the child.

"She has a beautiful face," said Trotty.

"Why, yes!" replied the other in a low voice, as he gently turned it up with both his hands towards his own, and looked upon it steadfastly. "I've thought so, many times. I've thought so, when my hearth was very cold, and cupboard very bare. I thought so t'other night, when we were taken like two thieves. But they—they shouldn't try the little face too often, should they, Lilian? That's hardly fair upon a man!"

He sunk his voice so low, and gazed upon her with an air so stern and strange, that Toby, to divert the current of his thoughts, inquired if his wife were living.

"I never had one," he returned, shaking his head. "She's my brother's child: an orphan. Nine year old, though you'd hardly think it; but she's tired and worn out now. They'd have taken care on her, the Union[17]; eight and twenty mile away from where we live; between four walls (as they took care of my old father when he couldn't work no more, though he didn't trouble 'em long); but I took her instead, and she's lived with me ever since. Her mother had a friend once, in London here. We are trying to find her, and to find work too; but it's a large place. Never mind. More room for us to walk about in, Lilly!"

Meeting the child's eyes with a smile which melted Toby more than tears, he shook him by the hand.

"I don't so much as know your name," he said, "but I've opened my heart free to you, for I'm thankful to you; with good reason. I'll take your advice, and keep clear of this——"

"Justice," suggested Toby.

"Ah!" he said. "If that's the name they give him. This Justice. And to-morrow will try whether there's better fortun' to be met with, somewheres near London. Good night. A Happy New Year!"

"Stay!" cried Trotty, catching at his hand, as he relaxed his grip. "Stay! The New Year never can be happy to me, if we part like this. The New Year never can be happy to me, if I see the child and you, go wandering away, you don't know where, without a shelter for your heads. Come home with me! I'm a poor man, living in a poor place; but I can give you lodging for one night and never miss it. Come home with me! Here! I'll take her!" cried Trotty, lifting up the child. "A pretty one! I'd carry twenty times her weight, and never know I'd got it. Tell me if I go too quick for you. I'm very fast. I always was!" Trotty said this, taking about six of his trotting paces to one stride of his fatigued companion; and with his thin legs quivering again, beneath the load he bore.

"Why, she's as light," said Trotty, trotting in his speech as well as in his gait; for he couldn't bear to be thanked, and dreaded a moment's pause; "as light as a feather. Lighter than a Peacock's feather—a great deal lighter. Here we are, and here we go! Round this first turning to the right, Uncle Will, and past the pump, and sharp off up the passage to the left, right opposite the public-house. Here we are, and here we go. Cross over, Uncle Will, and mind the kidney pieman at the corner! Here we are and here we go! Down the Mews here, Uncle Will, and stop at the black door, with 'T. Veck, Ticket Porter' wrote upon a board; and here we are and here we go, and here we are indeed, my precious Meg, surprising you!"

With which words Trotty, in a breathless state, set the child down before his daughter in the middle of the floor. The little visitor looked once at Meg; and doubting nothing in that face, but trusting everything she saw there; ran into her arms.

"Here we are and here we go!" cried Trotty, running round the room and choking audibly. "Here! Uncle Will! Here's a fire you know! Why don't you come to the fire? Oh here we are and here we go! Meg, my precious darling, where's the kettle? Here it is and here it goes, and it'll bile in no time!"

Trotty really had picked up the kettle somewhere or other in the course of his wild career, and now put it on the fire: while Meg, seating the child in a warm corner, knelt down on the ground before her, and pulled off her shoes, and dried her wet feet on a cloth. Aye, and she laughed at Trotty too —so pleasantly, so cheerfully, that Trotty could have blessed her where she kneeled: for he had seen that, when they entered, she was sitting by the fire in tears.

"Why father!" said Meg. "You're crazy to-night, I think. I don't know what the Bells would say to that. Poor little feet. How cold they are!"

"Oh they're warmer now!" exclaimed the child. "They're quite warm now!"

"No, no, no," said Meg. "We haven't rubbed 'em half enough. We're so busy. So busy! And when they're done, we'll brush out the damp hair; and when that's done, we'll bring some colour to the poor pale face with fresh water; and when that's done, we'll be so gay, and brisk, and happy—!"

The child, in a burst of sobbing, clasped her round the neck; caressed her fair cheek with its hand; and said, "Oh Meg! oh dear Meg!"

Toby's blessing could have done no more. Who could do more!

"Why father!" cried Meg, after a pause.

"Here I am and here I go, my dear," said Trotty.

"Good Gracious me!" cried Meg. "He's crazy! He's put

the dear child's bonnet on the kettle, and hung the lid behind the door!"

"I didn't go to do it, my love," said Trotty, hastily repairing this mistake. "Meg, my dear?"

Meg looked towards him and saw that he had elaborately stationed himself behind the chair of their male visitor, where with many mysterious gestures he was holding up the sixpence he had earned.

"I see, my dear," said Trotty, "as I was coming in, half an ounce of tea lying somewhere on the stairs; and I'm pretty sure there was a bit of bacon too. As I don't remember where it was, exactly; I'll go myself and try to find 'em."

With this inscrutable artifice, Toby withdrew to purchase the viands he had spoken of, for ready money, at Mrs. Chickenstalker's; and presently came back, pretending he had not been able to find them, at first, in the dark.

"But here they are, at last," said Trotty, setting out the tea-things, "all correct! I was pretty sure it was tea, and a rasher. So it is. Meg, my Pet, if you'll just make the tea, while your unworthy father toasts the bacon, we shall be ready, immediate. It's a curious circumstance," said Trotty, proceeding in his cookery, with the assistance of the toasting-fork, "curious, but well known to my friends, that I never care, myself, for rashers, nor for tea. I like to see other people enjoy 'em," said Trotty, speaking very loud, to impress the fact upon his guest, "but to me, as food, they're disagreeable."

Yet Trotty sniffed the savour of the hissing bacon—ah!—as if he liked it; and when he poured the boiling water in the tea-pot, looked lovingly down into the depths of that snug cauldron, and suffered the fragrant steam to curl about his nose, and wreathe his head and face in a thick cloud. However, for all this, he neither ate nor drank, except at the very beginning, a mere morsel for form's sake, which he appeared to eat with infinite relish, but declared was perfectly uninteresting to him.

No. Trotty's occupation was, to see Will Fern and Lilian eat and drink; and so was Meg's. And never did spectators at a city dinner or court banquet find such high delight in seeing others feast: although it were a monarch or a pope: as those two did, in looking on that night. Meg smiled at Trotty, Trotty laughed at Meg. Meg shook her head and made belief to clap her hands, applauding Trotty; Trotty conveyed, in dumb-show, unintelligible narratives of how and when and where he had found their visitors, to Meg; and they were happy. Very happy.

"Although," thought Trotty, sorrowfully, as he watched Meg's face; "that match is broken off, I see!"

"Now, I'll tell you what," said Trotty after tea. "The little one, she sleeps with Meg, I know."

"With good Meg!" cried the child, caressing her. "With Meg."

"That's right," said Trotty. "And I shouldn't wonder if she kiss Meg's father, won't she? *I*'m Meg's father."

Mightily delighted Trotty was, when the child went timidly towards him; and having kissed him, fell back upon Meg again.

"She's as sensible as Solomon," said Trotty. "Here we come, and here we—no, we don't—I don't mean that—I—what was I saying, Meg, my precious?"

Meg looked towards their guest, who leaned upon her chair, and with his face turned from her, fondled the child's head, half hidden in her lap.

"To be sure," said Toby. "To be sure! I don't know what I'm rambling on about, to-night. My wits are wool-gathering, I think. Will Fern, you come along with me. You're tired to death, and broken down for want of rest. You come along with me."

The man still played with the child's curls, still leaned upon Meg's chair, still turned away his face. He didn't speak, but in his rough coarse fingers, clenching and expanding in the fair hair of the child, there was an eloquence that said enough.

"Yes, yes," said Trotty, answering unconsciously what he saw expressed in his daughter's face. "Take her with you,

Meg. Get her to bed. There! Now Will, I'll show you where you lie. It's not much of a place: only a loft: but having a loft, I always say, is one of the great conveniences of living in a mews; and till this coach-house and stable gets a better let, we live here cheap. There's plenty of sweet hay up there, belonging to a neighbour; and it's as clean as hands and Meg can make it. Cheer up! Don't give way. A new heart for a New Year, always!"

The hand released from the child's hair, had fallen, trembling, into Trotty's hand. So Trotty, talking without intermission, led him out as tenderly and easily as if he had been a child himself.

Returning before Meg, he listened for an instant at the door of her little chamber; an adjoining room. The child was murmuring a simple Prayer before lying down to sleep; and when she had remembered Meg's name, "Dearly, Dearly" so her words ran—Trotty heard her stop and ask for his.

It was some short time before the foolish little old fellow could compose himself to mend the fire, and draw his chair to the warm hearth. But when he had done so, and had trimmed the light, he took his newspaper from his pocket, and began to read. Carelessly at first, and skimming up and down the columns; but with an earnest and a sad attention, very soon.

For this same dreaded paper re-directed Trotty's thoughts into the channel they had taken all that day, and which the day's events had so marked out and shaped. His interest in the two wanderers had set him on another course of thinking, and a happier one, for the time; but being alone again, and reading of the crimes and violences of the people, he relapsed into his former train.

In this mood, he came to an account (and it was not the first he had ever read) of a woman who had laid her desperate hands not only on her own life but on that of her young child.[18] A crime so terrible, and so revolting to his soul, dilated with the love of Meg, that he let the journal drop, and fell back in his chair, appalled.

"Unnatural and cruel!" Toby cried. "Unnatural and cruel! None but people who were bad at heart: born bad: who had no business on the earth: could do such deeds. It's too true, all I've heard to-day; too just, too full of proof. We're Bad!"

The Chimes took up the words so suddenly—burst out so loud, and clear, and sonorous—that the Bells seemed to strike him in his chair.

And what was that, they said?

"Toby Veck, Toby Veck, waiting for you Toby! Toby Veck, Toby Veck, waiting for you Toby! Come and see us, come and see us, Drag him to us, drag him to us, Haunt and hunt him, haunt and hunt him, Break his slumbers, break his slumbers! Toby Veck Toby Veck, door open wide, Toby, Toby Veck Toby Veck, door open wide Toby—" then fiercely back to their impetuous strain again, and ringing in the very bricks and plaster on the walls.

Toby listened. Fancy, fancy! His remorse for having run away from them that afternoon! No, no. Nothing of the kind. Again, again, and yet a dozen times again. "Haunt and hunt him, haunt and hunt him, Drag him to us, drag him to us!" Deafening the whole town!

"Meg," said Trotty softly: tapping at her door. "Do you hear anything?"

"I hear the Bells, father. Surely they're very loud tonight."

"Is she asleep?" said Toby, making an excuse for peeping in.

"So peacefully and happily! I can't leave her yet though, father. Look how she holds my hand!"

"Meg," whispered Trotty. "Listen to the Bells!"

She listened, with her face towards him all the time. But it underwent no change. She didn't understand them.

Trotty withdrew, resumed his seat by the fire, and once more listened by himself. He remained here a little time.

It was impossible to bear it; their energy was dreadful.

"If the tower-door is really open," said Toby, hastily laying aside his apron, but never thinking of his hat, "what's to hinder me from going up into the steeple and satisfying myself? If it's shut, I don't want any other satisfaction. That's enough."

He was pretty certain as he slipped out quietly into the street that he should find it shut and locked, for he knew the door well, and had so rarely seen it open, that he couldn't reckon above three times in all. It was a low arched portal, out-side the church, in a dark nook behind a column; and had such great iron hinges, and such a monstrous lock, that there was more hinge and lock than door.

But what was his astonishment when, coming bare-headed to the church; and putting his hand into this dark nook, with a certain misgiving that it might be unexpectedly seized, and a shivering propensity to draw it back again; he found that the door, which opened outwards, actually stood ajar!

He thought, on the first surprise, of going back; or of getting a light, or a companion; but his courage aided him immediately; and he determined to ascend alone.

"What have I to fear?" said Trotty. "It's a church! Besides, the ringers may be there, and have forgotten to shut the door."

So he went in; feeling his way as he went, like a blind man; for it was very dark. And very quiet, for the Chimes were silent.

The dust from the street had blown into the recess; and lying there, heaped up, made it so soft and velvet-like to the foot, that there was something startling even in that. The narrow stair was so close to the door, too, that he stumbled at the very first; and shutting the door upon himself, by striking it with his foot, and causing it to rebound back heavily, he couldn't open it again.

This was another reason, however, for going on. Trotty groped his way, and went on. Up, up, up, and round and round; and up, up, up; higher, higher, higher up!

It was a disagreeable staircase for that groping work; so low and narrow, that his groping hand was always touching something; and it often felt so like a man or ghostly figure standing up erect and making room for him to pass without discovery, that he would rub the smooth wall upward searching for its face, and downward searching for its feet, while a chill tingling crept all over him. Twice or thrice, a door or niche broke the monotonous surface; and then it seemed a gap as wide as the whole church; and he felt on the brink of an abyss, and going to tumble headlong down; until he found the wall again.

Still up, up, up; and round and round; and up, up, up; higher, higher, higher up!

At length, the dull and stifling atmosphere began to freshen: presently to feel quite windy: presently it blew so strong, that he could hardly keep his legs. But he got to an arched window in the tower, breast-high, and holding tight, looked down upon the house-tops, on the smoking chimneys, on the blur and blotch of lights (towards the place where Meg was wondering where he was and calling to him perhaps), all kneaded up together in a leaven of mist and darkness.

This was the belfry, where the ringers came. He had caught hold of one of the frayed ropes which hung down through apertures in the oaken roof. At first he started; thinking it was hair; then trembled at the very thought of waking the deep Bell. The Bells themselves were higher. Higher, Trotty, in his fascination, or in working out the spell upon him, groped his way. By ladders now, and toilsomely, for it was steep, and not too certain holding for the feet.

Up, up, up; and climb and clamber; up, up, up; higher, higher, higher up!

Until, ascending through the floor, and pausing with his head just raised above its beams, he came among the Bells. It was barely possible to make out their great shapes in the gloom; but there they were. Shadowy, and dark, and dumb.

A heavy sense of dread and loneliness fell instantly upon him, as he climbed into this airy nest of stone and metal. His head went round and round. He listened, and then raised a wild "Halloa!"

Halloa! was mournfully protracted by the echoes.

Giddy, confused, and out of breath, and frightened, Toby looked about him vacantly, and sunk down in a swoon.

THIRD QUARTER.

BLACK are the brooding clouds and troubled the deep waters, when the Sea of Thought, first heaving from a calm, gives up its Dead. Monsters uncouth and wild, arise in premature, imperfect resurrection; the several parts and shapes of different things are joined and mixed by chance; and when, and how, and by what wonderful degrees, each separates from each, and every sense and object of the mind resumes its usual form and lives again, no man—though every man is every day the casket of this type of the Great Mystery—can tell.

So; when and how the darkness of the night-black steeple changed to shining light; when and how the solitary tower was peopled with a myriad figures; when and how the whispered "Haunt and hunt him," breathing monotonously through his sleep or swoon, became a voice exclaiming in the waking ears of Trotty, "Break his slumbers;" when and how he ceased to have a sluggish and confused idea that such things were, companioning a host of others that were not; there are no dates or means to tell. But: awake, and standing on his feet upon the boards where he had lately lain: he saw this Goblin Sight.

He saw the tower, whither his charmed footsteps had brought him, swarming with dwarf phantoms, spirits, elfin creatures of the Bells. He saw them leaping, flying, dropping, pouring from the Bells without a pause. He saw them, round him on the ground; above him, in the air; clambering from him, by the ropes below; looking down upon him, from the massive iron-girded beams; peeping in upon him, through the chinks and loopholes in the walls; spreading away and away from him in enlarging circles, as the water ripples give way to a huge stone that suddenly comes plashing in among them. He saw them, of all aspects and all shapes. He saw them ugly, handsome, crippled, exquisitely formed. He saw them young, he saw them old, he saw them kind, he saw them cruel, he saw them merry, he saw them grim; he saw them dance, and heard them sing; he saw them tear their hair, and heard them howl. He saw the air thick with them. He saw them come and go, incessantly. He saw them riding downward, soaring upward, sailing off afar, perching near at hand, all restless and all violently active. Stone, and brick, and slate, and tile, became transparent to him as to them. He saw them *in* the houses, busy at the sleepers' beds. He saw them soothing people in their dreams; he saw them beating them with knotted whips; he saw them yelling in their ears; he saw them playing softest music on their pillows; he saw them cheering some with the songs of birds and the perfume of flowers; he saw them flashing awful faces on the troubled rest of others, from enchanted mirrors which they carried in their hands.

He saw these creatures, not only among sleeping men but waking also, active in pursuits irreconcilable with one another, and possessing or assuming natures the most opposite. He saw one buckling on innumerable wings to increase his speed; another loading himself with chains and weights, to retard his. He saw some putting the hands of clocks forward, some putting the hands of clocks backward, some endeavouring to stop the clock entirely. He saw them representing, here a marriage ceremony, there a funeral; in this chamber an election, and in that a ball; ** everywhere, restless and untiring motion.

Bewildered by the host of shifting and extraordinary figures, as well as by the uproar of the Bells, which all this while were ringing, Trotty clung to a wooden pillar for support, and turned his white face here and there, in mute and stunned astonishment.

As he gazed, the Chimes stopped. Instantaneous change! The whole swarm fainted; their forms collapsed, their speed deserted them; they sought to fly, but in the act of falling died and melted into air. No fresh supply succeeded them. One straggler leaped down pretty briskly from the surface of the Great Bell, and alighted on his feet, but he was dead and gone before he could turn round. Some few of the late company who had gambolled in the tower, remained there, spinning over and over a little longer; but these became at every turn more faint, and few, and feeble, and soon went the way of the rest. The last of all was one small hunchback, who had got into an echoing corner, where he twirled and twirled, and floated by himself a long time; showing such perseverance, that at last he dwindled to a leg and even to a foot, before he finally retired; but he vanished in the end, and then the tower was silent.

Then and not before, did Trotty see in every Bell a bearded figure of the bulk and stature of the Bell—incomprehensibly, a figure and the Bell itself. Gigantic, grave, and darkly watchful of him, as he stood rooted to the ground.

Mysterious and awful figures! Resting on nothing; poised in the night air of the tower, with their draped and hooded heads merged in the dim roof; motionless and shadowy. Shadowy and dark, although he saw them by some light belonging to themselves—none else was there—each with its muffled hand upon its goblin mouth.

He could not plunge down wildly through the opening in the floor, for all power of motion had deserted him. Otherwise he would have done so—aye, would have thrown himself, head-foremost, from the steeple-top, rather than have seen them watching him with eyes that would have waked and watched although the pupils had been taken out.

Again, again, the dread and terror of the lonely place, and of the wild and fearful night that reigned there, touched him like a spectral hand. His distance from all help; the long, dark, winding, ghost-beleaguered way that lay between him and the earth on which men lived; his being high, high, high, up there, where it had made him dizzy to see the birds fly in the day; cut off from all good people, who at such an hour were safe at home and sleeping in their beds; all this struck coldly through him, not as a reflection but a bodily sensation. Meantime his eyes and thoughts and fears, were fixed upon the watchful figures; which, rendered unlike any figures of this world by the deep gloom and shade enwrapping and enfolding them, as well as by their looks and forms and supernatural hovering above the floor, were nevertheless as plainly to be seen as were the stalwart oaken frames, cross-pieces, bars and beams, set up there to support the Bells. These hemmed them, in a very forest of hewn timber; from the entanglements, intricacies, and depths of which, as from among the boughs of a dead wood blighted for their Phantom use, they kept their darksome and unwinking watch.

A blast of air—how cold and shrill!—came moaning through the tower. As it died away, the great Bell, or the Goblin of the Great Bell, spoke.

"What visitor is this!" it said. The voice was low and deep, and Trotty fancied that it sounded in the other figures as well.

"I thought my name was called by the Chimes!" said Trotty, raising his hands in an attitude of supplication. "I hardly know why I am here, or how I came. I have listened to the Chimes these many years. They have cheered me often."

"And have you thanked them?" said the Bell.

"A thousand times!" said Trotty.

"How?"

"I am a poor man," faltered Trotty, "and could only thank them in words."

"And always so?" inquired the Goblin of the Bell. "Have you never done us wrong in words?"

"No!" cried Trotty eagerly.

"Never done us foul, and false, and wicked wrong, in words?" pursued the Goblin of the Bell.

Trotty was about to answer, "Never!" But he stopped, and was confused.

"The voice of Time," said the Phantom, "cries to man, Advance! Time is for his advancement and improvement; for his greater worth, his greater happiness, his better life; his progress onward to that goal within its knowledge and its view, and set there, in the period when Time and He began. Ages of darkness, wickedness, and violence, have come and gone: millions uncountable, have suffered, lived, and died: to point the way Before him. Who seeks to turn him back, or stay him on his course, arrests a mighty engine which will strike the meddler dead; and be the fiercer and the wilder, ever, for its momentary check!"

"I never did so to my knowledge, Sir," said Trotty. "It was quite by accident if I did. I wouldn't go to do it, I'm sure."

"Who puts into the mouth of Time, or of its servants," said the Goblin of the Bell, "a cry of lamentation for days which have had their trial and their failure, and have left deep traces of it which the blind may see—a cry that only serves the Present Time, by showing men how much it needs their help when any ears can listen to regrets for such a Past —who does this, does a wrong. And you have done that wrong to us, the Chimes."

Trotty's first excess of fear was gone. But he had felt tenderly and gratefully towards the Bells, as you have seen; and when he heard himself arraigned as one who had offended them so weightily, his heart was touched with penitence and grief.

"If you knew," said Trotty, clasping his hands earnestly —"or perhaps you do know—if you know how often you have kept me company; how often you have cheered me up when I've been low; how you were quite the plaything of my little daughter Meg (almost the only one she ever had) when first her mother died, and she and me were left alone—you won't bear malice for a hasty word!"

"Who hears in us, the Chimes, one note bespeaking disregard, or stern regard, of any hope, or joy, or pain, or sorrow, of the many-sorrowed throng; who hears us make response to any creed that gauges human passions and affections, as it gauges the amount of miserable food on which humanity may pine and wither; does us wrong. That wrong you have done us!" said the Bell.

"I have!" said Trotty. "Oh forgive me!"

"Who hears us echo the dull vermin of the earth: the Putters Down of crushed and broken natures, formed to be raised up higher than such maggots of the time can crawl or can conceive," pursued the Goblin of the Bell:

"who does so, does us wrong. And you have done us wrong!"

"Not meaning it," said Trotty. "In my ignorance. Not meaning it!"

"Lastly, and most of all," pursued the Bell. "Who turns his back upon the fallen and disfigured of his kind; abandons them as Vile; and does not trace and track with pitying eyes the unfenced precipice by which they fell from Good—grasping in their fall some tufts and shreds of that lost soil, and clinging to them still when bruised and dying in the gulf below; does wrong to Heaven and Man, to Time and to Eternity. And you have done that wrong!"

"Spare me," cried Trotty, falling on his knees; "for Mercy's sake!"

"Listen!" said the Shadow.

"Listen!" cried the other Shadows.

"Listen!" said a clear and child-like voice, which Trotty thought he recognised as having heard before.

The organ sounded faintly in the church below. Swelling by degrees, the melody ascended to the roof, and filled the choir and nave. Expanding more and more, it rose up, up; up, up; higher, higher, higher up; awakening agitated hearts within the burly piles of oak, the hollow bells, the iron-bound doors, the stairs of solid stone; until the tower walls were insufficient to contain it, and it soared into the sky.

No wonder that an old man's breast could not contain a sound so vast and mighty. It broke from that weak prison in a rush of tears; and Trotty put his hands before his face.

"Listen!" said the Shadow.

"Listen!" said the other Shadows.

"Listen!" said the child's voice.

A solemn strain of blended voices, rose into the tower.

It was a very low and mournful strain: a Dirge: and as he listened, Trotty heard his child among the singers.

"She is Dead!" exclaimed the old man. "Meg is dead! Her Spirit calls to me. I hear it!"

"The Spirit of your child bewails the dead, and mingles

with the dead—dead hopes, dead fancies, dead imaginings of youth," returned the Bell, "but she is living. Learn from her life, a living truth. Learn from the creature dearest to your heart, how bad the Bad are born. See every bud and leaf plucked one by one from off the fairest stem, and know how bare and wretched it may be. Follow her! To Desperation!"

Each of the shadowy figures stretched its right arm forth, and pointed downward.

"The Spirit of the Chimes is your companion," said the figure. "Go! It stands behind you!"

Trotty turned, and saw—the child? The child Will Fern had carried in the street; the child whom Meg had watched, but now, asleep!

"I carried her myself, to-night," said Trotty. "In these arms!"

"Show him what he calls himself," said the dark figures, one and all.

The tower opened at his feet. He looked down, and beheld his own form, lying at the bottom, on the outside: crushed and motionless.

"No more a living man!" cried Trotty. "Dead!"

"Dead!" said the figures all together.

"Gracious Heaven! And the New Year—"

"Past," said the figures.

"What!" he cried, shuddering. "I missed my way, and coming on the outside of this tower in the dark, fell down—a year ago?"

"Nine years ago!" replied the figures

As they gave the answer, they recalled their outstretched hands; and where their figures had been, there the Bells were.

And they rung; their time being come again. And once again, vast multitudes of phantoms sprung into existence; once again, were incoherently engaged, as they had been before; once again, faded on the stopping of the Chimes; and dwindled into nothing.

"What are these?" he asked his guide. "If I am not mad, what are these?"

"Spirits of the Bells. Their sound upon the air," returned the child. "They take such shapes and occupations as the hopes and thoughts of mortals, and the recollections they have stored up, give them."

"And you," said Trotty wildly. "What are you?"

"Hush, hush!" returned the child. "Look here!"

In a poor, mean room; working at the same kind of embroidery which he had often, often seen before her; Meg, his own dear daughter, was presented to his view. He made no effort to imprint his kisses on her face; he did not strive to clasp her to his loving heart; he knew that such endearments were for him no more. But he held his trembling breath; and brushed away the blinding tears, that he might look upon her; that he might only see her.

Ah! Changed. Changed. The light of the clear eye, how dimmed. The bloom, how faded from the cheek. Beautiful she was, as she had ever been, but Hope, Hope, Hope, oh where was the fresh Hope that had spoken to him like a voice!

She looked up from her work, at a companion. Following her eyes, the old man started back.

In the woman grown, he recognised her at a glance. In the long silken hair, he saw the self-same curls; around the lips, the child's expression lingering still. See! In the eyes, now turned inquiringly on Meg, there shone the very look that scanned those features when he brought her home!

Then what was this, beside him!

Looking with awe into its face, he saw a something reigning there: a lofty something, undefined and indistinct, which made it hardly more than a remembrance of that child—as yonder figure might be—yet it was the same: the same: and wore the dress.

Hark. They were speaking!

"Meg," said Lilian, hesitating. "How often you raise your head from your work to look at me!"

"Are my looks so altered, that they frighten you?" asked Meg.

"Nay dear! But you smile at that, yourself! Why not smile, when you look at me, Meg?"

"I do so. Do I not?" she answered: smiling on her.

"Now you do," said Lilian, "but not usually. When you think I'm busy, and don't see you, you look so anxious and so doubtful, that I hardly like to raise my eyes. There is little cause for smiling in this hard and toilsome life, but you were once so cheerful."

"Am I not now!" cried Meg, speaking in a tone of strange alarm, and rising to embrace her. "Do *I* make our weary life more weary to you, Lilian!"

"You have been the only thing that made it life," said Lilian, fervently kissing her; "sometimes the only thing that made me care to live so, Meg. Such work, such work! So many hours, so many days, so many long, long nights of hopeless, cheerless, never-ending work—not to heap up riches, not to live grandly or gaily, not to live upon enough, however coarse; but to earn bare bread; to scrape together just enough to toil upon, and want upon, and keep alive in us the consciousness of our hard fate! Oh Meg, Meg!" she raised her voice and twined her arms about her as she spoke, like one in pain. "How can the cruel world go round, and bear to look upon such lives!"

"Lilly!" said Meg, soothing her, and putting back her hair from her wet face. "Why Lilly! You! So pretty and so young!"

"Oh Meg!" she interrupted, holding her at arm's-length, and looking in her face imploringly. "The worst of all, the worst of all! Strike me old, Meg! Wither me, and shrivel me, and free me from the dreadful thoughts that tempt me in my youth!"

Trotty turned to look upon his guide. But the Spirit of the child had taken flight. Was gone.

Neither did he himself remain in the same place; for Sir Joseph Bowley, Friend and Father of the Poor, held a great festivity at Bowley Hall, in honour of the natal day of Lady Bowley. And as Lady Bowley had been born on New Year's

Day (which the local newspapers considered an especial pointing of the finger of Providence to number One, as Lady Bowley's destined figure in Creation), it was on a New Year's Day that this festivity took place.

Bowley Hall was full of visitors. The red-faced gentleman was there, Mr. Filer was there, the great Alderman Cute was there—Alderman Cute had a sympathetic feeling with great people, and had considerably improved his acquaintance with Sir Joseph Bowley on the strength of his attentive letter: indeed had become quite a friend of the family since then—and many guests were there. Trotty's ghost was there, wandering about, poor phantom, drearily; and looking for its guide.

There was to be a great dinner in the Great Hall. At which Sir Joseph Bowley, in his celebrated character of Friend and Father of the Poor, was to make his great speech. Certain plum puddings were to be eaten by his Friends and Children in another Hall first; and at a given signal, Friends and Children flocking in among their Friends and Fathers, were to form a family assemblage, with not one manly eye therein unmoistened by emotion.

But there was more than this to happen. Even more than this. Sir Joseph Bowley, Baronet and Member of Parliament, was to play a match at skittles—real skittles—with his tenants.[19]

"Which quite reminds one," said Alderman Cute, "of the days of old King Hal, stout King Hal, bluff King Hal.[20] Ah. Fine character!"

"Very," said Mr. Filer, dryly.** "For marrying women and murdering 'em. Considerably more than the average number of wives by the bye."

"You'll marry the beautiful ladies, and not murder 'em, eh?" said Alderman Cute to the heir of Bowley, aged twelve. "Sweet boy! We shall have this little gentleman in Parliament now," said the Alderman, holding him by the shoulders, and looking as reflective as he could, "before we know where we are. We shall hear of his successes at the poll; his speeches in the House; his overtures from Governments; his brilliant achievements of all kinds; ah! we shall make our little orations about him in the Common Council, I'll be bound; before we have time to look about us!"

"Oh, the difference of shoes and stockings!" Trotty thought. But his heart yearned towards the child, for the love of those same shoeless and stockingless boys, predestined (by the Alderman) to turn out bad, who might have been the children of poor Meg.

"Richard," moaned Trotty, roaming among the company, to and fro; "where is he? I can't find Richard! Where is Richard?"

Not likely to be there, if still alive! But Trotty's grief and solitude confused him; and he still went wandering among the gallant company; looking for his guide, and saying, "Where is Richard? Show me Richard!"

He was wandering thus, when he encountered Mr. Fish, the confidential Secretary: in great agitation.

"Bless my heart and soul!" cried Mr. Fish. "Where's Alderman Cute? Has anybody seen the Alderman?"

Seen the Alderman? Oh dear! Who could ever help seeing the Alderman? He was so considerate, so affable; he bore so much in mind the natural desire of folks to see him; that if he had a fault, it was the being constantly On View. And wherever the great people were, there, to be sure, attracted by the kindred sympathy between great souls, was Cute.

Several voices cried that he was in the circle round Sir Joseph. Mr. Fish made way there; found him; and took him secretly into a window near at hand. Trotty joined them. Not of his own accord. He felt that his steps were led in that direction.

"My dear Alderman Cute," said Mr. Fish. "A little more this way. The most dreadful circumstance has occurred. I have this moment received the intelligence. I think it will be best not to acquaint Sir Joseph with it till the day is over. You understand Sir Joseph, and will give me your opinion. The most frightful and deplorable event!"

"Fish!" returned the Alderman. "Fish! My good fellow, what is the matter? Nothing revolutionary, I hope! No—no attempted interference with the magistrates?"

"Deedles, the banker," gasped the Secretary. "Deedles, Brothers—who was to have been here to-day—high in office in the Goldsmiths' Company—"

"Not stopped!" exclaimed the Alderman. "It can't be!"

"Shot himself."

"Good God!"

"Put a double-barrelled pistol to his mouth, in his own counting-house," said Mr. Fish, "and blew his brains out. No motive. Princely circumstances!"

"Circumstances!" exclaimed the Alderman. "A man of noble fortune. One of the most respectable of men. Suicide, Mr. Fish! By his own hand!"

"This very morning," returned Mr. Fish.

"Oh the brain, the brain!" exclaimed the pious Alderman, lifting up his hands. "Oh the nerves, the nerves; the mysteries of this machine called Man! Oh the little that unhinges it: poor creatures that we are! Perhaps a dinner, Mr. Fish. Perhaps the conduct of his son, who, I have heard, ran very wild, and was in the habit of drawing bills upon him without the least authority! A most respectable man. One of the most respectable men I ever knew! A lamentable instance, Mr. Fish. A public calamity! I shall make a point of wearing the deepest mourning. A most respectable man! But there is One above. We must submit, Mr. Fish. We must submit!"

What, Alderman! No word of Putting Down? Remember, Justice, your high moral boast and pride. Come, Alderman! Balance those scales. Throw me into this, the empty one, No Dinner, and Nature's Founts in some poor woman, dried by starving misery and rendered obdurate to claims for which her offspring *has* authority in holy mother Eve. Weigh me the two: you Daniel, going to judgment, when your day shall come! Weigh them, in the eyes of suffering thousands, audience (not unmindful) of the grim farce you play. Or supposing that you strayed from your five wits—it's not so far to go, but that it might be—and laid hands upon that throat of yours, warning your fellows (if you have a fellow) how they croak their comfortable wickedness to raving heads and stricken hearts. What then?

The words rose up in Trotty's breast, as if they had been spoken by some other voice within him. Alderman Cute pledged himself to Mr. Fish that he would assist him in breaking the melancholy catastrophe to Sir Joseph, when the day was over. Then, before they parted, wringing Mr. Fish's hand in bitterness of soul, he said, "The most respectable of men!" And added that he hardly knew: not even he: why such afflictions were allowed on earth.

"It's almost enough to make one think, if one didn't know better," said Alderman Cute, "that at times some motion of a capsizing nature was going on in things, which affected the general economy of the social fabric. Deedles Brothers!"

The skittle-playing came off with immense success. Sir Joseph knocked the pins about quite skilfully; Master Bowley took an innings at a shorter distance also; and everybody said** that now, when a Baronet and the Son of a Baronet played at skittles, the country was coming round again, as fast as it could come.

At its proper time, the Banquet was served up. Trotty involuntarily repaired to the Hall with the rest, for he felt himself conducted thither by some stronger impulse than his own free will. The sight was gay in the extreme; the ladies were very handsome; the visitors delighted, cheerful, and good-tempered. When the lower doors were opened, and the people flocked in, in their rustic dresses, the beauty of the spectacle was at its height; but Trotty only murmured more and more, "Where is Richard? He should help and comfort her! I can't see Richard!"

There had been some speeches made; and Lady Bowley's health had been proposed;** and Sir Joseph Bowley had returned thanks, and had made his great speech, showing by various pieces of evidence that he was the born Friend and Father, and so forth; and had given as a Toast, his Friends and Children, and the Dignity of Labor; when a slight disturbance at the bottom of the Hall attracted Toby's notice. After some confusion, noise, and opposition, one man broke through the rest, and stood forward by himself.

Not Richard. No. But one whom he had thought of, and had looked for, many times. In a scantier supply of light, he might have doubted the identity of that worn man, so old, and grey, and bent; but with a blaze of lamps upon his gnarled and knotted head, he knew Will Fern as soon as he stepped forth.

"What is this!" exclaimed Sir Joseph, rising. "Who gave this man admittance? This is a criminal from prison! Mr. Fish, Sir, *will* you have the goodness—"

"A minute!" said Will Fern. "A minute! My Lady, you was born on this day along with a New Year. Get me a minute's leave to speak."

She made some intercession for him and Sir Joseph took his seat again, with native dignity.

The ragged visitor—for he was miserably dressed—looked round upon the company, and made his homage to them with a humble bow.

"Gentlefolks!" he said. "You've drunk the Labourer.[21] Look at me!"

"Just come from jail," said Mr. Fish.

"Just come from jail," said Will. "And neither for the first time, nor the second, not the third, nor yet the fourth."

Mr. Filer was heard to remark testily, that four times was over the average; and he ought to be ashamed of himself.

"Gentlefolks!" repeated Will Fern. "Look at me! You see I'm at the worst. Beyond all hurt or harm; beyond your help; for the time when your kind words or kind actions could have done ME good,"—he struck his hand upon his breast, and shook his head, "is gone, with the scent of last year's beans or clover on the air. Let me say a word for these," pointing to the labouring people in the hall; "and when you're met together, hear the real Truth spoke out for once."

"There's not a man here," said the host, "who would

have him for a spokes-
man."

"Like enough, Sir Joseph.
I believe it. Not the less
true, perhaps, is what I say.
Perhaps that's a proof on it.
Gentlefolks, I've lived many
a year in this place. You
may see the cottage from the
sunk fence over yonder. I've
seen the ladies draw it in
their books a hundred times.
It looks well in a picter, I've
heerd say; but there an't
weather in picters, and may-
be 'tis fitter for that, than for a place to live in. Well! I
lived there. How hard—how bitter hard, I lived there, I
won't say. Any day in the year, and every day, you can judge
for your own selves."

He spoke as he had spoken on the night when Trotty
found him in the street. His voice was deeper and more

husky, and had a trembling in it now and then; but he never raised it, passionately, and seldom lifted it above the firm stern level of the homely facts he stated.

" 'Tis harder than you think for, gentlefolks, to grow up decent: commonly decent: in such a place. That I growed up a man and not a brute, says something for me—as I was then. As I am now, there's nothing can be said for me or done for me. I'm past it."

"I am glad this man has entered," observed Sir Joseph, looking round serenely. "Don't disturb him. It appears to be Ordained. He is an Example: a living example. I hope and trust, and confidently expect, that it will not be lost upon my Friends here."

"I dragged on," said Fern, after a moment's silence, "somehow. Neither me nor any other man knows how; but so heavy, that I couldn't put a cheerful face upon it, or make believe that I was anything but what I was. Now, gentlemen —you gentlemen that sits at Sessions—when you see a man with discontent writ on his face, you says to one another, 'he's suspicious. I has my doubts,' says you, 'about Will Fern. Watch that fellow!' I don't say, gentlemen, it ain't quite nat'ral, but I say 'tis so; and from that hour, whatever Will Fern does, or lets alone—all one—it goes against him."

Alderman Cute stuck his thumbs in his waistcoat-pockets, and leaning back in his chair, and smiling, winked at a neighbouring chandelier. As much as to say, "Of course! I told you so. The common cry! Lord bless you, we are up to all this sort of thing—myself and human nature."

"Now, gentlemen," said Will Fern, holding out his hands, and flushing for an instant in his haggard face. "See how your laws are made to trap and hunt us when we're brought to this. I tries to live elsewhere. And I'm a vagabond. To jail with him! I comes back here. I goes a-nutting in your woods, and breaks—who don't?—a limber branch or two. To jail with him! One of your keepers sees me in the broad day, near my own patch of garden, with a gun. To jail with him!

I has a nat'ral angry word with that man, when I'm free again. To jail with him! I cuts a stick. To jail with him! I eats a rotten apple or a turnip. To jail with him! It's twenty mile away; and coming back, I begs a trifle on the road. To jail with him! At last, the constable, the keeper—anybody—finds me anywhere, a doing anything. To jail with him, for he's a vagrant, and a jail-bird known; and jail's the only home he's got."

The Alderman nodded sagaciously, as who should say, "A very good home too!"

"Do I say this to serve MY cause!" cried Fern. "Who can give me back my liberty, who can give me back my good name, who can give me back my innocent niece? Not all the Lords and Ladies in wide England. But, gentlemen, gentlemen, dealing with other men like me, begin at the right end. Give us, in mercy, better homes when we're a lying in our cradles; give us better food when we're a working for our lives; give as kinder laws to bring us back when we're a going wrong; and don't set Jail, Jail, Jail, afore us, everywhere we turn. There an't a condescension you can show the Labourer then, that he won't take, as ready and as grateful as a man can be; for he has a patient, peaceful, willing heart. But you must put his rightful spirit in him first; for whether he's a wreck and ruin such as me, or is like one of them that stand here now, his spirit is divided from you at this time. Bring it back, gentlefolks, bring it back! Bring it back, afore the day comes when even his Bible changes in his altered mind, and the words seem to him to read, as they have sometimes read in my own eyes—in Jail: 'Whither thou goest, I can Not go; where thou lodgest, I do Not lodge; thy people are Not my people; Nor thy God my God!' "[22]

A sudden stir and agitation took place in the Hall. Trotty thought at first, that several had risen to eject the man; and hence this change in its appearance. But another moment showed him that the room and all the company had vanished from his sight, and that his daughter was again before him, seated at her work. But in a poorer, meaner garret than

before; and with
no Lilian by her side.
The frame at which
she had worked, was
put away upon a shelf
and covered up. The
chair in which she
had sat, was
turned against
the wall. A
history was
written in

these little things, and in Meg's grief-worn face. Oh! who could fail to read it!

Meg strained her eyes upon her work until it was too dark to see the threads; and when the night closed in, she lighted her feeble candle and worked on. Still her old father was invisible about her; looking down upon her; loving her—how dearly loving her!—and talking to her in a tender voice about the old times, and the Bells. Though he knew, poor Trotty, though he knew she could not hear him.

A great part of the evening had worn away, when a knock came at her door. She opened it. A man was on the threshold. A slouching, moody, drunken sloven: wasted by intemperance and vice: and with his matted hair and unshorn beard in wild disorder: but with some traces on him, too, of having been a man of good proportion and good features in his youth.

He stopped until he had her leave to enter; and she, retiring a pace or two from the open door, silently and sorrowfully looked upon him. Trotty had his wish. He saw Richard.

"May I come in, Margaret?"

"Yes! Come in. Come in!"

It was well that Trotty knew him before he spoke; for with any doubt remaining on his mind, the harsh discordant voice would have persuaded him that it was not Richard but some other man.

There were but two chairs in the room. She gave him hers, and stood at some short distance from him, waiting to hear what he had to say.

He sat, however, staring vacantly at the floor; with a lustreless and stupid smile. A spectacle of such deep degradation, of such abject hopelessness, of such a miserable downfall, that she put her hands before her face and turned away, lest he should see how much it moved her.

Roused by the rustling of her dress, or some such trifling sound, he lifted his head, and began to speak as if there had been no pause since he entered.

"Still at work, Margaret? You work late."

"I generally do."

"And early?"

"And early."

"So she said. She said you never tired; or never owned that you tired. Not all the time you lived together. Not even when you fainted, between work and fasting. But I told you that, the last time I came."

"You did," she answered. "Again I implored you to tell me nothing more; and you made me a solemn promise, Richard, that you never would."

"A solemn promise," he repeated, with a drivelling laugh and vacant stare. "A solemn promise. To be sure. A solemn promise!" Awakening, as it were, after a time; in the same manner as before; he said with sudden animation,

"How can I help it, Margaret? What am I to do? She has been to me again!"

"Again!" cried Meg, clasping her hands. "Oh, does she think of me so often! Has she been again!"

"Twenty times again," said Richard. "Margaret, she haunts me. She comes behind me in the streets, and thrusts it in my hand. I hear her foot upon the ashes when I'm at my work (ha, ha! that an't often), and before I can turn my head, her voice is in my ear, saying, 'Richard, don't look round. For heaven's love, give her this!' She brings it where I live; she sends it in letters; she taps at the window and lays it on the sill. What *can* I do? Look at it!"

He held out in his hand a little purse, and clinked the money it enclosed.

"Hide it," said Meg. "Hide it! When she comes again, tell her, Richard, that I love her in my soul. That I never lie down to sleep, but I bless her, and pray for her. That in my solitary work, I never cease to have her in my thoughts. That she is with me, night and day. That if I died tomorrow, I would remember her with my last breath. But that I cannot look upon it!"

He slowly recalled his hand, and crushing the purse together, said with a kind of drowsy thoughtfulness:

"I told her so. I told her so, as plain as words could speak. I've taken this gift back and left it at her door, a dozen times since then. But when she came at last, and stood before me, face to face, what could I do?"

"You saw her!" exclaimed Meg. "You saw her! Oh, Lilian, my sweet girl! Oh, Lilian, Lilian!"

"I saw her," he went on to say, not answering, but engaged in the same slow pursuit of his own thoughts. "There she stood: trembling! 'How does she look, Richard? Does she ever speak of me? Is she thinner? My old place at the table: what's in my old place? And the frame she taught me our old work on—has she burnt it, Richard?' There she was. I heard her say it."

Meg checked her sobs, and with the tears streaming from her eyes, bent over him to listen. Not to lose a breath.

With his arms resting on his knees; and stooping forward in his chair, as if what he said were written on the ground in some half legible character, which it was his occupation to decipher and connect; he went on.

"'Richard, I have fallen very low; and you may guess how much I have suffered in having this sent back, when I can bear to bring it in my hand to you. But you loved her once, even in my memory, dearly. Others stepped in between you; fears, and jealousies, and doubts, and vanities, estranged you from her; but you did love her, even in my memory!' I suppose I did," he said, interrupting himself for a moment. "I did! That's neither here nor there. 'Oh Richard, if you ever did; if you have any memory for what is gone and lost, take it to her once more. Once more! Tell her how I begged and prayed. Tell her how I laid my head upon your shoulder, where her own head might have lain, and was so humble to you, Richard. Tell her that you looked into my face, and saw the beauty which she used to praise, all gone: all gone: and in its place, a poor, wan, hollow cheek, that she would weep to see. Tell her everything, and take it back, and she will not refuse again. She will not have the heart!'"

So he sat musing, and repeating the last words, until he woke again, and rose.

"You won't take it, Margaret?"

She shook her head, and motioned an entreaty to him to leave her.

"Good night, Margaret."

"Good night!"

He turned to look upon her; struck by her sorrow, and perhaps by the pity for himself which trembled in her voice. It was a quick and rapid action; and for the moment some flash of his old bearing kindled in his form. In the next he went as he had come. Nor did this glimmer of a quenched fire seem to light him to a quicker sense of his debasement.

In any mood, in any grief, in any torture of the mind or body, Meg's work must be done. She sat down to her task, and plied it. Night, midnight. Still she worked.

She had a meagre fire, the night being very cold; and rose at intervals to mend it. The Chimes rang half-past twelve while she was thus engaged; and when they ceased she heard a gentle knocking at the door. Before she could so much as wonder who was there, at that unusual hour, it opened.

Oh Youth and Beauty, happy as ye should be, look at this! Oh Youth and Beauty, blest and blessing all within your reach, and working out the ends of your Beneficent Creator, look at this!

She saw the entering figure; screamed its name; cried "Lilian!"

It was swift, and fell upon its knees before her: clinging to her dress.

"Up, dear! Up! Lilian! My own dearest!"

"Never more, Meg; never more! Here! Here! Close to you, holding to you, feeling your dear breath upon my face!"

"Sweet Lilian! Darling Lilian! Child of my heart—no mother's love can be more tender—lay your head upon my breast!"

"Never more, Meg. Never more! When I first looked

into your face, you knelt before me. On my knees before you, let me die. Let it be here!"

"You have come back. My Treasure! We will live together, work together, hope together, die together!"

"Ah! Kiss my lips, Meg; fold your arms about me; press me to your bosom; look kindly on me; but don't raise me. Let it be here. Let me see the last of your dear face upon my knees!"

Oh Youth and Beauty, happy as ye should be, look at this! Oh Youth and Beauty, working out the ends of your Beneficent Creator, look at this!

"Forgive me, Meg! So dear, so dear! Forgive me! I know you do, I see you do, but say so, Meg!"

She said so, with her lips on Lilian's cheek. And with her arms twined round—she knew it now—a broken heart.

"His blessing on you, dearest love. Kiss me once more! He suffered her to sit beside His feet, and dry them with her hair.[23] Oh Meg, what Mercy and Compassion!"

As she died, the Spirit of the child returning, innocent and radiant, touched the old man with its hand, and beckoned him away.

FOURTH QUARTER.

SOME new remembrance of the ghostly figures in the Bells; some faint impression of the ringing of the Chimes; some giddy consciousness of having seen the swarm of phantoms reproduced and reproduced until the

LINTON SC

recollection of them lost itself in the confusion of their numbers; some hurried knowledge, how conveyed to him he knew not, that more years had passed; and Trotty, with the Spirit of the child attending him, stood looking on at mortal company.

Fat company, rosy-cheeked company, comfortable company. They were but two, but they were red enough for ten. They sat before a bright fire, with a small low table between them; and unless the fragrance of hot tea and muffins lingered longer in that room than in most others, the table had seen service very lately. But all the cups and saucers being clean, and in their proper places in the corner-cupboard; and the brass toasting-fork hanging in its usual nook and spreading its four idle fingers out as if it wanted to be measured for a glove; there remained no other visible tokens of the meal just finished, than such as purred and washed their whiskers in the person of the basking cat, and glistened in the gracious, not to say the greasy, faces of her patrons.

This cosy couple (married, evidently) had made a fair division of the fire between them, and sat looking at the glowing sparks that dropped into the grate; now nodding off into a doze; now waking up again when some hot fragment, larger than the rest, came rattling down, as if the fire were coming with it.

It was in no danger of sudden extinction, however; for it gleamed not only in the little room, and on the panes of window-glass in the door, and on the curtain half drawn across them, but in the little shop beyond. A little shop, quite crammed and choked with the abundance of its stock; a perfectly voracious little shop, with a maw as accommodating and full as any shark's. Cheese, butter, firewood, soap, pickles, matches, bacon, table-beer, peg-tops, sweetmeats, boys' kites, bird-seed, cold ham, birch brooms, hearthstones, salt, vinegar, blacking, red-herrings, stationery, lard, mushroom-ketchup, staylaces, loaves of bread, shuttlecocks, eggs, and slate pencil: everything was fish that came to the net of this greedy little shop, and all these articles were in its net.

How many other kinds of petty merchandise were there, it would be difficult to say; but balls of packthread, ropes of onions, pounds of candles, cabbage-nets, and brushes, hung in bunches from the ceiling, like extraordinary fruit; while various odd canisters emitting aromatic smells, established the veracity of the inscription over the outer door, which informed the public that the keeper of this little shop was a licensed dealer in tea, coffee, tobacco, pepper, and snuff.

Glancing at such of these items as were visible in the shining of the blaze, and the less cheerful radiance of two smoky lamps which burnt but dimly in the shop itself, as though its plethora sat heavy on their lungs; and glancing, then, at one of the two faces by the parlour-fire; Trotty had small difficulty in recognising in the stout old lady, Mrs. Chickenstalker: always inclined to corpulency, even in the days when he had known her as established in the general line, and having a small balance against him in her books.

The features of her companion were less easy to him. The great broad chin, with creases in it large enough to hide a finger in; the astonished eyes, that seemed to expostulate with themselves for sinking deeper and deeper into the yielding fat of the soft face; the nose afflicted with that disordered action of its functions which is generally termed The Snuffles; the short thick throat and labouring chest, with other beauties of the like description; though calculated to impress the memory, Trotty could at first allot to nobody he had ever known: and yet he had some recollection of them too. At length, in Mrs. Chickenstalker's partner in the general line, and in the crooked and eccentric line of life, he recognised the former porter of Sir Joseph Bowley; an apoplectic innocent, who had connected himself in Trotty's mind with Mrs. Chickenstalker years ago, by giving him admission to the mansion where he had confessed his obligations to that lady, and drawn on his unlucky head such grave reproach.

Trotty had little interest in a change like this, after the changes he had seen; but association is very strong sometimes; and he looked involuntarily behind the parlour-door, where the accounts of credit customers were usually kept in chalk. There was no record of his name. Some names were there, but they were strange to him, and infinitely fewer than of old; from which he augured that the porter was an advocate of ready-money transactions, and on coming into the business had looked pretty sharp after the Chickenstalker defaulters.

So desolate was Trotty, and so mournful for the youth and promise of his blighted child, that it was a sorrow to him, even to have no place in Mrs. Chickenstalker's ledger.

"What sort of a night is it, Anne?" inquired the former porter of Sir Joseph Bowley, stretching out his legs before the fire, and rubbing as much of them as his short arms could reach; with an air that added, "Here I am if it's bad, and I don't want to go out if it's good."

"Blowing and sleeting hard," returned his wife; "and threatening snow. Dark. And very cold."

"I'm glad to think we had muffins," said the former porter, in the tone of one who had set his conscience at rest. "It's a sort of night that's meant for muffins. Likewise crumpets. Also Sally Lunns."[24]

The former porter mentioned each successive kind of eatable, as if he were musingly summing up his good actions. After which he rubbed his fat legs as before, and jerking them at the knees to get the fire upon the yet unroasted parts, laughed as if somebody had tickled him.

"You're in spirits, Tugby, my dear," observed his wife.

The firm was Tugby, late Chickenstalker.

"No," said Tugby. "No. Not particular. I'm a little elewated. The muffins came so pat!"

With that he chuckled until he was black in the face; and had so much ado to become any other colour, that his fat legs took the strangest excursions into the air. Nor were they reduced to anything like decorum until Mrs. Tugby had thumped him violently on the back, and shaken him as if he were a great bottle.

"Good gracious, goodness, lord-a-mercy bless and save

227

the man!" cried Mrs. Tugby, in great terror. "What's he doing?"

Mr. Tugby wiped his eyes, and faintly repeated that he found himself a little elewated.

"Then don't be so again, that's a dear good soul," said Mrs. Tugby, "if you don't want to frighten me to death, with your struggling and fighting!"

Mr. Tugby said he wouldn't, but his whole existence was a fight; in which, if any judgment might be founded on the constantly-increasing shortness of his breath, and the deepening purple of his face, he was always getting the worst of it.

"So it's blowing, and sleeting, and threatening snow; and is dark, and very cold: is it, my dear?" said Mr. Tugby, looking at the fire, and reverting to the cream and marrow of his temporary elevation.

"Hard weather indeed," returned his wife, shaking her head.

"Aye, aye! Years," said Mr. Tugby, "are like Christians in that respect. Some of 'em die hard; some of 'em die easy. This one hasn't many days to run, and is making a fight for it. I like him all the better. There's a customer, my love!"

Attentive to the rattling door, Mrs. Tugby had already risen.

"Now then!" said that lady, passing out into the little shop. "What's wanted? Oh! I beg your pardon, Sir, I'm sure. I didn't think it was you."

She made this apology to a gentleman in black, who, with his wristbands tucked up, and his hat cocked loungingly on one side, and his hands in his pockets, sat down astride on the table-beer barrel, and nodded in return.

"This is a bad business upstairs, Mrs. Tugby," said the gentleman. "The man can't live."

"Not the back-attic can't!" cried Tugby, coming out into the shop to join in the conference.

"The back-attic, Mr. Tugby," said the gentleman, "is coming down stairs fast; and will be below the basement very soon."

Looking by turns at Tugby and his wife, he sounded the barrel with his knuckles for the depth of beer, and having found it, played a tune upon the empty part.

"The back-attic, Mr. Tugby," said the gentleman: Tugby having stood in silent consternation for some time: "is Going."

"Then," said Tugby, turning to his wife, "he must Go, you know, before he's Gone."

"I don't think you can move him," said the gentleman, shaking his head. "I wouldn't take the responsibility of saying it could be done myself. You had better leave him where he is. He can't live long."

"It's the only subject," said Tugby, bringing the butter-scale down upon the counter with a crash, by weighing his fist on it, "that we've ever had a word upon; she and me; and look what it comes to! He's going to die here, after all. Going to die upon the premises. Going to die in our house!"

"And where should he have died, Tugby?" cried his wife.

"In the workhouse," he returned. "What are workhouses made for?"

"Not for that," said Mrs. Tugby, with great energy. "Not for that. Neither did I marry you for that. Don't think it, Tugby. I won't have it. I won't allow it. I'd be separated first, and never see your face again. When my widow's name stood over that door, as it did for many many years: this house being known as Mrs. Chickenstalker's far and wide, and never known but to its honest credit and its good report: when my widow's name stood over that door, Tugby, I knew him as a handsome, steady, manly, independent youth; I knew her as the sweetest-looking, sweetest-tempered girl, eyes ever saw; I knew her father (poor old creetur, he fell down from the steeple walking in his sleep, and killed himself), for the simplest, hardest-working, childest-hearted man, that ever drew the breath of life; and when I turn them out of house and home, may angels turn me out of Heaven. As they would! And serve me right!"

Her old face, which had been a plump and dimpled one

before the changes which had come to pass, seemed to shine out of her as she said these words; and when she dried her eyes, and shook her head and her handkerchief at Tugby, with an expression of firmness which it was quite clear was not to be easily resisted, Trotty said, "Bless her! Bless her!"

Then he listened, with a panting heart, for what should follow. Knowing nothing yet, but that they spoke of Meg.

If Tugby had been a little elevated in the parlour, he more than balanced that account by being not a little depressed in the shop, where he now stood staring at his wife, without attempting a reply; secretly conveying, however—either in a fit of abstraction or as a precautionary measure—all the money from the till into his own pockets, as he looked at her.

The gentleman upon the table-beer cask, who appeared to be some authorised medical attendant upon the poor, was far too well accustomed, evidently, to little differences of opinion between man and wife, to interpose any remark in this instance. He sat softly whistling, and turning little drops of beer out of the tap upon the ground, until there was a perfect calm: when he raised his head, and said to Mrs. Tugby, late Chickenstalker.

"There's something interesting about the woman, even now. How did she come to marry him?"

"Why that," said Mrs. Tugby, taking a seat near him, "is not the least cruel part of her story, Sir. You see they kept company, she and Richard, many years ago. When they were a young and beautiful couple, everything was settled, and they were to have been married on a New Year's Day. But, somehow, Richard got it into his head, through what the gentlemen told him, that he might do better, and that he'd soon repent it, and that she wasn't good enough for him, and that a young man of spirit had no business to be married. And the gentleman frightened her, and made her melancholy, and timid of his deserting her, and of her children coming to the gallows, and of its being wicked to be man and wife, and a good deal more of it. And in short, they lingered and lingered, and their trust in one another was broken, and so at last was the match. But the fault was his. She would have married him, Sir, joyfully. I've seen her heart swell, many times afterwards, when he passed her in a proud and careless way; and never did a woman grieve more truly for a man, than she for Richard when he first went wrong."

"Oh! he went wrong, did he?" said the gentleman, pulling out the vent-peg of the table-beer, and trying to peep down into the barrel through the hole.

"Well, sir, I don't know that he rightly understood himself, you see. I think his mind was troubled by their having broke with one another; and that but for being ashamed before the gentlemen, and perhaps for being uncertain too, how she might take it, he'd have gone through any suffering or trial to have had Meg's promise and Meg's hand again. That's my belief. He never said so; more's the pity! He took to drinking, idling, bad companions: all the fine resources that were to be so much better for him than the Home he might have had. He lost his looks, his character, his health, his strength, his friends, his work: everything!"

"He didn't lose everything, Mrs. Tugby," returned the gentleman, "because he gained a wife; and I want to know how he gained her."

"I'm coming to it, Sir, in a moment. This went on for years and years; he sinking lower and lower; she enduring, poor thing, miseries enough to wear her life away. At last, he was so cast down, and cast out, that no one would employ or notice him; and doors were shut upon him, go where he would. Applying from place to place, and door to door; and coming for the hundredth time to one gentleman who had often and often tried him (he was a good workman to the very end); that gentleman, who knew his history, said, 'I believe you are incorrigible; there is only one person in the world who has a chance of reclaiming you; ask me to trust you no more, until she tries to do it.' Something like that, in his anger and vexation."

"Ah!" said the gentleman. "Well?"

"Well, Sir, he went to her, and kneeled to her; said it was so; said it ever had been; and made a prayer to her to save him."

"And she?—Don't distress yourself, Mrs. Tugby."

"She came to me that night to ask me about living here. 'What he was once to me,' she said, 'is buried in a grave; side by side with what I was to him. But I have thought of this; and I will make the trial. In the hope of saving him; for the love of the light-hearted girl (you remember her) who was to have been married on a New Year's Day; and for the love of her Richard.' And she said he had come to her from Lilian, and Lilian had trusted to him, and she never could forget that. So they were married; and when they came home here, and I saw them, I hoped that such prophecies as parted them when they were young, may not often fulfil themselves as they did in this case, or I wouldn't be the makers of them for a Mine of Gold."

The gentleman got off the cask, and stretched himself: observing

"I suppose he used her ill, as soon as they were married?"

"I don't think he ever did that," said Mrs. Tugby, shaking her head, and wiping her eyes. "He went on better for a short time: but his habits were too old and strong to be got rid of; he soon fell back a little; and was falling fast back, when his illness came so strong upon him. I think he has always felt for her. I am sure he has. I've seen him, in his crying fits and tremblings, try to kiss her hand; and I have heard him call her 'Meg,' and say it was her nineteenth birthday. There he has been lying now, these weeks and months. Between him and her baby, she has not been able to do her old work; and by not being able to be regular, she has lost it, even if she could have done it. How they have lived, I hardly know!"

"*I* know," muttered Mr. Tugby; looking at the till, and round the shop, and at his wife; and rolling his head with immense intelligence. "Like Fighting Cocks!"

He was interrupted by a cry—a sound of lamentation—

from the upper story of the house. The gentleman moved hurriedly to the door.

"My friend," he said, looking back, "you needn't discuss whether he shall be removed or not. He has spared you that trouble, I believe."

Saying so, he ran up stairs, followed by Mrs. Tugby; while Mr. Tugby panted and grumbled after them at leisure: being rendered more than commonly short-winded by the weight of the till, in which there had been an inconvenient quantity of copper. Trotty, with the child beside him, floated up the staircase like mere air.

"Follow her! Follow her! Follow her!" He heard the ghostly voices in the Bells repeat their words as he ascended. "Learn it, from the creature dearest to your heart!"

It was over. It was over. And this was she, her father's pride and joy! This haggard, wretched woman, weeping by the bed, if it deserved that name, and pressing to her breast, and hanging down her head upon, an infant. Who can tell how spare, how sickly, and how poor an infant! Who can tell how dear!

"Thank God!" cried Trotty, holding up his folded hands. "Oh, God be thanked! She loves her child!"

The gentleman, not otherwise hard-hearted or indifferent to such scenes, than that he saw them every day, and knew that they were figures of no moment in the Filer sums— mere scratches in the working of those calculations—laid his hand upon the heart that beat no more, and listened for the breath, and said, "His pain is over. It's better as it is!" Mrs. Tugby tried to comfort her with kindness. Mr. Tugby tried philosophy.

"Come, come!" he said, with his hands in his pockets, "you mustn't give way, you know. That won't do. You must fight up. What would have become of me if *I* had given way when I was porter; and we had as many as six runaway carriage-doubles[25] at our door in one night! But I fell back upon my strength of mind, and didn't open it!"

Again Trotty heard the voices, saying, "Follow her!" He

turned towards his guide, and saw it rising from him, passing through the air. "Follow her!" it said. And vanished.

He hovered round her; sat down at her feet; looked up into her face for one trace of her old self; listened for one note of her old pleasant voice. He flitted round the child: so wan, so prematurely old, so dreadful in its gravity, so plaintive in its feeble, mournful, miserable wail. He almost worshipped it. He clung to it as her only safeguard; as the last unbroken link that bound her to endurance. He set his father's hope and trust on the frail baby; watched her every look upon it as she held it in her arms; and cried a thousand times, "She loves it! God be thanked, she loves it!"

He saw the woman tend her in the night; return to her when her grudging husband was asleep, and all was still; encourage her, shed tears with her, set nourishment before her. He saw the day come, and the night again; the day, the night; the time go by; the house of death relieved of death; the room left to herself and to the child; he heard it moan and cry; he saw it harass her, and tire her out, and when she slumbered in exhaustion, drag her back to consciousness, and hold her with its little hands upon the rack; but she was constant to it, gentle with it, patient with it. Patient! Was its loving mother in her inmost heart and soul, and had its Being knitted up with hers as when she carried it unborn.

All this time, she was in want; languishing away, in dire and pining want. With the baby in her arms, she wandered here and there, in quest of occupation; and with its thin face lying in her lap, and looking up in hers, did any work for any wretched sum; a day and night of labour for as many farthings as there were figures on the dial. If she had quarrelled with it; if she had neglected it; if she had looked upon it with a moment's hate; if, in the frenzy of an instant, she had struck it! No. His comfort was, She loved it always.

She told no one of her extremity, and wandered abroad in the day lest she should be questioned by her only friend: for any help she received from her hands, occasioned fresh disputes between the good woman and her husband; and it was new bitterness to be the daily cause of strife and discord, where she owed so much.

She loved it still. She loved it more and more. But a change fell on the aspect of her love. One night.

She was singing faintly to it in its sleep, and walking to and fro to hush it, when her door was softly opened, and a man looked in.

"For the last time," he said.

"William Fern!"

"For the last time."

He listened like a man pursued: and spoke in whispers.

"Margaret, my race is nearly run. I couldn't finish it, without a parting word with you. Without one grateful word."

"What have you done?" she asked: regarding him with terror.

He looked at her, but gave no answer.

After a short silence, he made a gesture with his hand, as if he set her question by; as if he brushed it aside; and said,

"It's long ago, Margaret, now: but that night is as fresh in my memory as ever 'twas. We little thought, then," he added, looking round, "that we should ever meet like this. Your child, Margaret? Let me have it in my arms. Let me hold your child."

He put his hat upon the floor, and took it. And he trembled as he took it, from head to foot.

"Is it a girl?"

"Yes."

He put his hand before its little face.

"See how weak I'm grown, Margaret, when I want the courage to look at it! Let her be a moment. I won't hurt her. It's long ago; but—What's her name?"

"Margaret," she answered, quickly.

"I'm glad of that," he said. "I'm glad of that."

He seemed to breathe more freely; and after pausing for an instant, took away his hand, and looked upon the infant's face. But covered it again, immediately.

"Margaret!" he said; and gave her back the child. "It's Lilian's."

"Lilian's!"

"I held the same face in my arms when Lilian's mother died and left her."

"When Lilian's mother died and left her!" she repeated, wildly.

"How shrill you speak! Why do you fix your eyes upon me so? Margaret!"

She sunk down in a chair, and pressed the infant to her breast, and wept over it. Sometimes she released it from her embrace, to look anxiously in its face: then strained it to her bosom again. At those times: when she gazed upon it: then it was that something fierce and terrible began to mingle with her love. Then it was that her old father quailed.

"Follow her!" was sounded through the house. "Learn it, from the creature dearest to your heart!"

"Margaret," said Fern, bending over her, and kissing her upon the brow: "I thank you for the last time. Good night. Good bye. Put your hand in mine, and tell me you'll forget me from this hour, and try to think the end of me was here."

"What have you done!" she asked again.

"There'll be a Fire to-night[26]," he said, removing from her. "There'll be Fires this winter-time, to light the dark nights, East, West, North, and South. When you see the distant sky red, they'll be blazing. When you see the distant sky red, think of me no more; or, if you do, remember what a Hell was lighted up inside of me, and think you see its flames reflected in the clouds. Good night. Good bye!"

She called to him; but he was gone. She sat down stupefied, until her infant roused her to a sense of hunger, cold, and darkness. She paced the room with it the livelong night, hushing it and soothing it. She said at intervals, "like Lilian, when her mother died and left her!" Why was her step so quick, her eye so wild, her love so fierce and terrible, whenever she repeated those words?

"But it is Love," said Trotty. "It is Love. She'll never cease to love it. My poor Meg!"

She dressed the child next morning with unusual care—ah vain expenditure of care upon such squalid robes!—and once more tried to find some means of life. It was the last day of the Old Year. She tried till night, and never broke her fast. She tried in vain.

She mingled with an abject crowd, who tarried in the snow, until it pleased some officer appointed to dispense the public charity (the lawful charity; not that once preached upon a Mount), to call them in, and question them, and say to this one, "go to such a place," to that one, "come next week;" to make a foot-ball of another wretch, and pass him here and there, from hand to hand, from house to house, until he wearied and lay down to die[27]; or started up and robbed, and so became a higher sort of criminal, whose claims allowed of no delay. Here, too, she failed. She loved her child, and wished to have it lying on her breast. And that was quite enough.

It was night: a bleak, dark, cutting night: when, pressing the child close to her for warmth, she arrived outside the house she called her home. She was so faint and giddy, that she saw no one standing in the doorway until she was close upon it, and about to enter. Then she recognised the master of the house, who had so disposed himself—with his person it was not difficult—as to fill up the whole entry.

"Oh!" he said, softly. "You have come back?"

She looked at the child, and shook her head.

"Don't you think you have lived here long enough without paying any rent? Don't you think that, without any money, you've been a pretty constant customer at this shop, now?" said Mr. Tugby.

She repeated the same mute appeal.

"Suppose you try and deal somewhere else," he said. "And suppose you provide yourself with another lodging. Come! Don't you think you could manage it?"

She said in a low voice, that it was very late. To-morrow.

"Now I see what you want," said Tugby; "and what you

mean. You know there are two parties in this house about you, and you delight in setting 'em by the ears. I don't want any quarrels; I'm speaking softly to avoid a quarrel; but if you don't go away, I'll speak out loud, and you shall cause words high enough to please you. But you shan't come in. That I am determined."

She put her hair back with her hand, and looked in a sudden manner at the sky, and the dark lowering distance.

"This is the last night of an Old Year: and I won't carry ill-blood and quarrellings and disturbances into a New One, to please you nor anybody else," said Tugby, who was quite a retail Friend and Father. "I wonder you an't ashamed of yourself, to carry such practices into a New Year. If you haven't any business in the world, but to be always giving way, and always making disturbances between man and wife, you'd be better out of it. Go along with you."

"Follow her! To desperation!"

Again the old man heard the voices. Looking up, he saw the figures hovering in the air, and pointing where she went, down the dark street.

"She loves it!" he exclaimed, in agonised entreaty for her. "Chimes! She loves it still!"

"Follow her!" The shadow swept upon the track she had taken, like a cloud.

He joined in the pursuit; he kept close to her; he looked into her face. He saw the same fierce and terrible expression mingling with her love, and kindling in her eyes. He heard her say, "Like Lilian! To be changed like Lilian!" and her speed redoubled.

Oh, for something to awaken her! For any sight, or sound, or scent, to call up tender recollections in a brain on fire! For any gentle image of the Past to rise before her!

"I was her father! I was her father!" cried the old man, stretching out his hands to the dark shadows flying on above. "Have mercy on her, and on me! Where does she go? Turn her back! I was her father!"

But they only pointed to her, as she hurried on; and said,

"To desperation! Learn it from the creature dearest to your heart!"

A hundred voices echoed it. The air was made of breath expended in those words. He seemed to take them in, at every gasp he drew. They were everywhere, and not to be escaped. And still she hurried on; the same light in her eyes, the same words in her mouth, "Like Lilian! To be changed like Lilian!"

All at once she stopped.

"Now, turn her back!" exclaimed the old man, tearing his white hair. "My child! Meg! Turn her back! Great Father, turn her back!"

In her own scanty shawl, she wrapped the baby warm. With her fevered hands she smoothed its limbs, composed its face, arranged its mean attire. In her wasted arms she folded it, as though she never would resign it more. And with her dry lips, kissed it in a final pang, and last long agony of Love.

Putting its tiny hand up to her neck, and holding it there, within her dress: next to her distracted heart, she set its sleeping face against her: closely, steadily, against her: and sped onward to the river.

To the rolling River, swift and dim, where Winter Night sat brooding like the last dark thoughts of many who had sought a refuge there before her. Where scattered lights upon the banks gleamed sullen, red, and dull, as torches that were burning there, to show the way to Death. Where no abode of living people cast its shadow on the deep, impenetrable, melancholy shade.

To the River! To that portal of Eternity, her desperate footsteps tended with the swiftness of its rapid waters running to the sea. He tried to touch her as she passed him, going down to its dark level; but the wild distempered form, the fierce and terrible love, the desperation that had left all human check or hold behind, swept by him like the wind.

He followed her. She paused a moment on the brink, before the dreadful plunge. He fell down on his knees, and in a shriek addressed the figures in the Bells now hovering above them.

"I have learnt it!" cried the old man. "From the creature dearest to my heart! Oh, save her, save her!"

He could wind his fingers in her dress; could hold it! As the words escaped his lips he felt his sense of touch return, and knew that he detained her.

The figures looked down steadfastly upon him.

"I have learnt it!" cried the old man. "Oh, have mercy on me in this hour, if, in my love for her, so young and good, I slandered Nature in the breasts of mothers rendered desperate! Pity my presumption, wickedness, and ignorance. and save her!"

He felt his hold relaxing. They were silent still.

"Have mercy on her!" he exclaimed, "as one in whom this dreadful crime has sprung from Love perverted; from the strongest, deepest Love we fallen creatures know! Think what her misery must have been, when such seed bears such fruit! Heaven meant her to be Good. There is no loving mother on the earth who might not come to this, if such a life had gone before. Oh, have mercy on my child, who, even at this pass, means mercy to her own, and dies herself, and perils her Immortal Soul, to save it!"

She was in his arms. He held her now. His strength was like a giant's.

"I see the spirit of the Chimes among you!" cried the old man, singling out the child, and speaking in some inspiration, which their looks conveyed to him. "I know that our Inheritance is held in store for us by Time. I know there is a Sea of Time to rise one day, before which all who wrong us or oppress us will be swept away like leaves. I see it, on the flow! I know that we must trust and hope, and neither doubt ourselves, nor doubt the Good in one another. I have learnt it from the creature dearest to my heart. I clasp her in my arms again. Oh Spirits, merciful and good, I take your lesson to my breast along with her! Oh Spirits, merciful and good, I am grateful!"

He might have said more, but the Bells; the old familiar Bells; his own dear, constant, steady friends, the Chimes;

began to ring the joy-peals for a New Year, so lustily, so merrily, so happily, so gaily, that he leapt upon his feet, and broke the spell that bound him.

"And whatever you do, father," said Meg, "don't eat tripe again, without asking some doctor whether it's likely to agree with you; for how you *have* been going on, Good gracious!"

She was working with her needle, at the little table by the fire; dressing her simple gown with ribbons for her wedding. So quietly happy, so blooming and youthful, so full of beautiful promise, that he uttered a great cry as if it were an Angel in his house; then flew to clasp her in his arms.

But he caught his feet in the newspaper, which had fallen on the hearth; and somebody came rushing in between them.

"No!" cried the voice of this same somebody; a generous and jolly voice it was! "Not even you. Not even you. The first kiss of Meg in the New Year is mine. Mine! I have been waiting outside the house, this hour, to hear the Bells and claim it. Meg, my precious prize, a happy year! A life of happy years, my darling wife!"

And Richard smothered her with kisses.

You never in all your life saw anything like Trotty after this. I don't care where you have lived or what you have seen; you never in all your life saw anything at all approaching him! He sat down in his chair and beat his knees and cried; he sat down in his chair and beat his knees and laughed; he sat down in his chair and beat his knees and laughed and cried together; he got out of his chair and hugged Meg; he got out of his chair and hugged Richard; he got out of his chair and hugged them both at once; he kept running up to Meg, and squeezing her fresh face between his hands and kissing it, going from her backwards not to lose sight of it, and running up again like a figure in a magic lantern; and whatever he did, he was constantly sitting himself down in this chair, and never stopping in it for one single moment; being—that's the truth—beside himself with joy.

"And to-morrow's your wedding-day, my Pet!" cried Trotty. "Your real, happy wedding-day!"

"To-day!" cried Richard, shaking hands with him. "To-day. The Chimes are ringing in the New Year. Hear them!"

They WERE ringing! Bless their sturdy hearts, they WERE ringing! Great Bells as they were; melodious, deep-mouthed, noble Bells; cast in no common metal; made by no common founder; when had they ever Chimed like that, before!

"But to-day, my Pet," said Trotty. "You and Richard had some words to-day."

"Because he's such a bad fellow, father," said Meg. "An't you, Richard? Such a headstrong, violent man! He'd have made no more of speaking his mind to that great Alderman, and putting *him* down I don't know where, than he would of——"

"—Kissing Meg," suggested Richard. Doing it too!

"No. Not a bit more," said Meg. "But I wouldn't let him, father. Where would have been the use!"

"Richard, my boy!" cried Trotty. "You was turned up Trumps originally; and Trumps you must be till you die! But you were crying by the fire to-night, my Pet, when I came home! Why did you cry by the fire?"

"I was thinking of the years we've passed together, father. Only that. And thinking you might miss me, and be lonely."

Trotty was backing off to that extraordinary chair again, when the child, who had been awakened by the noise, came running in half-dressed.

"Why, here she is!" cried Trotty, catching her up. "Here's little Lilian! Ha ha ha! Here we are and here we go! Oh here we are and here we go again! And here we are and here we go! And Uncle Will too!" Stopping in his trot to greet him heartily. "Oh, Uncle Will, the Vision that I've had to-night, through lodging you! Oh, Uncle Will, the obligations that you've laid me under, by your coming, my good friend!"

Before Will Fern could make the least reply, a Band of Music burst into the room, attended by a flock of neighbours, screaming "A Happy New Year, Meg!" "A Happy Wedding!" "Many of 'em!" and other fragmentary good wishes of that sort. The Drum (who was a private friend of Trotty's) then stepped forward, and said:

"Trotty Veck, my boy! It's got about, that your daughter is going to be married to-morrow. There an't a soul that knows you that don't wish you well, or that knows her and don't wish her well. Or that knows you both, and don't wish you both all the happiness the New Year can bring. And here we are, to play it in and dance it in, accordingly."

Which was received with a general shout. The Drum was rather drunk, by-the-bye; but never mind.

"What a happiness it is, I'm sure," said Trotty, "to be so esteemed! How kind and neighbourly you are! It's all along of my dear daughter. She deserves it!"

They were ready for a dance in half a second (Meg and Richard at the top); and the Drum was on the very brink of leathering away with all his power; when a combination of prodigious sounds was heard outside, and a good-humoured comely woman of some fifty years of age, or thereabouts, came running in, attended by a man bearing a stone pitcher of terrific size, and closely followed by the marrow-bones and cleavers[28], and the bells: not *the* Bells, but a portable collection, on a frame.

Trotty said, "It's Mrs. Chickenstalker!" And sat down, and beat his knees again.

"Married, and not tell me, Meg!" cried the good woman. "Never! I couldn't rest on the last night of the Old Year without coming to wish you joy. I couldn't have done it, Meg. Not if I had been bed-ridden. So here I am; and as it's New Year's Eve, and the Eve of your wedding too, my dear, I had a little flip[29] made, and brought it with me."

Mrs. Chickenstalker's notion of a little flip, did honour to her character. The pitcher steamed and smoked and reeked like a volcano; and the man who had carried it, was faint.

"Mrs. Tugby!" said Trotty, who had been going round and round her, in an ecstasy. "I *should* say, Chickenstalker—Bless your heart and soul! A happy New Year, and many of 'em! Mrs. Tugby,"

said Trotty when he had saluted her; "I *should* say, Chickenstalker—This is William Fern and Lilian."

The worthy dame, to his surprise, turned very pale and very red.

"Not Lilian Fern whose mother died in Dorsetshire!"[30] said she.

Her uncle answered "Yes," and meeting hastily, they exchanged some hurried words together; of which the upshot was, that Mrs. Chickenstalker shook him by both hands; saluted Trotty on his cheek again, of her own free will; and took the child to her capacious breast.

"Will Fern!" said Trotty, pulling on his right-hand muffler. "Not the friend you was hoping to find?"

"Ay!" returned Will, putting a hand on each of Trotty's shoulders. "And like to prove a'most as good a friend, if that can be, as one I found."

"Oh!" said Trotty. "Please to play up there. Will you have the goodness!"

To the music of the band, the bells, the marrow-bones and cleavers; all at once; and while the Chimes were yet in lusty operation out of doors; Trotty, making Meg and Richard second couple, led off Mrs. Chickenstalker down the dance, and danced it in a step unknown before or since; founded on his own peculiar trot.

Had Trotty dreamed? Or are his joys and sorrows, and the actors in them, but a dream; himself a dream; the teller of this tale a dreamer, waking but now? If it be so, oh Listener, dear to him in all his visions, try to bear in mind the stern realities from which these shadows come; and in your sphere—none is too wide, and none too limited for such an end—endeavour to correct, improve, and soften them. So may the New Year be a Happy one to You, Happy to many more whose Happiness depends on You! So may each Year be happier than the last, and not the meanest of our brethren or sisterhood debarred their rightful share, in what our Great Creator formed them to enjoy.

THE END

APPENDIX A

The Deleted 'Young England' Passages from
The Chimes

ABOUT the end of October 1844 Dickens, nearing the end of the writing of *The Chimes*, replied to some criticisms Forster had made of those parts of the story he had already seen: 'As you dislike the Young England gentleman,' he wrote,

I shall knock him out and replace him by a man . . . who recognizes no virtue in anything but the good old times. . . . A real good old city tory, in a blue coat and bright buttons and a white cravat and with a tendency of blood to the head.

(Forster, *Life of Dickens*, ed. J. W. T. Ley, 1928, p. 355).

This was done but the passages satirizing Young England found in the manuscript of *The Chimes* have, I think, enough vigour about them to be worth rescuing from oblivion and I have accordingly reproduced them here.

'Young England' was a tiny splinter group of Peel's Tories, a few young aristocratic MPs from Eton and Cambridge, steeped in the novels of Scott, whose romantic remedy for the distress of the working classes – or 'Order of the Peasantry', as they preferred to call them – was a return to a state of feudalism (or rather, what they imagined feudalism to have been), the restoration of the throne, church and aristocracy as the real and effective governing institutions of the country. Too much power, they believed, had become vested in the predominantly middle-class House of Commons, and the natural protectors of the poor – a *noblesse oblige* aristocracy and an almsgiving church – needed to be recalled to their duties. Peel was unsympathetic to these nostalgic views and Disraeli, now thirty-seven years old and disappointed in his expectations of government office in 1841, emerged as the group's leader, partly, no doubt, in order to embarrass his chief. 'Young England' addressed itself mainly to the young, the 'New Generation' (to quote the sub-title of Disraeli's *Coningsby*, a 'Young England' manifesto in fictional form) and, by dint of much publishing and speech-making, contrived to make a great noise in the country. Lord John Manners's volume *England's Trust and Other Poems* (1841) which contained the notorious couplet,

> Let wealth and commerce, laws and learning die
> But leave us still our old Nobility!

was followed by his *Plea for National Holy-days* (1843), Disraeli's *Coningsby* (1844) and the Hon. George Smythe's *Historic Fancies* (1844). One of Smythe's 'fancies' was the revival of the royal custom of touching sick people for the King's Evil as a symbolic manifestation of closer relations between Throne and People.

'Young England' was hardly likely to appeal to Dickens, whose general view of the past is expressed in *The Chimes* by the Great Bell – 'Ages of darkness, wickedness, and violence' – and nearly every word uttered by the 'Young England gentleman' in the following passages is a gibe at some aspect of the group's activities and beliefs. Even his white waistcoat is significant for this was, we learn from *Punch* (28 December 1844, p. 142), the uniform of 'Young England':

> Oh! the vests of Young England are perfectly white,
> And they're cut very neatly and sit very tight,
> And they serve to distinguish our Young Englishmen
> From the juvenile MANNERS to CONINGSBY BEN.

In the second passage, when the 'Young England gentleman' languishes about the regenerative power of 'Stained Glass Windows and Enormous Candlesticks', Dickens is, of course, tilting at 'Young England's' links with the Oxford Movement (Lord John Manners was much influenced by his close friend, Faber). He had already, not long before, satirized the Movement in an article written for the *Examiner* (3 June 1843) and entitled, 'Report of the Commissioners Appointed to Inquire into the Condition of the Persons Variously Engaged in the University of Oxford':

A vast number of witnesses being interrogated as to what they understood by the words Religion and Salvation, answered Lighted Candles. Some said water; some, bread; others, little boys; others mixed the water, lighted candles, bread and little boys all up together, and called the compound Faith.

Similarly, in the sixth passage the 'youngish sort of gentleman's' enthusiasm for the skittles match played between Sir Joseph and his tenants is another palpable hit. About this time, we learn from an anonymous pamphlet published in 1872 and called *Lord John Manners. A Political and Literary Sketch*, Disraeli and Manners were busily urging their aristocratic friends to found cricket-clubs for their tenants and were themselves

[going] about from place to place engaging with great spirit and good nature in a variety of manly sports with the labouring population; until it almost seemed that we were to witness the renewal of those scenes of mirth and jollity, which had earned for this country, in olden times, the enviable, but, alas! no longer applicable title of Merrie England.

Note: *Words enclosed in square brackets denote those which remain in the text. Page references in Roman numerals are to the manuscript and those in Arabic are to the relevant page in this edition. I have not indicated any of the current revision in the manuscript passages. The version shown, therefore, is the final one arrived at by Dickens in manuscript.*

1. [One was a low-spirited gentleman of middle age, of a meagre habit, and a disconsolate face. ... The other,] a pleasant-looking youngish sort of gentleman, in a white waistcoat ... (*pp. xiii and 166*)

2. ["And what do you say?" asked the Alderman jocosely]

of the youngish sort of gentleman in the white waistcoat. ["You have heard friend Filer. What do *you* say?".]

"My dear Alderman Cute," returned the gentleman, with an exhausted smile. ["What *is* to be said]! Look at this Serf!"—meaning Trotty. "Where is his Faith in the Ideal and the Vague! Can the Elements of its Regeneration struggle from beneath the withering influences of the Out-of-Drawing and the Common-Place! Oh refer," said the youngish sort of gentleman, "Refer to Strutt's Costumes and see what such a man was once."

["He hadn't in his very best circumstances a shirt to his back, nor a stocking to his foot; and there was scarcely a vegetable in all England for him to put into his mouth," said Mr. Filer. "I can prove it by tables."]

"He had Faith in the Elementary Sir!" returned the youngish sort of gentleman. "He had Faith in Smithfield if you mean that" growled Mr. Filer. "and something too much of it."

"The Fires of Smithfield by whomsoever lighted: and the kindlers were of no one class: were at least associated with the Glowing and the Picturesque!" observed the other. "They have been quenched in Pig-markets; and this"—meaning Trotty again, "is the Degraded actuality that has sprung up from among the Steaming Swine. Restore" said the youngish sort of gentleman, "the Good Old Times, the Grand Old Times, the Great Old Times! Raise up this trodden worm into a man by the mysterious but certain agency (it always has been so) of Stained Glass Windows and Enormous Candlesticks"—he languished for a moment here, as contemplating his own face in a bright silver one. "Then his Regeneration is accomplished. Until then, Behold him!"

[It is possible that poor] old [Trotty's faith in] the Vague [was not entirely destroyed for he] certainly [felt vague enough at that moment . . .] (*pp. xiv and 168–9*)

3. [". . . It's a mathematical certainty."]

"What do *you* say?" enquired the alderman: [mightily diverted:] of the youngish sort of gentleman.

"My dear alderman Cute what is to be said! The Nuptials of these people in the old Times would have been a Pastoral thing; a Subject for the Painter: a little Pageant symbolical of the union between the Real and the Impossible. But now—in Saint Giles' church—or Providence chapel—!" the gentleman shrugged his shoulders and sighed bitterly.

Alderman Cute [laid his right forefinger on the side of his nose . . .] (*pp. xvi and 171*)

4. [. . . in this chamber an election, and in that a ball.] Before one sofa where the youngish sort of gentleman (Trotty recognized him by his waistcoat) lay dozing, a small party were enjoying rustic sports, while another rather larger party were being hanged on trees in the background and a third were having brazen collars soldered round their necks as the born vassals of an undeniably picturesque Baron; singing at the same time "oh the good old times, the grand old times, the glorious old Feudal times, the Genuine Genteel Millennium!" (*pp. xxxvi and 202*)

5. [". . . bluff King Hal. Ah! Fine character!"
"Very," said Mr. Filer dryly.]
"He did his appointed work, Sir," said the youngish sort of gentleman.
"What was that?" asked Mr. Filer. ["Marrying women and murdering 'em? Considerably more than the average number of Wives, by the bye."]
"It was his Mission, Sir." returned the youngish sort of gentleman. "And he fulfilled it." (*pp. xlii and 210*)

6. [and everybody said] (the youngish sort of gentleman especially) [that now, when a Baronet . . . played at skittles, the country was coming round again.] (*pp. xlv and 213*)

7. [Lady Bowley's health had been proposed] and the youngish sort of gentleman had given it (he was a good speaker, the youngish sort of gentleman) [and Sir Joseph Bowley had returned thanks . . .] (*pp. xlv and 213*)

APPENDIX B

The descriptive headlines added to *A Christmas Carol* and
The Chimes in the Charles Dickens edition, 1868

A CHRISTMAS CAROL

STAVE ONE

Out upon Merry Christmas!
God bless you, merry gentleman!
Scrooge's Fireside
The Ghost
The Ghost's departure

STAVE TWO

Another unearthly Visitor
Scrooge's School-Days
The Fezziwig Ball
Scrooge's old Love
Expecting a Third Visitor

STAVE THREE

Christmas Shops
At Bob Cratchit's
Tiny Tim and Mr Scrooge
Over Land and Sea
Games at Forfeits
Ignorance and Want

STAVE FOUR

A Death has occurred
Ghoules

APPENDIX

FOURTH QUARTER

Mr. Tugby's back-attic going
The Back-attic gone
Love and Fear
Love and Desperation
To be married To-morrow

NOTES TO
A CHRISTMAS CAROL

1. In his preface to the recent Folio Society publication of the *Carol* manuscript in facsimile, Frederick B. Adams Jr notes that Dickens here digressed into the following sprightly remarks on the character of Hamlet:

   > Perhaps you think that Hamlet's intellects were strong. I doubt it. If you could have such a son tomorrow, depend upon it, you would find him a poser. He would be a most impracticable fellow to deal with, and however creditable he might be to his family, after his decease, he would prove a special incumbrance in his lifetime, trust me.

   These sentences were deleted before proof stage.

2. *'came down'*. A pun on the literal and slang meanings of 'come down'. In the slang sense the phrase means to give money.

3. *what the knowing ones call 'nuts' to Scrooge*. The old expression that something was 'nuts to' someone meant that it was a source of pleasure to them (v. O.E.D. s.v. 'nut', sense 5a).

4. *the Union workhouses*. The Poor Law Amendment Act of 1834, the working of which Dickens had attacked so fiercely in *Oliver Twist*, had divided England and Wales up into twenty-one districts; in each of these a commissioner was empowered to form 'poor law unions' by grouping parishes together for administrative purposes and to build workhouses for the reception of the destitute. The term 'Union' came to be used as a synonym for 'workhouse' (cf. note 17 to *The Chimes*, below).

5. *decrease the surplus population*. The belief that England had too many mouths to feed had been worrying people ever since the appearance of Malthus's *Essay on the Principle of Population* in 1803. Malthus made it clear whom he regarded as 'surplus' when he wrote (p. 531):

   > A man who is born into a world already possessed, if he cannot get subsistence from his parents, on whom he has a just demand, and if society do not want his labour, has no claim of *right* to the smallest portion of food, and, in fact, has no business to be where he is. At nature's mighty feast there is no vacant cover for him. She tells him to be gone ...

6. *Saint Dunstan ... his familiar weapons*. Writing about St Dunstan (924–88) in his *Child's History of England* Dickens recounts the legend referred to here in the following way:

[Dunstan] was an ingenious smith, and worked at a forge in a little cell ... he used to tell the most extraordinary lies about demons and spirits who, he said, came there to persecute him. For instance, he related that one day when he was at work, the devil looked in at the little window, and tried to tempt him to lead a life of idle pleasure; whereupon, having his pincers in the fire, red hot, he seized the devil by the nose, and put him to such pain, that his bellowings were heard for miles and miles. Some people are inclined to think this nonsense a part of Dunstan's madness ... but I think not. I observe that it induced the ignorant people to consider him a holy man, and that it made him very powerful. Which was exactly what he always wanted.

7. *next morning.* Boxing Day was treated as an ordinary working day until it was made a Bank Holiday by Act of Parliament in 1871. (H)

8. *dip.* A tallow candle.

9. *like the ancient Prophet's rod.* An allusion to the Book of Exodus, chapter 7, verse 12, which describes how Aaron's rod, transformed into a serpent, swallowed up the serpents similarly produced by Pharaoh's magicians.

10. *The Ward.* A constable of the watch which patrolled the streets of London at night until the institution of the Metropolitan Police in 1829.

11. *a mere United States security.* During the early 1830s individual States of the Union (not the Federal Government) borrowed lavishly from foreign capitalists, especially English ones, to finance such public works as railway and canal building. The American financial crisis of 1837 forced many states to repudiate their debts, a proceeding vehemently reprobated in the English press. (H)

12. *Not a latent echo in the house ... but fell upon the heart of Scrooge.* In her lecture, 'The Middle Years: from the *Carol* to *Copperfield*' (published by the Dickens Fellowship in *Dickens Memorial Lectures 1970*), Kathleen Tillotson notes of this description, 'The whole impression, and half the details, come from Tennyson's "Mariana"'. 'Mariana' was first published in Tennyson's *Poems chiefly Lyrical* in 1830.

13. *Valentine ... and his wild brother, Orson.* The story of two brothers, one of whom is carried off by a bear and reared as a wild man in the woods while the other is brought up as a knight at court, is first found in an early French romance. It appeared in England in the sixteenth century and was one of the traditional nursery tales that Dickens delighted to recall.

14. *And what's his name. ... And the Sultan's Groom. ... What right had he to be married to the Princess?* The incidents Scrooge alludes to here occur in 'The Story of Noor-ed-Deen and his Son, and of

Shems-ed-Deen and his Daughter' in *The Arabian Nights* (chapter four of E. W. Lane's edition). The brothers Noor-ed-Deen and Shems-ed-Deen, joint Viziers to the Sultan of Cairo, quarrel bitterly and Noor-ed-Deen departs to the city of El-Basrah where he prospers and begets a son, Hasan. After his death Hasan's life is in danger but his beauty, as he lies sleeping on his father's tomb, attracts a passing Jinneeyeh (female Genie) who shows him to a Genie. The Genie tells her that the daughter of the Vizier of Cairo, Shems-ed-Deen, is equally beautiful but is about to be forcibly married to an ugly humpbacked groom of the Sultan's, the Sultan having been enraged by her father's refusal to marry her to anyone but the son of his lost and now yearned-for brother, Noor-ed-Deen, if he should ever appear. The two Genii transport Hasan to Cairo where he displaces the humpbacked groom at the bridal ceremony while the latter is compelled by the Genii to remain upside-down all night. But the Genii had to return Hasan to El-Basrah when dawn appeared and they took him up, undressed as he was, to transport him there. Their passage was intercepted, however, by a fiery shooting-star which burnt one of them. The other hastily deposited Hasan, still sleeping, at the point where this happened 'and as destiny had appointed, this place was Damascus: so she placed him by one of the gates of this city and flew away'. Dickens refers to this story also in the first of his Christmas Stories, 'A Christmas Tree', written for publication in *Household Words* in 1850: 'Tarts are made according to the recipe of the Vizier's son of Bussorah [El-Basrah] who turned pastrycook after he was set down in his drawers at the gate of Damascus.'

15. *Friday, running for his life to the little creek.* Dickens also recalls this episode from *Robinson Crusoe* (another of the books which he devoured as a child) in his essay, 'Nurse's Stories' (1860), collected in *The Uncommercial Traveller*: 'No face is ever reflected in the waters of the little creek which Friday swam across when pursued by his two brother cannibals with sharpened stomachs.'

16. *A Welch wig.* A cap made of knitted worsted, as worn by Sol Gills in *Dombey and Son*. (H)

17. *organ of benevolence.* A term borrowed from the Victorian pseudo-science of phrenology, the basic premise of which was that intellectual and moral character could be gauged from the shape of the skull which phrenologists divided into some forty sections or 'organs', each one being the seat of a mental or moral faculty. The 'organ of benevolence' was located at the top of the forehead.

18. *Fezziwig 'cut'.* According to the O.E.D. (s.v. 'cut', sense 30) to 'cut' in dancing means 'to spring from the ground and, while in the air, to twiddle the feet one in front of the other alternately, with great rapidity'.

19. *the celebrated herd in the poem.* An allusion to Wordsworth's poem, 'Written in March' in which occur the lines:

> 'The cattle are grazing,
> Their heads never raising;
> There are forty feeding like one!' (H)

20. *spontaneous combustion.* This was a medical myth widely received in the early nineteenth century, the idea being that the chemical elements of the human body could become so corrupted that the victim could suddenly perish in a self-generated conflagration. Dickens's causing Krook in *Bleak House* to die in this way involved him in controversy with G. H. Lewes.

21. *twelfth-cakes.* Large cakes, frosted and decorated, made to be eaten on Twelfth Night.

22. *Norfolk biffins.* Norfolk cooking-apples which have been baked slowly and are a rusty red in colour. Often mentioned with gusto by Dickens. (H)

23. *for Christmas daws to peck at.* An allusion to *Othello*, Act I, Scene 1, lines 63–4.

24. *dinners to the bakers' shops.* On Sundays and on Christmas Day, when bakers were legally forbidden to bake bread, people would take their joints of meat, etc., to the bake-houses to cook. (H)

25. *to close these places on the Seventh Day.* Between 1832 and 1837 Sir Andrew Agnew had made repeated attempts to introduce a Sunday Observance Bill in the House of Commons. This Bill would not only have closed the bakeries on Sundays but would also have prohibited many of the people's recreations while leaving the wealthier classes unaffected. In June 1836, under the pseudonym of 'Timothy Sparks', Dickens had published a vigorous attack on Agnew entitled *Sunday under Three Heads. As it is; As Sabbath Bills would make it; As it might be made.* In it he describes a working man emerging from a bakery on Sunday

> with the reeking dish, in which a diminutive joint of mutton simmers above a vast heap of half-browned potatoes ... the dinner is borne into the house amidst a shouting of small voices, and jumping of fat legs, which would fill Sir Andrew Agnew with astonishment; as well it might, seeing that Baronets, generally speaking, eat pretty comfortable dinners all the week through, and cannot be expected to understand what people feel, who only have a meat dinner on one day out of every seven.

26. *vain man in his little brief authority.* An allusion to *Measure for Measure*, Act II, Scene 2, lines 117–18.

27. *Old Scratch.* Formerly, a nickname for the devil (from the Old Norse word *skratta*, a goblin).

28. *set him in the midst of them.* See St Matthew, chapter 18, verse 2.

29. *Laocoön.* The Trojan priest who attempted to dissuade his countrymen from dragging the wooden horse into Troy. The goddess Athene caused two great serpents to emerge from the sea which entwined themselves round Laocoön and his two sons and crushed them all to death. Dickens had doubtless seen replicas of the famous sculpture in the Vatican depicting this event. (H)

30. *Walk-ER.* A Victorian cockney expression, known to Sam Weller, indicating amused incredulity. (H)

31. *Joe Miller. Joe Miller's Jests* by John Mottley was first published in 1739, the name being taken from a Drury Lane actor who had a reputation as a humorist.

32. *bishop.* Bishop is made by pouring heated red wine over bitter oranges and then adding sugar and spices. The liquor is purple, the colour of a bishop's cassock, hence the name. (H)

NOTES TO
THE CHIMES

1. *steeple of an old church.* 'It's a great thing to have my title,' Dickens wrote to Forster from Genoa, 'and see my way to work the bells . . . I see nothing but the old London belfry I have set them in . . .' The belfry illustrated by Doyle and Stanfield is that of St Dunstan-in-the-West, Fleet Street. Presumably they were acting on Dickens's instructions but St Dunstan's in 1844 was not an old church. The medieval church (mentioned in *Barnaby Rudge*) had been pulled down in 1830 and the present edifice built by John Shaw, the high tower (no steeple) being regarded as his masterpiece. (H)

2. *ticket-porter.* A London street-porter licensed by the City Corporation. Mayhew describes them as a dying breed in Vol. 3 of his *London Labour and the London Poor* (1861): 'They usually, but not always, wear white aprons, and display their tickets as badges,' he notes. Contemporary reviewers of *The Chimes* frequently commented on how untypical a ticket-porter Trotty Veck was, e.g. the *Morning Post* (23 December 1844):

> Trotty Veck is not a ticket-porter of the common stamp. [He has] no monopoly to carry goods at fixed high prices [nor] . . . impunity to knock down all living obstructions to his way . . . instead of being 'up to a thing or two,' poor Toby Veck is ready to do anything for anybody at anybody's price.

3. *pettitoes.* pigs' trotters. 'Polonies' are pork sausages and 'chitter-lings' the small intestines of a pig, goose, etc.

4. *his sledge-hammer daily rung.* The *Chimes* manuscript shows that Dickens's first choice of name for the young blacksmith was Clement (St Clement was the patron saint of blacksmiths, cf. Joe Gargery's song, 'Old Clem', in *Great Expectations*), but it was soon changed to the more likely name of Richard.

5. *He knew them, Cute did.* In the character of Alderman Cute Dickens is lampooning Sir Peter Laurie (1778–1861), a noted Middlesex magistrate. Laurie enjoyed a great reputation for jocularity and shrewd common sense; he was also celebrated for his ability to talk to offenders brought before him in their own language.

6. *the bills of mortality.* At the end of the sixteenth century the London Company of Parish Clerks began to issue regular returns of the deaths occurring in the 109 parishes in and around London; this area came to be known as 'within the bills of mortality'.

7. *Consequently he's a robber.* In Mr Filer's speech 'proving' that Trotty must have stolen his tripe from someone else Dickens is hitting back at the *Westminster Review*, organ of the political economists, which had annoyed him in June 1844 by remarking of the *Christmas Carol*, 'Who went without turkey and punch in order that Bob Cratchit might get them – for, unless there were turkeys and punch in surplus, some one must go without – is a disagreeable reflection kept wholly out of sight [by Dickens].'

8. *the good old times!* Dickens had long been infuriated by praisers of the 'good old days'. 'If ever I destroy myself,' he wrote to Douglas Jerrold on 3 May 1843, 'it will be in the bitterness of hearing those infernal and damnably good old times extolled.' He lost few opportunities in his writings of attacking this form of cant, e.g. *American Notes* (1843), chapter three:

   those good old customs of the good old times which made England, even so recently as in the reign of the Third King George, in respect of her criminal code and prison regulations, one of the most bloody-minded and barbarous countries on the earth.

9. *Strutt's Costumes. A Complete View of the Dress and Habits of the People of England* by the antiquary Joseph Strutt was published in 1796–9 and a new edition appeared in 1842. In his painting of the Dickens children done in that year (for Dickens and his wife to take with them to America) Maclise represents one of the children studying this work.

10. *no right or business to be married.* Political economists in the early nineteenth century directed a great deal of propaganda towards the working classes to persuade them to abstain from marriage until they had enough income to support a family, e.g. the fourth tale

in Mrs Marcet's *John Hopkins's Notions on Political Economy* (1833) in which the Hopkinses, impoverished by their swarming family, persuaded their twenty-two-year-old son to postpone marrying his sweetheart. Dickens's apparent encouragement in *The Chimes* of early marriages among the poor was much criticized and a little story called *The Wedding Bells* was anonymously published the following Christmas, expressly designed to refute him on this point.

11. *the church-service*. The phrase 'all sick persons and young children' occurs in the Litany in the Book of Common Prayer. In *American Notes*, chapter six, Dickens refers to it as 'that beautiful passage'.

12. *Put suicide Down*. In 1841 Sir Peter Laurie had begun a campaign to put a stop to the crime of attempted suicide among the poor (which had become very prevalent) by sentencing offenders brought before him to prison and hard labour, and had thereby incurred much odium on humanitarian grounds. In the autumn of 1844 he sent for trial a woman accused of trying to poison herself, observing:

> he had no doubt she would be transported. He had put an end to persons attempting to drown themselves; he would now try the same cure for attempted poisoning. He had no doubt that those who took poison did not do so for the purpose of self-destruction, but for the purpose of exciting sympathy; and such morbid charity was more calculated to do injury than anything else.
>
> *Report quoted in* Punch, *5 October 1844*.

13. *the Poor Man's Friend*. One of Dickens's targets in portraying Sir Joseph Bowley, MP, was undoubtedly the Whig ex-Chancellor Lord Brougham who had been by turns a vociferous champion of Queen Caroline, the Reform Bill, education for the people, and other popular causes. He preened himself on his philanthropy but, during a speech in the Lords on the Factory Bill in 1844, he seemed to give a striking example of how superficial his concern for the people was. Supporters of the Bill, which aimed to limit working hours in factories to ten hours a day had argued that the children of women factory-workers suffered from malnutrition as their mothers had no leisure to feed them; Brougham observed that peeresses and MPs' wives were also often prevented 'by their various avocations' from suckling *their* children but he 'had never heard that any mischief resulted from the practice'. For this crass comparison he was bitterly attacked in *Punch* (6 April 1844) by Douglas Jerrold, who makes great play with the phrase 'the poor man's friend' in his article (entitled 'Lord Brougham on Wet-Nurses').

14. *dispensation of an all-wise Providence*. Cf. Lord Brougham's

attribution, in the Lords debate referred to in note 13, of the sufferings of the poor to 'the mysterious decrees and inscrutable dispensations of Providence'.

15. *pinking and eyelet-holing.* Ornamenting material by cutting small holes and shapes in it (usually to display a rich lining or undergarment of contrasting colour).

16. *music on the new system.* In 1843 John Curwen published his *Grammar of Vocal Music* which set out a new system of musical notation, without staves and notes, based on the principles of solfeggio and solmization (tonic sol-fa). (H)

17. *the Union.* Cf. note 4 to the *Carol*, above.

18. *laid her desperate hands, not only on her own life, but on that of her young child.* Dickens is here alluding to the case of Mary Furley, tried and sentenced for infanticide on 16 April 1844. In her evidence, reported in *The Times* on 17 April, she said that she had quitted the Whitechapel workhouse because of the brutal ill-treatment suffered there by her young child; she had tried to support herself and the baby by sewing shirts but, since the most she was able to earn that way was 5¼d. a day, she had borrowed a few shillings to buy ribbons to make up dress-caps for sale. This money was stolen from her and she then frantically resolved to drown herself and the child rather than return to the workhouse. When they were pulled out of the Thames the child was dead. Sentencing her to death, the judge remarked, 'Your act, which would have been at any time cruel, is rendered more so by the fact of the crime being committed by you – the mother of the child.' After a public outcry, in which Dickens joined (see his 'Threatening Letter to Thomas Hood from an Ancient Gentleman', *Hood's Magazine*, May 1844), her sentence was commuted to seven years' transportation. The most horrific part of Trotty's vision of Meg's future in the Fourth Quarter of *The Chimes* was clearly directly inspired by the Furley case.

19. *play at match at skittles . . . with his tenants.* This touch is all that remains of the cancelled satire on 'Young England' found in the *Chimes* manuscript. See Appendix A.

20. *bluff King Hal.* In his *Child's History of England*, chapter 28, Dickens remarks, 'We now come to King Henry the Eighth, whom it has been too much the fashion to call "Bluff King Hal" and "Burly King Harry" and other fine names; but whom I shall take the liberty of calling, plainly, one of the most detestable villains that ever drew breath.' After recounting the 'horrors' of Henry's reign, Dickens concludes, 'He was a most intolerable ruffian, a disgrace to human nature, and a blot of blood and grease upon the History of England.'

21. *you've drunk the Labourer.* 'The health of the labourer' was a

traditional toast at agricultural dinners. The cruel absurdity of this ritual when the farmers and landowners who performed it grudged their labourers even starvation wages was widely remarked on. In January 1844 the *Economist* commented,

> Take the first smock-frock labourer one meets as a specimen of 'a bold peasantry, their country's pride'; and see what a being, mentally and physically, the government of the oligarchy has made him. . . . Consider the irony of the Duke of Richmond, and grandees, who have reduced the man to this state, drinking his health at agricultural dinners as the pride and main-stay of the country.

22. *Whither thou goest, I can Not go.* . . . A reversal of the promise Ruth made to Naomi (Book of Ruth, chapter I, verse 16).

23. *and dry them with her hair.* Lilian is, of course, referring to Mary Magdalene, the 'patron saint' of penitent prostitutes. See St Luke, chapter 7, verse 38.

24. *Sally Lunns.* A light sweet teacake containing sultanas or currants served hot and eaten with butter. Apparently named after the woman who first made them in Bath, about the end of the eighteenth century.

25. *runaway carriage-doubles.* A favourite diversion of London street-urchins in Victorian times was to knock at the street door of grand houses and then run off (this is the subject of a famous cartoon by Cruikshank). A 'carriage-double' could be a double knock signifying the arrival of visitors in their own carriage.

26. *There'll be a Fire tonight.* Rick-burning, a wild revenge taken by agricultural labourers on farmers who would not pay them a living wage, was a subject of much concern at this time. The *Annual Register* (1844) noted that 102 cases were reported during 1843 whereas the average figure for 1838–42 had been only 49. Offenders were savagely punished; the spring of 1844 had seen Gifford White, an eighteen-year-old Huntingdonshire labourer, transported *for life* merely for threatening to commit arson if he and his fellow-labourers were not supplied with work. (This case inspired Hood to write his 'Lay of the Labourer', in *Hood's Magazine*, November 1844).

27. *wearied and lay down to die.* Almost certainly, Dickens is here alluding to a famous passage on Carlyle's *Past and Present* (1843) which describes an Irish widow in Edinburgh who

> went forth with her three children, bare of all resource, to solicit help from the Charitable Establishments of that City. At this Charitable Establishment and then at that she was refused; referred from one to the other, helped by none – till she had exhausted them all; till her strength and heart failed her: she sank down in typhus-fever; died, and infected her

Lane with fever, so that 'seventeen other persons' died of fever there in consequence.

28. *marrow-bones and cleavers*. The shin-bone of an ox striking a butcher's cleaver provided 'rough music' at weddings and other festivities in humble life. (H)

29. *a little flip*. A drink made of egg beaten up in spiced ale with a little spirit added. A favourite beverage with Mrs Micawber in *Copperfield*. (H)

30. *Dorsetshire*. Dickens changed Will Fern's native county in the proofs from Hertfordshire to Dorsetshire, doubtless because of the particular notoriety of Dorset at this time as a county where the peasantry existed in the utmost squalor and poverty. See a letter signed 'A Dorsetshire Landlord' in *Lloyd's Weekly London Newspaper* (28 April 1844), which asserted that if the farm-labourers' condition were not swiftly ameliorated, it 'must ... produce a revolution not less frightful than that which France has been subjected to'. Lord Ashley was quoted in the *Northern Star* (16 December 1843) as warning a Sturminster agricultural dinner that Dorset was 'becoming a by-word in men's mouths'.

MORE ABOUT PENGUINS

Penguinews, which appears every month, contains details of all the new books issued by Penguins as they are published. From time to time it is supplemented by *Penguins in Print*, which is a complete list of all available books published by Penguins. (There are well over four thousand of these.)

A specimen copy of *Penguinews* will be sent to you free on request. For a year's issues (including the complete lists) please send 50p if you live in the United Kingdom, or 75p if you live elsewhere. Just write to Dept EP, Penguin Books Ltd, Harmondsworth, Middlesex, enclosing a cheque or postal order, and your name will be added to the mailing list.

Note: *Penguinews* and *Penguins in Print* are not available in the U.S.A. or Canada

CHARLES DICKENS

DOMBEY AND SON

With an Introduction by Raymond Williams

'Dombey and Son' is both a family and a firm; and this ambiguity is at the heart of Dickens's novel. For Mr Dombey pride of position and mercantile reputation are gods to which all human feelings must be sacrificed. But his cruelties to his wife and daughter, as Raymond Williams points out in his introduction, are not presented within a narrow framework of individual morality. In *Dombey and Son* Dickens is attempting something new in English fiction, to look beyond isolated errors and vices to their breeding ground within society. What is seen, and challenged, is a system which breeds misery.

The bustling teeming streets of mid-Victorian London come vividly alive in this novel, which is an imaginative response to the fact of the city. But year by year the new railway technology is remaking London in its own image. In his descriptive passages – and in the plot itself – Dickens responds to the real contradictions of Britain's new industrial power: its potential for shaping lives, for creation and destruction, for life and death.

OUR MUTUAL FRIEND

Edited by Stephen Gill

Our Mutual Friend, like all Dickens's later works, is a rich and complex pattern of theme and symbol, which yet retains all the comic exuberance that characterized his writing from *The Pickwick Papers* onwards. It begins, like *Little Dorrit*, as a satire on wealth and its corrupting power, symbolized by the inheritance of a dust-heap and represented by the changing fortunes of Boffin, the Golden Dustman, and by the brilliant portrayal of the upstart Veneerings and their circle. But in the subsidiary story of Eugene Wrayburn and Bradley Headstone, Stephen Gill detects a new transformation of the Dickensian genius, towards a greater inwardness and a fascination with extreme situations. In the last novel he completed, Dickens seemed to be about to make yet another advance in the practice of his art.

CHARLES DICKENS

OLIVER TWIST

With an Introduction by Angus Wilson

Oliver Twist, Dickens's second novel, has recognizable antecedents in the Gothic romance and the Newgate Novel and in popular melodrama. But out of these elements the 25-year-old writer created an entirely new kind of novel, scathing in its exposure of contemporary cruelties, always exciting, and clothed in an unforgettable atmosphere of mystery and pervasive evil. Its major characters – Fagin, Bill Sykes, the Artful Dodger – have become creatures of myth, and its great scenes have lost none of their power to terrify and move.

MARTIN CHUZZLEWIT

Edited by P. N. Furbank

Martin Chuzzlewit (1843–4) is Charles Dickens's comic masterpiece – an opinion shared by Dickens himself who, when he began the novel 'never had so much confidence in his powers', and when he had finished it was convinced it was 'in a hundred points immeasurably the best of my stories'. A study in selfishness and hypocrisy, the plot of *Martin Chuzzlewit* moves from the sunniest farcicality to the grimmest reaches of criminal psychology, from the domestic and parochial villainy of Mr Pecksniff to the public villainy of the Anglo-Bengalee Assurance company.

Also available

AMERICAN NOTES
BARNABY RUDGE
BLEAK HOUSE
GREAT EXPECTATIONS
LITTLE DORRIT
THE OLD CURIOSITY SHOP
THE PICKWICK PAPERS
A TALE OF TWO CITIES
THE MYSTERY OF EDWIN DROOD

CHARLES DICKENS

DAVID COPPERFIELD

Edited by Trevor Blount

David Copperfield (1849–50) was Dickens's 'favourite child' and the book in which he revealed most of himself and particularly of his early life. But, as Trevor Blount writes in his introduction, Dickens 'did more than transliterate autobiography. He fashioned himself anew in what he wrote, and in so doing achieved simultaneously the sanity and distinction of art, and the warmth and quickness of joyous life.' Above all in this novel he created some of his most famous characters – Micawber, Uriah Heep, Steerforth – creatures whom, in Chesterton's words, 'we would not forget if we could, creatures whom we could not forget if we would, creatures who are more actual than the man who made them'.

HARD TIMES

Edited by David Craig

Hard Times, which has never achieved the popularity and seldom the recognition of Dickens's other novels, is his withering portrait of a Lancashire mill-town in the 1840s. In the persons of Gradgrind and Bounderby he powerfully stigmatized the prevalent philosophy of Utilitarianism which, whether in school or factory, allowed human beings to be caged in a dreary scenery of brick terraces and foul chimneys, to be enslaved by machines, and reduced to numbers.

'It has a kind of perfection as a work of art that we don't associate with Dickens – a perfection that is one with the sustained and complete seriousness for which among his productions it is unique. . . . The prose is that of one of the greatest masters of English, and the dialogue – very much a test in such an undertaking – is consummate; beautifully natural in its stylization' – F. R. Leavis in *The Great Tradition*.

THE PENGUIN ENGLISH LIBRARY

Some Recent Volumes